SO! THE DRESDEN-DOLL TYPE, WAS SHE?

A bright young lady, just out of school, and entirely unfitted to face the world. He didn't actually say so, but the implication was clear. She was a typical rich man's daughter—fragile, protected, secure in her own little corner, and believing it was the world. It was all there, not in so many words, but with the meaning clearly between the lines. This was what that fresh young reporter had thought of her and dared to write about in *The Leola Record*! On the surface the piece seemed to flatter and praise. What credit he gave her for leaving her "gay city life" to bury herself in quiet little Leola! An Allard had come home. And so forth. She would like to wring his neck with her own hands. He had made a complete fool of her. Everyone in Leola would be laughing. Well, she'd show Tom Webb a thing or two. . . .

A Long Time Coming

A LONG TIME COMING

A novel for young people

by PHYLLIS A. WHITNEY

A SIGNET BOOK

NEW AMERICAN LIBRARY

TIMES MIRROR

SIGNET AND MENTOR BOOKS ARE ALSO AVAILABLE AT DIS-
COUNTS IN BULK QUANTITY FOR INDUSTRIAL OR SALES-
PROMOTIONAL USE. FOR DETAILS, WRITE TO PREMIUM
MARKETING DIVISION, NEW AMERICAN LIBRARY, INC., 1301
AVENUE OF THE AMERICAS, NEW YORK, NEW YORK 10019.

Acknowledgment

The quotation by Carl Sandburg on page 1 is from THE
PEOPLE, YES. Used by permission of Harcourt Brace Jovano-
vich, Inc.

The quotation by Stephen Vincent Benét on page 235 is from
"Prayer" in WE STAND UNITED AND OTHER RADIO
SCRIPTS, published by Rinehart & Company, Inc. Copyright,
1942, by Stephen Vincent Benét.

 SIGNET TRADEMARK REG. U.S. PAT. OFF. AND FOREIGN COUNTRIES
REGISTERED TRADEMARK—MARCA REGISTRADA
HECHO EN CHICAGO, U.S.A.

SIGNET, SIGNET CLASSICS, MENTOR, PLUME AND MERIDIAN BOOKS
are published by The New American Library, Inc.,
1301 Avenue of the Americas, New York, New York 10019

FIRST PRINTING, JANUARY, 1976

1 2 3 4 5 6 7 8 9

PRINTED IN THE UNITED STATES OF AMERICA

For Wilma Jones
with gratitude for the kind assistance
which made this book possible

Contents

A Note from the Author

ONE EVENING LAST WINTER MY HUSBAND PLACED AN open magazine on top of the book I was reading, his way of saying, "This is worth while." The magazine was *Nation's Business* and the title on the turned-up page read "No Migrant Problem Here"; the article was by André Fontaine.

For the moment the title meant nothing to me, but I was drawn to the pictures: photographs of bright-eyed, smiling people of Mexican descent. There were other pictures, too, the alert faces of typical Americans, and the trusting faces of children.

The article proved to be the factual account of how one small Midwestern town and the migrants who came each year to work in the fields had progressed from animosity and ill feeling to a common ground of trust and healthy cooperation. As I read, I experienced that surge of excitement which comes when I find an idea really worth writing about. Here was a story that *had* to be told.

In the following weeks, I wrote letters to some of the people mentioned in the article, I searched eagerly for more articles and books that had been written on this subject, and eventually I made the decision to go and see for myself.

Some months later, I stepped from a cool, air-conditioned train into the broiling midsummer heat of the little Illinois town of the article. For days I talked with the townspeople, the workers in church mission groups, the management in the canneries, shop people, and the migrants themselves. I visited their camp nursery schools and saw take place some of the small incidents that appear in *A Long Time Coming*. I was made welcome by the townspeople and treated with great natural courtesy by several migrant families. I came away enormously moved.

As it always happens in a search of this kind, a mere beginning led to finding much more material than could be used in one book. Stories from Florida, Texas, New Jersey, California, Michigan, and New York accumulated until I saw quite clearly that here were a problem and a solution that have no one locale. This might have happened anywhere.

So in my story I have purposely avoided using a real town. Leola is a made-up name for what is really a composite of many towns. The characters are also fictional, except that they hold attitudes which are truly typical of those found in many parts of our country today. All this has been brought together in a story that is "real" in the sense that the characters have become alive to me, as I hope they will live for you, the reader. Yes, this is a story about young people, for it is the young people who have most at stake and who can do the most about the future.

—*Phyllis A. Whitney*

A LONG TIME COMING

Man is a long time coming,
Man will yet win.
Brother may yet line up with brother.
—*Carl Sandburg*

Runaway

Christie opened the cab door and got out at the entrance to the big Chicago railroad station. Behind her Mrs. O'Regan paid the fare, tipping the driver cautiously. In her role of guardian, housekeeper, adviser, and soft-hearted critic, Agnes O'Regan had been paying what bills it was possible to pay for the Allards as long as Christie could remember. Sometimes Christie suspected that she paid out of her own savings.

When Agnes was ready, Christie picked up the smart calf suitcase that had been her mother's and walked toward the doors with Agnes hurrying in her wake. Now that she was on her way, Christie wanted to hasten this departure. The sooner she put Chicago behind her, the sooner she might forget the hurtful things connected with it.

She was glad now that she was slipping away without letting anyone know the time of her leaving. It would have been too upsetting to have pitying friends here at the station. Agnes had understood that.

"Wait a second, darlin'," Agnes said. "You need a bit of smoothing down."

Christie stopped and let Agnes flick imaginary specks from her navy-blue shantung suit, tuck a wisp of fair hair back under her straw, as if Christie were a little girl of ten, instead of a young woman of eighteen.

"I'm all right," Christie protested. "Agnes, you'll remember the agreement we made, won't you? This isn't a parting for good. You're going to your folks in New York for now, but we'll see each other again. So let's make it quick and easy. If you stay till I board the train, there'll be oceans of tears, and—and——" Her voice broke and she couldn't go on.

Agnes scowled at her fiercely, though her own nose was pink and she was sniffing. "I'm a woman of my word, as well you know. But I'd like to have a look at this Mexican girl you'll be accompanying to the town of Leola."

"We're a half-hour early, so she probably won't be here yet," Christie said. "Besides, you don't have to worry. Aunt Amelia would never ask me to do anything that wasn't all right. And as soon as I reach Leola, I'll be going right to Aunt Amelia's house."

She walked into the station, with Agnes trotting after her, little and fierce and protective. It was cooler in here, away from the July heat of Chicago pavements. The great, vaulted ceiling made a distant, hushed roar of the clang of gates, the shuffle of feet, the shouting and general hum of human beings on their way from here to somewhere else.

For an instant Christie felt the old tingle of anticipation go through her. She had always loved to travel with Eve. Then she remembered that there was nothing exciting to anticipate any more and winced away from the thought of her mother. Resolutely she walked toward an empty section on one of the long, brown-varnished benches.

"What's a worry to me," Agnes grumbled, "is who's to look after you while you look after some Mexican riffraff just turned seventeen."

"How do you know she's riffraff?" Christie asked, seating herself on the bench with the suitcase at her feet.

"She ran away from home, didn't she?" Agnes perched beside her on the edge of the bench.

"But she wants to go back and I'm glad to help, since Aunt Amelia has asked me to."

"A lucky thing it is you're going to your aunt." The flowers on Agnes's hat nodded in solemn approval. "A good woman she is—Miss Amelia Allard—though with strong ideas. Your poor mother would be happy to see you in her hands."

Christie knew what would happen if Agnes got off on the subject of her mother at this last moment. She put an

4

arm around Agnes's shoulders and gave her a quick squeeze.

"Remember, this isn't good-bye, Agnes. You'll write to me and I'll write to you, and you're not to worry one bit. But you know if you stay we'll both be in tears, and—and I don't want that."

Mrs. O'Regan scowled away a redcap who paused beside Christie's suitcase, and then got briskly to her feet.

"It's right you are, darlin'. I'll be on my way now. Remember, you'll carry your own bag these days, and don't be forgetting it. You have to save every penny now."

Christie nodded. Her mother's debts had been alarming. The furnishings of the big North Shore apartment had been sold and the apartment subleased. The car was gone, and Eve's furs—almost everything. But somehow Christie couldn't worry about possessions or money now. Not in the face of other, deeper pangs; the loss of her mother and that other loss which hurt so much to think about. Phil. . . .

Agnes bent to kiss her and left the wet stain of tears on her cheek. Christie swallowed and clung to her for a last frightened moment. In all her life she had never been completely on her own before. This time it was Agnes who drew gently away and tried to adopt a matter-of-fact manner.

"It's just for a while, darlin'. Now remember—if you see that good-for-nothing father of yours down there in Leola, just you give him the back of your hand."

Christie dabbed her eyes with a small white handkerchief, one of her mother's that she'd put in her pocket for comfort. "Don't worry, I won't see him. Aunt Amelia says he never comes to Leola any more, even though he was born there." The father whom she had not seen since she was nine years old was the least of her worries just now.

Agnes gave her a last hug and kiss and went off toward the door as fast as she could go. Christie stared at her mother's suitcase and fought the desire to run after Agnes.

The suitcase reminded her of her mother again, and the

stab of hurt returned. Once more she felt a sense of unreality about everything that was happening. It just couldn't be that Eve was gone. She'd been so pretty and bright and gay. She'd always seemed so young that sometimes people called them sisters. That was why Eve had not wanted Christie to call her "Mommy" or "Mother", but had insisted on the shortening of her real name, Evelyn.

It was Eve's heart that had given out, old Dr. Stevens said. He had told her she played too hard, danced too hard. But she never listened to him. Who wanted to be a dull old woman, she laughed, and went right on with her feverish search after what she called "living." Though sometimes, as Christie grew older, she wondered if her mother had ever really found the thing she searched for so restlessly. Now she'd never have another chance.

Aunt Amelia had come up from Leola for Christie's graduation and had left urging her to come to the little country town for a few months till she could decide what she wanted to do. Perhaps if it hadn't been for the letter from Phil Cunningham, Christie might have tried to stay in Chicago where she had grown up.

The thought of Phil's letter reminded her of something she must do before she left the station. In a few moments she would walk over to the information counter to see if the Mexican girl was there. But first she had to end something once and for all. She had to go out of Chicago without a single trace of Phil left anywhere, except in her heart.

She snapped open her white handbag and reached into it for Phil's letter. She didn't need to read it again; she knew the words by heart. What had happened was very simple. He had gone into the Air Force early in the year and was stationed in Texas. There he had met a girl. Three weeks ago he had married her.

Christie's cheeks burned at the memory of the words she had poured out on paper to Phil after her mother's death. She and Phil had been so much together before he went away. They'd gone to parties, read the same books, taken long walks along the shore of Lake Michigan. He'd kissed her in the moonlight and it had meant everything to Christie.

6

But now she knew it had not meant everything to him. His letter was kind, and it had stabbed with every word. To lose Eve, and then Phil——the ache of loneliness inside her was something she could not escape, could not still.

Abruptly she tore the envelope and its contents across, and then again and again, until it was no more than confetti in her lap. A station attendant with a broom and dustpan was sweeping near by and she brushed the scraps into the pan, dusted her skirt free of them. The ache had not been brushed away, but she picked up her suitcase and walked across the station, her heels clicking firmly on the hard floor.

The information booth stood in the middle of the station. As Christie walked toward it she saw the Mexican girl waiting for her, a plump woman beside her, probably the relative Aunt Amelia had mentioned. The girl wore a white blouse with a round neck and puffed sleeves, and a brightly figured yellow-and-green cotton skirt. Her thick black hair went up from her forehead in a pompadour and hung about her shoulders at the back. Green earrings dangled from her ears. She was striking in a sullen sort of way. At the moment her big dark eyes seemed to stare at nothing. She merely waited, outwardly passive. Her plump relative, on the contrary, was looking anxiously about the station.

This was a problem Christie hardly knew how to meet, but she stepped up to the counter and spoke to the girl. "You're Aurora Gomez, aren't you? My aunt Amelia in Leola asked me to look you up before we board the train. I'm Christie Allard."

The girl's gaze flicked over her briefly, almost scornfully, it seemed to Christie. But the older woman took care of the matter of words. She broke into effusive and relieved thanks, said she must get back to her job, told Aurora sharply that she should be a better daughter to her parents, and went off, leaving Christie with this girl, a year younger than herself, who looked as if she might be anything but friendly.

The big clock that ruled the life of the station ticked ahead one minute and the loud-speaker suddenly bawled

7

through the echoing cavern. Automatically, those who waited for trains tensed and listened, struggling to understand the garbled sounds. Christie caught only the word "Leola" among the list of stops and the final direction that the train was waiting at Gate 10.

"Have you any baggage?" she asked Aurora.

The girl shrugged and held up a square of yellow cotton that had been knotted to hold her few possessions.

"Come along then," Christie said. "We can get aboard."

For just a moment Aurora looked as if she might not agree to come aboard. Then her shoulders drooped, she let the bundle dangle limply from her hand, and walked beside Christie to the gate where a trainman was examining tickets. Aurora fished hers from the pocket of her skirt and the two girls went through the gate and down the platform.

Christie let Aurora go ahead of her into one of the coaches and gave her the seat by the window. The Mexican girl moved limply, without interest or objection. But when Christie wanted to put her bundle up on the baggage rack beside her own suitcase, Aurora clung to it.

"Is good here," she said, and held it in her lap.

Christie settled down in the blue-covered seat and put her head back against the white seat cover. Outside the lighted car the gray daylight of the station pressed dismally against the window. Baggage trucks rumbled by and shouts came to them dimly through double panes of glass. The seats were filling up now.

Christie felt increasingly baffled by the girl beside her. Aunt Amelia had explained that Father Cudahy of St. Ann's Church had heard that Christine Allard was coming to town from Chicago. He had thought it might be easier and more pleasant for Aurora if she could come home in the company of another girl so nearly her own age. So he had gone to Mr. Bennett, the minister of Aunt Amelia's church, to see if some arrangement could be made.

Mr. Bennett, it seemed, roomed at Aunt Amelia's, and Christie found herself hoping that he wouldn't be too stuffy and ministerial. She hadn't gone to Sunday school since she'd been a little girl, and Eve had not bothered about church because she liked to sleep till noon on Sundays.

At any rate, through one church and another, Christie had been asked to accompany to Leola this girl who had for some reason run away, but was now willing to go home. If the ride was to be a pleasant one, she would have to make friends with Aurora, who would apparently make no effort of her own on this score. Besides, she was curious about the girl.

"I love to ride on trains," she began brightly. "There's always a feeling of adventure about going somewhere— anywhere. Don't you think so?"

Aurora stared at her own slender hands, and Christie found herself noting the roughness of the skin, the broken nails on which traces of scarlet polish remained.

"To stay in one place, that is better," Aurora said.

This was puzzling from a girl who had certainly not wanted to stay in one place.

Christie tried again. "Don't you like trains?"

Aurora shrugged. "It makes not much difference to me."

Eve's delicately evasive ways had never suited Christie. When she wanted to know something, she always asked straight out.

"How did you get from Leola to Chicago?"

Briefly, Aurora lifted her hand and pointed the thumb.

Christie was startled. Hitchhiking for a girl sounded appalling. She shifted quickly to a safer subject.

"Have you lived in Leola very long?"

For the first time the Mexican girl turned her head to look directly at Christie. Plainly it was her turn to be surprised.

"You are kidding?" she said curtly.

Outside on the platform there was the muted shout of "A-a-ll a-bo-ard!" The train jerked, and the platform began to slide slowly past.

"Why should I be kidding?" Christie asked. She was beginning to feel more and more uncomfortable with this strange girl. "I've never been to Leola. I don't know anything about it."

"You do not know about it and your name is Allard? What a laugh! Maybe you don't know about Allard canned vegetables?"

Of course she knew about them, Christie thought impatiently. You couldn't go to a grocery store without seeing Allard vegetables on the shelves. She also knew that the Allard plant was in Leola and that her grandfather had owned it. But all this didn't clarify Aurora's scorn.

"My father is with the Sage and Thorpe Company. They're publishers in New York City," she explained. "I don't suppose he has much to do with the Allard Company in Leola."

"It is only that he owns it," Aurora said.

Fresh, cool air began to circulate through the car as the conditioning unit went to work. Christie drew a deep breath. After the sticky heat of Chicago, it felt wonderful. For a little while she was silent, watching gray city slums run past the window, thinking about Aurora's words.

She knew so little about her father, really. Since her parents' divorce so long ago, Eve had been bitter against him, blamed him for everything. Of late years she'd hardly mentioned him at all. So it was a surprise to Christie to learn that he still had interests in Leola.

Obviously there was a resentment toward the Allards on Aurora's part, though Christie was at a loss to see why, and she cast about for another opening clue to the puzzle of the girl beside her.

"Did you grow up in Mexico, Aurora? When did you come to the United States?"

This time she got a swift and unexpected reaction. Aurora turned toward her in the seat, indignation lighting her eyes.

"So! You think I am Mexican, yes? Pay attention then. I am American just like you, just like the Allards. My father, my mother, they were born in the Valley, in Texas. I was born in Texas and my small sister as well. Also the twins who died, they were born in the United States. And all, all of us are American!"

Christie blinked at the suddenness of the attack. She was aware of heads across the aisle turning to look at

10

them, and she made a hasty calming motion with her hand.

"Well, all right, Aurora Gomez. So you're American."

"United States American!" Aurora insisted.

"All right," Christie repeated mildly. "United States American. What other kind is there?"

Aurora switched her course without pausing for breath. "You Anglos!" she fairly spat out the phrase, as if it were her worst insult. "Always you think you are all the world. Mexico, too, is in the Americas, and also South America."

"I'm sorry," Christie said. "I suppose we don't think about that as often as we should."

"I'll say!" said Aurora. And there the conversation ended.

Christie decided that she didn't care much one way or another. It was unlikely that the Gomez family and Aunt Amelia moved in the same circles. Leola would be a quiet, sleepy little Midwestern town in which Christie might escape the reminders that abounded in Chicago. She could vegetate there and be dull, perhaps forget. Eventually she would think about her future. Not college, since there was no money and she did not want to accept the offer which had come from her father after Eve's death. When she thought of the way he had treated her mother, she wanted nothing of him. Thanks to the insistence of her counsellor at school, she had taken a course in shorthand and typing, so when she came back to Chicago she could get a job. Aunt Amelia wouldn't expect her to work in a little town like Leola.

After an hour or so of monotonous travel, she began to get hungry. There was no proper diner on this train, but there was a snack car on ahead. Christie invited Aurora to join her in getting a sandwich and a glass of milk, but the girl refused, and as Christie swayed with the train up the aisle she found she was a little relieved to get away from her strange companion for a while.

Shortly before noon Aurora began to take her first interest in the farm country outside the train window. She looked out eagerly, recognizing landmarks as they slipped by.

"Almost we are there," she volunteered.

11

Christie got her suitcase down from the rack, settled her navy-blue straw more firmly on her hair, and pulled on white gloves. Aurora noted the gloves with grudging interest.

"They don't get dirty?" she asked.

"They're easy to wash," Christie explained. "Agnes washed—" she changed the phrase—"I wash them every time I wear them."

Aurora nodded solemnly. "With hot water." It was a statement, not a question, and again Christie was puzzled. Perhaps there was no hot water at Aurora's house, though such a condition was hard to imagine. At any rate, this was no time for a discussion of gloves.

"My aunt wired that she wouldn't be able to be at the station because of a meeting she had to attend," Christie explained. "But I'm going to take a cab to her house, so I'll drop you off on the way."

"Where I live is not your way," Aurora said.

"Then we'll go out of my way," Christie told her cheerfully. She knew Aunt Amelia's strong ideas about duty and she suspected that she had better not let Aurora out of her sight until she had been safely delivered to her home. Besides, she didn't mind going out of the way. In Leola time had no meaning, no urgency. There was nothing else she had to do.

The train was running through the fringes of town now and Christie looked out the window at wide, ordered streets and old trees. On the other side, things looked a bit more ramshackle, so that was probably the section she had read about in stories—"the wrong side of the tracks." Then the train began to slow down and Christie could hear the clanging of a crossroads bell as the train rolled to a stop beside a platform that bore the sign "Leola."

Aurora was behaving like a little girl. She might have run away from something in Leola that she did not like, but now she was obviously glad to be home. Christie could hardly pull her away from the window.

"That Rafael is out there!" Aurora cried excitedly. "That *Mexican* Rafael! The nerve of him to come!"

But Christie thought she sounded more pleased than angry. Looking out the windows as they went down the aisle, Christie could see a nice-looking boy on the platform. He wore a blue checked shirt outside his dungarees, and his black hair had been slicked back in shiny neatness. He looked up at the car windows with an eagerness that was engaging. Christie hoped that Aurora would treat him nicely.

The trainman set her suitcase on the platform and she went down the steps with Aurora right at her heels. The platform baked with heat beneath the noon-high sun, and quivering, steamy air rose to engulf them. It was a shock after the cool train.

The boy named Rafael came forward at once, but he did not touch Aurora or even hold out his hand, though his smile spread happiness across his face.

"Querida," he said. "Why did you go away?"

Aurora tossed her head and the green earrings tapped her cheeks. "That is no business of yours. And I am not *querida* to you."

For the first time Christie saw that Rafael was not alone. Behind him was a tanned young man who looked to be in his early twenties, a big fellow in gray slacks and a short-sleeved blue shirt.

He clapped Rafael on the shoulder and shook his head at Aurora. "Don't let her get you down. We know she's glad to see us. Hello, Aurora. Don't look so scared. I'm not going to scold you. But I think you're going to catch it from your papa."

Aurora, who was not looking in the least scared, smiled for the first time since Christie had met her. This large young man was apparently someone she liked and trusted. Christie waited behind her a little awkwardly, a sudden sense of loneliness sweeping through her. Even Aurora had someone to meet her, to care about her. The reasonable fact that Aunt Amelia had been unable to get to the station did not help Christie's feeling of strangeness at the moment.

Then the tall young man's gaze moved past Aurora to Christie and something appraising came into his eyes.

"You're Miss Allard, I believe? I'm John Macdonald from out at the plant. And this is Rafael Olivera. We're grateful to you for seeing Aurora back to town."

13

Christie sensed his lack of warmth and nodded to him briefly to hide her own uncertainty.

Rafael gave her a shy "Hello" and turned again to Aurora. "You will come with us, yes? Señor Mac has the car and when he has done the errands we will take you home."

"Can we give you a lift, too, Miss Allard?" John Macdonald asked with cool courtesy. It was as if he withheld judgment, waiting to see what stuff she was made of, and his manner made her want to show him how little she cared what he thought.

Near the curb stood an elderly cab, with a still more elderly driver peering hopefully out for a fare. Christie waved one white-gloved hand at him and he came to life and swung open the door.

"No, thank you," she told John Macdonald. "I'll get to Aunt Amelia's in no time in a taxi."

"And I will go with you," Aurora announced. "Already she has invited me," she told Rafael, and brushed past him with an impudent shrug of her shoulders. No one objected, though Rafael seemed disappointed. As the taxi pulled away from the curb, Christie looked out the rear window and saw that John Macdonald and Rafael were walking down the town's main business street. Rafael glanced regretfully over one shoulder. John Macdonald did not. Aurora, too, took a peek out the window and made a face at Rafael before she settled comfortably back in the cab's seat, more cheerful than she had been all morning.

"Where to?" the cab driver asked.

"To the Allard plant," Aurora told him.

2

Wrong Foot Forward

The train had pulled out, and the striped black-and-white gates at the crossing lifted as the taxi turned toward the west side of town.

"My goodness, but it's hot," Christie murmured, fanning herself with a handkerchief already damp.

"So?" said Aurora. "Always it is like this in the summer."

She seemed cheerful now and not at all sullen. Evidently the prospect of a scolding waiting for her from her father did not particularly trouble her.

On this side of the tracks the houses were smaller and more crowded together, the yards tiny. There were blocks of weed-grown fields where Queen Anne's lace spread its white crown. The streets still lay straight and orderly, with no unexpected turnings to break the monotony, and the ground boasted not the slightest roll to give interest to the land. But Christie had not come to Leola to be interested. The very monotony was soothing.

Aurora nudged her suddenly. "There! You can see the water tower now. The plant is ahead."

Christie looked through the windshield to see a number of long, low buildings crouched around a spider-legged water tower with the name ALLARD in huge black letters across it. It was odd to see her own name practically crowning the town of Leola. Not that she felt any sense of pride, since none of this had any real connection with her. In fact, it didn't look like anything to be proud of, the vista was too bare and ugly.

Aurora's excitement had turned her chattery. "I will tell you something. Never am I in a taxi before this day. This is why I would not go with that Rafael. For that reason and also because he will grow big in the head if I go with him. And that will not be good for such a one—no?" Her smile was brilliant, gay. She could be almost beautiful when her face lighted up like this.

Before Christie could comment, the taxi pulled up on the dirt road beside a gate in a high wire fence that stretched about the entire grounds. And Aurora was scrambling out of the cab.

"There is the mama!" she cried, tugging at Christie to make her look in the right direction. "She is coming, see?"

Inside the fence the grounds spread away, dirt and gravel and cinders, with only a tired patch of burnt-out grass here and there between stretches of miserable shanties. There were no trees, no shrubbery. From the door of a gray barracks-like structure, hidden until now by the buildings of the cannery, had come a large woman who strongly resembled the woman who had brought Aurora to the station in Chicago. She would have been on the plump side under ordinary circumstances, but now, plainly, she expected a baby, and she moved with an off-balance waddle.

Aurora flew toward her as she reached the gate, and the woman opened welcoming arms, crying and laughing at the same time. It was obvious that Mrs. Gomez was not going to scold her daughter, at least not immediately. Christie sat in the taxi wondering if Aurora would forget her and go off without a backward glance, or if she should wait to be noticed again, in order to say good-by.

But Aurora had not forgotten her. She turned about, dark eyes shining, and led her mother over to the cab. Mrs. Gomez made a quick movement of smoothing back her hair, the most she could do to dress up for company, and smiled warmly at Christie.

"*Gracias* señorita," she cried. "Much, much thanks. From my heart, *muchas gracias*."

Christie smiled weakly, embarrassed by thanks that were out of all proportion to the little she had done for Aurora.

"You will come into my house, please," Mrs. Gomez

invited. "You will do my house the so great honor, señorita."

Christie swallowed uncomfortably, her gaze on the unprepossessing building from which Mrs. Gomez had emerged, at the powdery dust and cinders of the grounds. She knew what dust and cinders would do to her blue suède shoes. At the same time, she could not hurt this friendly woman.

Aurora saved her the decision. She pulled her mother away hurriedly. "Not now, mamacita. Miss Allard must go to the house of her aunt." Then she turned back to Christie and somehow there was in her manner both pride and a look that dared the other girl to criticize.

"Thank you," she said with quiet dignity. "Good-by, Miss Allard."

"Why, you're welcome," Christie said awkwardly. "I'll be seeing you, Aurora."

Aurora gave her an odd look and walked into the camp with her mother, and Christie wondered why she had said anything so foolish. The most unlikely thing in the world was that she would ever see Aurora Gomez again, except by sheer chance.

She settled back in the cab and gave Aunt Amelia's address to the driver. As they drew away from the gate, Christie looked out the back window at the rows of unpainted wooden shacks. No wonder the girl had spoken so respectfully of hot water. In a place like this you'd probably haul cold water from a pump. She glanced again at the tower with the huge letters of the Allard name sprawled across it. No, she certainly wasn't proud of her connection with a place like this.

"Do people live in those shanties year after year?" she asked the cab driver.

"Why not?" He sounded surprised that she should question the obvious. "It's good enough for them Mexicans. Better than they're used to over the border. No use spoiling 'em, I say."

"I don't suppose they get spoiled very badly," Christie said, feeling mildly indignant.

"Let 'em do their job and get out. We don't want 'em hanging around Leola any longer than they need to."

"What do you mean—get out?" Christie asked.

"Hey, didn't somebody say your name was Allard? Don't you know anything about this place at all?"

Cab drivers, it seemed, were the same everywhere. They scolded you when they felt like it, and talked your ear off if you gave them a chance. This one went on without waiting for Christie to reply.

"That bunch at the plant are migrants. You know, they work the crops. Here today, gone tomorrow, and the silverware with 'em, if you don't watch out."

"I doubt that," said Christie, feeling prickly. She hadn't exactly liked Aurora, but she couldn't see her taking things that didn't belong to her. Now, however, she could understand why the other girl had said, "Are you kidding?" when she'd asked Aurora if she had always lived in Leola.

"Okay, okay." The driver shrugged the matter off as they bumped back across the tracks. "Anyway, I suppose you know the name of Allard used to be a pretty big one around here. The Allards are all gone now, except for Miss Amelia. And she makes up for a whole parcel of 'em put together. She still owns a good chunk of this town. You're Lawrence Allard's daughter, ain't you? Hope you're going to do better by us than he has, young lady."

Christie said nothing, wishing he would stop talking. But he went on and on as the car followed quiet, tree-shaded streets, passed expensive green lawns and verandas fringed by blue hydrangea bushes. Whether she welcomed a guided tour or not, the landmarks of Leola were pointed out to her. There was the public library. Old building, not so bad inside. Plenty of other fine old buildings in this town, like, for instance, the courthouse downtown. And over there now was the mansion where her grandfather had been born. It was the town museum now. Miss Amelia had loaned it to the town, said she couldn't rattle around alone in such a big place. Besides, it took an army of servants to run a place like that, and it was hard to get help these days, even with her money.

Christie looked at the big house with its sloping roofs

and old trees crowding around it, and wondered about her grandfather. Of course Eve had never talked much about the Allards, but she could remember her father telling stories about Josh Allard when she was small.

The cab turned down the next block and ran on a little farther. Here they were, the driver went on, and down that cross-street was the oldest, richest church in Leola. Her grandfather had been a deacon of that church and the Allards had always gone there. Until lately, when Miss Amelia had walked plumb out of it and never come back, thus scandalizing the whole town. He chuckled appreciatively as he drew the cab over to the curb. It was apparent that he had considerable respect for Miss Amelia Allard.

Christie was glad to be free of his chatter. She paid him quickly, added a tip that surprised him, and at the same moment winced as she remembered that Agnes had warned her against being too generous with tips. Then she got out of the cab and stood looking up at the wide-verandaed house that was Aunt Amelia's. A redheaded, overalled young gardener was on his knees in the yard, working around rosebushes with a trowel and fertilizer. On the top step of the veranda a grizzled, overly plump English bulldog lay half asleep in the shade.

At the slam of the cab door both gardener and bulldog looked up. The gardener grinned and the bulldog growled.

"Quiet, Fatso," the gardner said. "This is a friend."

He rose from his knees, wiping grubby hands on the seat of his overalls, and came toward her. He had a sprinkling of freckles across the bridge of his nose that matched the bright hue of his hair, and his eyes were patches of blue sky.

But Christie was weary and wanted to get off by herself as quickly as possible. She didn't want any more friendly townspeople talking her to death. Besides, out of the corner of her eye she could see the young man's grubby hand reaching toward the clean white calfskin handle of her suitcase.

She picked the bag up quickly and hurried past the

19

outstretched hand with a bright smile. "Thank you; don't trouble. It's not a bit heavy. My aunt said I could go right in."

She ran halfway up the steps before she realized that this elderly bulldog was the meanest-looking creature she had ever seen in her life and that he definitely did not approve of her. His bark had a man-eating sound, and she backed hastily down the steps, looking to the redhead for aid.

He addressed the bulldog in prompt and ringing tones. "Fatso, old fellow, I told you this was a friend. Now you lie down there and let her go by or it's going to be the worse for your soul."

Surprisingly, Fatso looked as though he understood every word. He grumbled deep in his throat, threw Christie a baleful look, and lay down full in her path. She tiptoed cautiously around him and approached the screen door of the house.

"He won't hurt you." The young man had gone back to his flower bed, but he still watched her. "Go right in, Miss Allard. Your room's upstairs. Your Aunt said she'd put a note on your door."

Christie mumbled "Thank you" with one eye on the dog, but Fatso only moved his eyes to watch her go by. The screen door was unlocked and she let herself into the house.

Again a sense of loneliness and strangeness enveloped her; a realization that the world she knew, the people she had loved, were gone completely. As she entered this house she would step into a new life, and suddenly she wanted only to run back to the love and safety of the old.

But of course there was nothing there to run back to. She could only go ahead. She blinked the hint of moisture from her eyes and crossed the hallway to the stairs rising at one side, darkly varnished around the carpeting. At her left was a big, old-fashioned living room, cheerful and comfortable. After her mother's taste for the modern, it seemed a little strange to Christie's eyes, but restful. Considering the heat outside, the house was wonderfully cool.

Christie mounted the stairs. In the upper hallway the

wallpaper wore pink nosegays and the carpet was moss-green. It was a big roomy house. She went past two closed doors, stepped into an upstairs sitting room, and saw another door opening off it. This door was ajar and a square of gray notepaper was fastened to the dark wood with a bit of cellophane tape.

Christie took the note from the door, carried her suitcase into the room, and closed the door gently behind her. In here the woodwork had been painted oyster white and the light wallpaper was strewn with tiny blue forget-me-nots. The rug on the floor was a soft gray-blue, the ruffled bedspread blue and white. In one corner the trunk sent ahead from Chicago waited for her like a friend out of the past. She set down the suitcase, pulled off her hat, and laid it between twin blue lamps on the maple dresser. Then she walked to the front window and looked out through organdy curtains.

The veranda roof sloped beneath the window and she could see the red-haired young man back at his work. A small maple rocker with a blue-patterned cushion invited her and she sat gratefully down by the window. The room was a far cry from the green-and-chartreuse modern bedroom Eve had designed for her, but somehow this seemed soothing and peaceful. Already it was a haven which belonged to her. It was so spick-and-span, so new that she was sure Aunt Amelia had done it over especially for her coming, and she felt touched by such thoughtfulness. Then, remembering the note, she unfolded the sheet of gray paper and read the words. They were as completely matter-of-fact as Aunt Amelia herself.

Dear Christine (Aunt Amelia never approved of nicknames):

I hope you will like your room and that you will enjoy it for as long as you care to stay. It is high time you came home to Leola and started being an Allard.

I shall be back around one o'clock for lunch. There will be just the four of us. You can help things along by making coffee and getting sandwich things out

of the refrigerator. Sorry I am unable to meet your
train. I have to meet a crisis instead.

Lovingly,
Aunt Amelia

Christie glanced at her watch. It was twelve-thirty, so she had better see if she could obey Aunt Amelia's directions. She located the bathroom first, combed back her fluffy blond hair and washed away some of the grime of travel. Then she went downstairs and explored the rear of the house.

There was a big bright dining room with French doors opening onto a small side porch. Beyond the dining room was a kitchen big enough to hold three of the one Agnes had had to work in at the North Shore apartment. Christie moved about uncertainly, wondering just what she was supposed to do, and who "the four of us" were who would be home for lunch. Her aunt and herself, of course. And probably the minister who roomed here—depressing thought. But who was the fourth? That redheaded gardener, perhaps? Maybe in Leola one invited the hired help in for meals. After all, this was a farming community.

Feeling a little better, and faintly amused at this story-book world, she opened the refrigerator door. Butter, they'd need—that was safe. And probably peanut butter and cheese spreads. She took things out of the icebox and placed them on the kitchen table, but she knew well enough what was really troubling her. Aunt Amelia had instructed her to make coffee. There was a coffeepot on the stove and she found the coffee can all too easily on a nearby shelf. But she hadn't the faintest idea what to do next. Probably, she thought, smiling wryly, she was the only eighteen-year-old girl in the town of Leola who had never in her life made a cup of coffee. Obviously, you put water and coffee together and ended up with the brew. But in what combination, she had no idea. Her mother had never taken the slightest interest in domestic matters, and Agnes had never liked anyone else "muddling around" her kitchen.

Christie remembered Phil's teasing, and how he used to

say Christie Allard couldn't even boil water. But Eve had said, "Darling, marry well and you won't have to." Eve and Phil, Phil and Eve. (If only she could stop remembering.) While she stood with the coffeepot in her hands, pondering the next step, the screen door slammed and someone came into the house. Was that Aunt Amelia already? Christie carried the pot over to the sink in order to look busy, and turned on the water. But it was not Aunt Amelia who addressed her from the kitchen doorway.

"Hello, Christine Allard," said a girl's voice behind her.

Christie shut off the water and turned around. The newcomer was a little older than herself. She was short and rather stocky and wore her brown hair combed back carelessly in a slightly longer than boyish bob. If her nose had started out the day with powder, the coating had long since been perspired off, and her lipstick had worn thin. Her brown loafers were covered with dust and she looked thoroughly tired and hot. But her smile was warm and welcoming. Christie found herself smiling back a little shyly.

"I'm Marge Molloy," the other girl said. "Welcome to Allard-town, Christine Allard."

If the smile hadn't been so genuine, Christie might have suspected a faint sarcasm in the words. But before she could decide, the girl hurried on.

"I see you're getting ready to make coffee. Go right ahead. I'll wash up and be with you in a minute. I don't know whether you've been told. I'm one of your aunt's roomers. Not that she needs to take in roomers, she just likes our company."

She waited for no answer, but hurried off toward the stairs, leaving Christie still in unwilling possession of the coffeepot. Well, a cookbook was the next step. But though she examined every shelf in view there was nothing in sight which would instruct her in the making of coffee. She set the pot firmly back on the stove and returned to searching the refrigerator.

In five minutes Marge Molloy joined her, face washed and shoes dusted. "How are things going?" she asked

23

cheerfully as she walked into the kitchen. "Oh, I thought you were starting the coffee?"

Christie turned from the refrigerator shamefacedly. "I suppose you'll think this is awful, but I've never made coffee in my life. I don't know how."

Marge's eyebrows went up. She made no comment, however, but went quickly to work measuring water into the coffeepot.

"You can set the table in the dining room," she said over her shoulder. "Miss Allard likes to observe the niceties, though I'd be happy to eat right here in the kitchen. Set a place for Alan Bennett, too, will you?"

"He's the minister, isn't he?" Christie asked as she headed for the dining-room door. Then she paused and looked around at Marge. "Is he—is he awfully—well, *like* a minister? I mean stuffy and terribly religious?"

There was a long silence from the stove as Marge measured coffee into the pot and lighted the burner under it.

"You sound as though you don't altogether approve of ministers," she said after a while.

Christie went into the dining room and began opening drawers in the mahogany sideboard, looking for a luncheon cloth and silverware.

"It isn't that," she called back. "It's just that I'd hate to have to be on my best behavior around some old sober-sides all the time."

There was a choked sound from the kitchen as if Marge were suddenly short of breath. Then she came into the dining room carrying cream and sugar, and her eyes were twinkling in a way that puzzled Christie.

"This is going to be an awful shock to you," Marge said. "But not only will you be eating lunch with a minister—brace yourself!—you'll also be eating it with a missionary. Me."

Christie dropped a spoon and bent to pick it up, hiding her blush. She couldn't have gotten off to a worse start with Marge Molloy if she had tried. But how could she have guessed? Missionaries went to darkest Africa. She had hardly expected to meet one in her aunt's kitchen.

"I—I'm sorry," she stammered. "I didn't know——"

24

"Okay," Marge said cheerfully. "Don't make it any worse. I forgive you and I'm sure Alan will, too. Suppose you go to the front door and tell him he'd better come in and wash up so we can sit down when your aunt gets here."

"The front door!" Christie repeated, the awful truth beginning to dawn on her. "You mean that young man out there, the one with the red hair——"

"Is Alan Bennett, our minister?" Marge said dryly. "Right. You catch on quickly."

"Oh, dear!" Christie wailed. "I thought he was just the gardener. I brushed right past him and wouldn't let him take my bag or anything."

"That might have hurt the gardener's feelings," Marge said, her tone sober, "but I imagine it gave Alan a laugh. Never mind, I'll go call him and you can do as the stories say, compose yourself."

But before Marge got as far as the front door, the screen opened again and closed in a quiet, ladylike fashion. There was no mistaking who had entered this time. Aunt Amelia was home.

3

Phone Call for Christie

One of the things Christie had always liked about her aunt was her straightforward matter-of-factness. Now Aunt Amelia greeted her with a peck on the cheek, the touch of a hand on her shoulder, and somehow Christie felt she had been as warmly welcomed to Leola as if her aunt's manner had been effusive.

The bulldog had followed his mistress into the house and now sat looking up at her adoringly, his stub of a tail thumping the floor. When she glanced his way, he snuffled and drooled a little in an excess of affection.

"Restrain yourself, Shelley," Aunt Amelia told him. "I've only been gone a couple of hours, you ridiculous old thing."

Shelley, whom the rest of the world apparently called Fatso, wriggled all over at being spoken to by his goddess.

Aunt Amelia ignored this adolation. "You've seen your room, of course?" she asked Christie.

"Yes, and I love it," Christie said. It seemed good to have someone in her life again who was "family." She hadn't realized how alone she had been feeling.

Aunt Amelia nodded and took off the old gray hat that was her favorite style and which sat loftily atop gray coronet braids. These braids had once grown on her own head but were now detachable. As always, she was neat and immaculate, and where others might wilt on a day like this, her gray silk frock managed to look as if she had just put it on. When she had pulled off the white kid gloves she wore for state occasions, she went upstairs to freshen up for lunch.

Marge paused on a trip to the dining room to nudge Fatso affectionately with her toe. "Isn't he the limit? I love to cuddle him, but it's no use, his heart belongs to Aunt Amelia."

Alan Bennett had been summoned indoors and had made a quick change. The overalls had been discarded for tan trousers and a sport shirt, and the grubbiness had been washed from his hands. Marge introduced him, and he held out a friendly hand to Christie.

"I didn't get a chance to welcome you properly earlier," he said. "You were a bit too quick for me."

Christie always hated the way her fair skin could burn with embarrassment. She put her hand into his, feeling thoroughly uncomfortable and not knowing what to say.

Aunt Amelia came downstairs and they sat down to an informal luncheon in the dining room. Christie unfolded her napkin, reached for her water glass, and found herself in the middle of the grace which Alan Bennett was saying. Since everyone else's head was bowed, she hoped her blunder hadn't been noticed.

26

Alan's words were brief, and in a moment the others looked up and began to talk as they assembled assorted sandwiches.

"Did you get Aurora Gomez back to town all right?" Alan asked Christie. "We're very grateful for your trouble."

She nodded. "It wasn't any trouble. She seemed anxious enough to get home. What made her run away in the first place?"

"Probably no one thing," Marge said. "Just a building up of resentment toward that kind of life."

"Nonsense!" Aunt Amelia looked up from cutting her large club sandwich into dainty wedges. "You probably coddle her, Marjory. These people should learn to make the best of what they have."

"Anyway, Christie," Marge said dryly, "you furnished her the thrill of her life this morning when you brought her out to camp in a cab. The whole place was buzzing with it and she's something of a heroine at the moment. As soon as this slack time ends she'll be out working in the field and the seven days' wonder will be over."

Christie sipped her coffee and looked at Marge, puzzled. "How did you know about the cab?"

"I was out at the camp nursery school when you arrived. It was all I could manage to keep that whole batch of kids from pouring outside to swarm around the taxi."

"Marjory," Aunt Amelia explained, "is with the Division of Home Missions of the National Council of Churches. I must say I don't wholly approve of what she is trying to do out at the Allard camp, but since your father is in full ownership, I have nothing to say."

Christie saw Marge and Alan exchange glances and sensed some undercurrent which she did not understand. Alan reached for the peanut butter jar and gently changed the subject.

"How did your meeting go this morning, Miss Allard?"

Aunt Amelia shook her head grimly. "No one had any brilliant ideas. Vandalism goes on constantly. Last night somebody got into the old Montgomery house out on the north edge of town and did a lot of damage. But all our town fathers do is wring their hands and scowl and brag about what will happen if ever they lay hands on the culprits. At least it's a beginning that several of them agree with me that the trouble stems from that eyesore of a Mexican slum right in the Allard Company's grounds."

Christie saw the light in Marge's eyes as the girl put down her coffee cup.

"That's too easy an out," Marge said indignantly. "The town of Leola has enough to be ashamed of without looking for a scapegoat. I'll agree that plenty needs to be mended out at the camp, but that's not the fault of the Mexican-Americans."

Somewhat to Christie's surprise, her aunt did not seem to resent Marge's sharp words. In fact, she looked as though she might enjoy a rousing good argument.

"What about the Olivera boy?" she demanded. "The police are already keeping an eye on him."

Alan broke in soothingly: "There's a way out of all this, so let's take it easy. I don't think the solution lies in making accusations or calling names."

Before Aunt Amelia could reply, the telephone in the living room rang and she excused herself and went to answer it.

Christie spoke her own bewilderment as her aunt went off. "What did she mean about the Olivera boy? I believe he was at the station this morning with John Macdonald to meet Aurora and he seemed a pleasant, quiet sort of person."

"That was Rafael," Alan said. "He's a fine boy. He comes over to the church to borrow books from me every now and then. And he never misses a service out at camp. His is one of the Protestant families. No, it's his twelve-year-old brother, Lopez, Miss Allard meant."

"Lopez would be all right, too, if he had a chance," Marge said.

Aunt Amelia came back into the room and nodded at her niece. "It's for you, Christine."

Christie rose in surprise. "I don't know anyone who would call me here."

"It's that new reporter from the Leola *Record*," her aunt explained. "He wants to interview you. I told him you were too tired to see him today, but I expect you'd better talk to him and make an appointment."

"But why ever would he want——?" Christie began as she moved toward the door and Marge answered her unfinished question.

"This is Allard-town, remember? And your last name is Allard."

Christie went into the living room and picked up the receiver. "Hello? This is Christine Allard."

"Hello," said an informal voice at the other end of the wire. "This is Tom Webb, star reporter. In Leola, Miss Allard, that means only reporter. When can I come out and get the story of your life?"

"I'm afraid my life hasn't much story to it," Christine said. "There isn't anything to tell."

"That's what you think." Tom Webb sounded as if he were used to getting what he wanted. "How about Saturday morning, that's tomorrow. Say ten o'clock?"

"You'll be wasting your time," Christine told him, amazed by his brashness.

There was a brief pause and then the voice went cheerily on. "That's all right. I'm paid to waste it. Do you want to make it ten o'clock?"

She was tempted to say "No," and hang up, but she suspected that if she did he'd turn up tomorrow morning at ten o'clock anyway. Besides, she didn't like his ready agreement that interviewing her would be a waste of time.

"All right," she said curtly. "Ten o'clock."

"Thanks a lot. See you tomorrow," he said, and rang off.

She hung up the receiver and went back to the dining room.

"I knew reporters in Chicago could be awfully fresh," she said, "but I don't see how a small-town newspaper can keep anyone like that."

"He's from Chicago," Marge told her, "and he's a good reporter. A lot of people think he's better than the *Record* has ever had before. Besides, the town ladies all like him. Well, back to work for me."

She carried her dishes out to the kitchen and the others followed her example. Alan said he had some calls to make that afternoon and further work to do on Sunday's sermon. Before he went off, he gave Christie a quick smile. "It's nice to have you here, Christine."

"The name's Christie," she said. "Please."

"Good," he agreed. "I like that better." And he breezed off to dress more formally for his calls.

Christie turned back to her aunt. "What on earth can I tell this Tom Webb tomorrow? There isn't any sense to his interviewing me."

Marge said dryly, "Maybe you can tell him about the wonderful job your father is doing out at the Allard plant."

The irritation that had been pricking Christine on and off ever since she'd left home that morning, plus the general weariness that had enveloped her in this wilting heat, spilled over suddenly.

"I haven't seen my father since I was nine years old," she told Marge. "I don't know anything about what he's doing at the Allard plant, and I wish people would stop looking at me as if I were responsible."

Marge's wide mouth spread in a grin. "You're not as quiet as you look, are you, Christie Allard? Sorry I stepped on your toes. Maybe that reporter will get a story after all. Well, I'm going back to camp."

"Let me drive you for once," Aunt Amelia said. "It's such a hot day and that's a long, dusty walk."

"No, thanks," said Marge airily. "You know my rules on that." And off she went with a last wave for Christie.

Aunt Amelia was scraping dishes, putting them into her electric dish washer, and Christie set about helping her. It seemed that her aunt had domestic help in a girl who came in twice a week, but otherwise she managed by herself.

"A fiddle for Marjory's rules!" Aunt Amelia said. "Yet I can't help respecting her attitude. When there's a real need she wouldn't hesitate to call on the mayor for a lift. But she wouldn't ask just for herself. She saves us all for emergencies. I can't approve of some of her notions, but I respect that girl. Tell me, Christine, what have you heard from your father since your mother's death?"

The sudden question took Christie by surprise. But

there was nothing she needed to conceal from Aunt Amelia.

"He wrote me a letter and said I could count on going on to college if I wanted to and that the checks for my support would keep right on coming. He said I could write him about my plans. Plans!"

She couldn't help the indignation that crept into the word. In all these years he'd never written to her at all. He'd simply gone out of her life and Eve's, except for the checks he had sent. A few years ago he had married again. Now he just popped up and wrote about sending her money, which of course she wasn't going to accept.

"He's probably concerned about you," her aunt said, wiping the sink dry with a dish cloth.

"Concerned!" Christie echoed. "I don't want his checks. I don't want anything from him at all!"

Aunt Amelia looked at her appraisingly. "Trouble with you is that you're all worn out, physically and emotionally. Why don't you run up to that new room of yours and take a nap?"

The last thing Christie felt was sleepy, but she welcomed the thought of getting away by herself. Her aunt was right. If she didn't try to relax, she might say things she didn't mean.

She agreed to the suggestion and went quickly out of the kitchen. Upstairs, as she crossed the sitting room, she noticed two framed photographs on a bookcase and paused to look at them. One was of a gray-haired woman with a straight mouth and decided chin line, who bore a strong resemblance to Aunt Amelia. The other picture showed a man's face, strong, unsmiling, with deep-set eyes. So this was the forceful old man who had left his stamp on Leola, made his name a respected one in the town? These two were her Allard grandparents and it seemed strange to think that she knew so little about them, when they were her father's parents.

She went into her room and lowered the shades on the front window and the one at the side. With the shades drawn to shut out the heat, it was relatively cool and restful in the blue dimness of forget-me-nots. She slipped out of her suit, kicked off her suède shoes, and got between cool sheets. She wished she could fall asleep. When she was asleep she could forget Chicago. Forget the emptiness that Eve had once filled. Forget Phil, who had been her companion through the last happy year or so. Sleeping helped, unless she dreamed. Then, sometimes, she woke up crying.

But now sleep would not come. Instead, old, unwanted memories returned. She was eight when her father first went away to his new job in the East. There had been letters from him, every week at first. Later, they'd begun to drop off a little. Then, when she was nine, he had come back to Chicago, come back at Christmastime. He had not stayed at the apartment, which had seemed strange to Christie. Eve had said he was just being "impossible." Two days before Christmas he had taken Christie downtown to the Loop and they'd gone to see Santa Claus at Marshall Field's, even though she was too old to believe in such things any more. They'd visited toy departments and then, for lunch, he took her to an elegant restaurant and talked to her in the grown-up way she had liked. It had been a serious conversation about her growing-up years and the things she must believe and hold to.

After lunch they walked down Michigan Avenue, looking at the beautiful bright windows, and her hand had been clasped as firmly in his as if she'd been a very little girl, instead of nine years old. Not until afterward did she realize that that visit had been a final good-by. He'd looked long into her eyes and he'd kissed her tenderly. And then he'd gone out of her life and had never come back. Not another letter had he written to her, leaving hers unanswered. For year after long year the hurt had been like a sickness inside her.

At first she had wanted to shut out the things Eve said against him, had wished that her mother wouldn't talk about him at all. She'd hated hearing about his selfishness, about how he had wanted to uproot his wife from the place which had always been home to her, just for the sake of his own ambition. And about how dull and serious he always was, though Christie had never found his seriousness dull.

32

But later, when he had not answered her letters, had not so much as sent her a present at Christmastime, or taken any interest in her, she had begun to believe that the things Eve said about him were true. She had ended up by feeling just the way her mother did. Agnes O'Regan had thrown her own influence onto the scale, too. Eve was Agnes's darling. She could do no wrong. And those who hurt her were violently disliked by Agnes. Hence the remark Agnes had made this morning in the station, that if ever Christie saw her father, she should give him the back of her hand. A good Irish phrase of repudiation. But Christie knew she was safe from seeing him here. Thanks to her father's lack of interest in the Allard Company, he was not likely to show up in Leola.

By making an effort she drew her thoughts away from him and turned them upon the new people she had met during this crowded day. The prickly Aurora. Marge Molloy, who spoke her mind frankly, but whom Christie had liked. The surprising redheaded young minister, Alan Bennett, who fitted no conception of any minister Christie had imagined. The reporter, Tom Webb, with his irritating manner on the phone. John Macdonald and the way his cool gray eyes had appraised her as if he did not approve of what he saw.

Tears came and she longed to be away from strange eyes which judged without knowing her; longed to be back within the protective circle of Eve's little world where the whole purpose of life was to be gay and happy, to have fun. Life here in Leola might not be so quiet as she had expected, and it certainly wasn't going to be any fun.

4

Tom Webb, Reporter

Christine was having a late lone breakfast in the kitchen Saturday morning when the doorbell rang to announce Tom Webb. Aunt Amelia, looming large in a lavender print frock, came out to summon her.

"Finish your coffee first. Mr. Webb can wait," she instructed.

Christie, who had been dreading the interview ever since getting out of bed, sipped her coffee slowly, postponing the moment of facing the reporter.

"I don't know what to say to him," she protested for the dozenth time.

"Don't worry; he'll ask questions," Aunt Amelia assured her. "Just don't answer any you don't care to answer. I'll be right there, and if he gets too inquisitive, I'll handle matters."

Thus reassured, Christie rose from the table. She had dressed for the morning in a crisp white cotton blouse and a swirly navy-blue skirt with red fish appliqued about its hem, a gift from whimsical Eve. She had put on barefoot peasant sandals to keep her as cool as reasonably possible. Aunt Amelia raised an eyebrow at the sandals, but only said, "At least you don't paint your toenails."

Christie walked into the living room ahead of her aunt and Tom Webb laid down the murder mystery Aunt Amelia had been reading and stood up.

"My favorite detective." He grinned.

Miss Amelia Allard ignored the comment and introduced Christie.

The reporter was rather stocky and not very tall. In his smile there was both a faint impudence and an engaging honesty. He looked Christie over quite frankly and she found herself resenting the inspection.

"Good morning, Miss Christine Allard," he said. "It's good to see another Chicagoan in our metropolis."

"Good morning," Christie said coolly, sitting down in an armchair which had its back to the light and left her in comfortable shadow.

Aunt Amelia chose a corner of the sofa, but sat as stiffly upright as if a board had been at her back. She waited and Christie waited, while Tom Webb took out a small notebook and flipped over the pages.

"How do you like Leola?" he asked. "I expect that's the first thing the town will want to know." He waited with his pencil poised as if he hung on her words, but Christie suspected a faint mockery in the pose. It was a little as if he were caricaturing a reporter at his own expense.

"I've just arrived," Christie said. "I don't know anything about Leola."

Tom Webb shook his head reproachfully. "Sorry, I can't use that at all."

Christie threw a quick look at her aunt, who seemed to see no necessity of coming to her aid.

"Well," she tried again, "I like your wide streets and big old trees."

"Likes—wide—streets," he mumbled, and scribbled in his book. Then he looked up. "How long are you planning to stay in Leola, Miss Allard?"

"As long as she likes," Aunt Amelia said quickly. "She is welcome to make this her home."

"I understand you've never been here before," Tom said, but his tone implied more than his words. Why, he seemed to be inquiring, had she never come to this town of her forebears?

Again Aunt Amelia answered for her. "It has never proved convenient for my niece to visit me until now."

Tom Webb glanced at Miss Allard and then back at Christie, and his thoughts were not concealed by his wry grin. Obviously he would have preferred Miss Amelia Allard's absence to her presence.

"After all," he said to Christie, "you're Lawrence Al-

35

lard's daughter and Josh Allard's granddaughter. Your grandfather practically built this town and he definitely built the Allard Company. You can't blame people for being interested in the fact that you've come to Leola for the first time. It seems to me it's a harmless enough curiosity which you shouldn't mind satisfying."

"My niece has nothing to conceal," Aunt Amelia said with dignity. "But neither she nor I care for publicity. She tried to make that clear to you on the telephone yesterday."

Christie's quick ear caught something like, "Oh, brother!" muttered beneath Tom Webb's breath, but her aunt did not hear. For the first time she began to enjoy the interview a little. This brash young reporter was up against no mean adversary in Aunt Amelia and she herself had no difficult part to play. She was only the ball they tossed back and forth. But she blessed her reliance on her aunt too soon.

From the veranda there came a bumping sound at the screen door, a snuffling and a snorting.

"Not now, Shelley," said Aunt Amelia. "We're busy. You can come in later."

But Fatso-Shelley was not to be shunted aside in such a manner. The snorting became more insistent and Aunt Amelia sighed and went to the door. She was back at once with a note in her hand, delivered by Fatso.

"The way they use that dog!" she said. "My next-door neighbor needs me and I'll have to run over for a few minutes." She glanced from Christie to Tom Webb and back again. "I'm sure you can handle this interview yourself, Christine. I'll be back before long."

She went off before Christie could object. Tom Webb brightened perceptibly and leaned back in his chair.

"Remarkable woman, your aunt," he said. "A woman with the courage of her convictions. She is so determined to intimidate me that she almost succeeds. Now, then—this is a lot better with just the two of us."

Christie regarded him uneasily and waited.

He flipped the notebook shut. "I always hate stage props. This was to impress your aunt. What I can't

36

remember in my head isn't worth remembering. Have you seen your father lately, Miss Allard?"

"No, I haven't," Christie said, and then added primly, "I don't wish to answer any personal questions."

Tom smiled, but his eyes were watchful. "As I understand it, your father had a blowup with your grandfather and never set foot in the town again. A lot of people think it strange that he inherited the plant at all. How old were you the last time you saw your father, Miss Allard?"

"Nine," said Christie. Let him make of that what he would.

To her relief he changed the subject. "Have you been out to the plant yet?"

Christie shook her head. "I only reached town yesterday."

"What about driving the Gomez girl to the camp from the train? You must have seen something of the place. What did you think of it?"

There was a step in the hallway and to Christie's relief Alan Bennett appeared in the door.

"Good morning, Christie," he said. " 'Morning, Tom. Do you need any help with this young man, Christie? I know how persistent he can be."

Tom grinned at the minister, unabashed. "I have to get my story, don't I? Everybody in Leola wants to know what Christine Allard is doing here in town and what she thinks of us."

"You might use the obvious," Alan Bennett said, "since it's the truth. Christie has just lost her mother. When Miss Allard asked her to come here for a visit until she decided what she wanted to do, she accepted. She doesn't know a thing about Leola yet because she hasn't been here twenty-four hours. I'll grant you that isn't a very colorful story, but it's all there is at the moment."

The young minister lounged in the doorway that led in from the hall, looking comfortable and easy.

Tom Webb seemed to know when he'd met his match.

"Okay," he said. "I'll see what airy nothings I can embroider to satisfy my panting public. All two of 'em." He turned back to the object of his interview. "So that's what

37

they call you? Christie. Only bit of human interest I've been able to pick up."

Alan laughed good-naturedly. "From what I've seen, you've made stories out of considerably less."

"Thanks," Tom said. "In the meantime, I suppose I can take a picture?"

There was no point in refusing, so Christie sat up stiffly in her chair, waiting for him to retrieve the camera and flash bulbs he had cached under the coffee table.

"Relax," he told her when he had the camera aloft, squinting into the finder.

But Christie could only stare at him tensely while he snapped the picture. He reproved her with a shake of his head.

"You look as though you wanted to bite me. Tell her a funny story, Mr. Bennett. I'm fresh out this morning."

Christie's gaze moved to the minister. He smiled in amusement mingled with sympathy. She smiled back and the bulb flashed.

"That's better," Tom said. "Thanks, Christie. I'll be back to see you when you know more about Leola. And when I can catch you without a bodyguard."

Christie said "Good-by" gravely, but Tom did not leave at once.

"There's just one more thing," he said. "And this time I'm not being funny and I'm not kidding. Since I've let you off so easily, perhaps you'll answer just one direct question for me. Are you likely to inherit any part of the Allard Company?" He stood there looking at her intently, his wry mouth unsmiling.

"Why, I don't know," Christie said, startled. "I—I don't see why I should."

"It might be a good idea for you to get out there and look things over sometime. Just in case. See what you think of Mr. Tidings and Company—he's the general manager. And of John Macdonald. Well, I'll have to run along now. Suppose we get together one of these days and talk Chicago."

It was just as well he didn't wait for an answer. His colossal cheekiness left Christie at a complete loss. She heard him whistling as he went down the street, and she stood up indignantly.

"What an impossible person! Thank you for helping me out, Mr. Bennett."

"I wish you'd call me Alan," the minister said. "I haven't the years to go with all this formality. And you're already Christie to me. But don't hold Tom's manner against him. There's something pretty solid about him. We see eye to eye on a number of things."

The screen door slammed just then and their discussion ended as Marge Molloy came limply into the room. Again her shoes were dusty and perspiration speckled her nose. She dropped wearily into a chair and fanned herself with a magazine from the coffee table.

"Trouble?" Alan asked. He left the support of the doorjamb and came into the room.

Christie didn't know whether to stay or to go. Neither of them was paying any attention to her, so probably it was all right to stay.

"Exactly one child showed up for nursery school this morning. One child out of forty-six."

"What's up?" Alan asked.

"I'm not sure, but I can guess. It's been managed subtly. All of a sudden all those parents who were so eager to have their children stay home from the fields and play games and learn a little English have whisked them right out from under my nose. Either the children are sick this morning, or their mothers have taken them out to the field."

"But why?" Alan demanded. "Why on earth——"

"You know," Marge said. "It's Tidings. Old Tidy. He hasn't got anything against the school except the cost of the building that John Macdonald wangled out of him. But you know the situation between him and Mac. Nobody's ever opposed Tidy's authority as general manager before. Mac was put on the job over his head and nothing would make Tidy happier than to see Mac fail. The workers are afraid of Tidy. If he lets it be known that he thinks it's better for the young children to stay with their mothers, and maybe do a little illegal work to help the budget along, who is going to argue with him?"

Restlessly Alan paced the length of the room and back. Christie saw his eyes rest briefly on her, and then shift away. Something disturbing appeared to be going on here in Leola that she didn't understand.

"What do you plan to do?" Alan asked of Marge.

"You know very well," Marge said. "Right now I'm hot and tired and angry and discouraged. But I've been all those things before. I was sent here to do a job in this town. I haven't been here long enough to get the full picture, but I'm beginning to see it. Pretty soon I'll know enough about who thinks what to start talking to people."

"I doubt that you can talk to Tidings," Alan said.

"I know that. If it weren't for what's at stake, I might feel sorry for him. He's a pretty sick man, both physically and emotionally. He has a twisted notion that there's something he has to prove, and a sensible appeal doesn't affect him."

"Never mind," Alan said, "there are plenty of us ready to back you up. Maybe I can help a little with my sermon Sunday. Anyway, how about you two girls coming over to church with me now to help me stuff envelopes?"

Marge excused herself and stood up. Christie did not find the prospect exciting, but since Alan had come to her help so recently, she couldn't very well refuse. She followed them into the hot sunlight and saw Aunt Amelia returning from next door.

5

The Church Without a View

Fatso waddled devotedly at Aunt Amelia's heels, remaining aloof when Marge bent to pat him.

"How did you come out with that impertinent young reporter, Christine?" Aunt Amelia asked.

"All right, I think," Christie said uncertaintly, "thanks to the way Mr. Bennett rescued me."

"Good," Aunt Amelia said. "Where are you off to now?"

Alan explained, and Aunt Amelia pushed Fatso away with her toe. "Do take this creature with you. He never gets enough exercise. Go with Marjory, Shelley. Don't be so ungrateful."

Miss Allard went on toward her own steps and Fatso, thus abandoned, sighed mournfully and waddled after Marge.

"I'm anxious to show you Glenview Church," Alan told Christie. "I assure you it's unique in this town and I'm very proud of it."

Christie wondered at Marge's chuckle, and decided to ask a question which had puzzled her ever since the cab driver's remark the day before. "I understand Aunt Amelia caused something of a scandal in town by leaving her regular church to come to Glenview. Can anybody tell me what happened?"

"I'd have given anything to see her the day she walked out," Marge said. "When it pleases her, she can do the most surprising about-face. She simply decided that the old church was growing too big, too rich, and too snobbish. She said she liked human beings and she thought God did, too. And she said Alan Bennett needed her support and that she felt he was a lot nearer to God in his preaching. So over to Glenview she came, and that was that. Sometimes I think she has a saving streak of Josh Allard in her after all. Though most people say she's like her mother."

Alan chuckled, remembering. "My congregation swelled by at least twenty of your aunt Amelia's followers the very next Sunday."

As they turned a corner and walked down the next block, Marge said, "Look, Christie, there's Glenview on ahead."

Christie looked down the usual straight Leola street, with its arching branches overhead. Down the block a flight of stone steps rose to a small roofed entryway, but that was all there was. No churchlike edifice rose against

41

the sky, though a church sign at the foot of the steps announced that this was Glenview Church and gave the minister's name and the time of Sunday service.

"The church that never grew up." Alan chuckled at her bewilderment. "They got the basement built just when the depression hit. Later there was a war shortage of materials. And all along there was never enough money in the small congregation to finish the building. But it's my first church and you'd better be respectful. I'm pretty fond of it."

As they came closer Christie saw that a wire fence enclosed a large space beyond the tiny entrance structure. No higher than the top of the fence rose the "roof" of Glenview Church. It was a roof that had once been intended for the floor of the building that was to rise above. Only the basement had been completed. From Glenview, she began to suspect, you would not have much of a view of anything except the sky overhead.

Alan led the way up the steps and unlocked the door. The 'entrance way that should have opened into the church proper was merely a tiny hallway from which a second flight of stairs led down to the basement. Apparently this was the church itself. Alan went down and the girls followed him, Fatso clumping after them. At the foot of the stairs Christie saw that various small rooms opened on one side, the church on the other. Alan led the way down an aisle in the latter and Christie saw small sections of wooden pews lined up across a big room to seat the congregation. Up in front was what must originally have been intended for the entertainment platform of a basement meeting and recreation room. But it was now the altar. At the left of the platform was a small room which Alan had turned into a study.

Fatso seemed to have been here before, because he snuffled over to what must have been a favorite corner and promptly went to sleep.

Bookshelves rose solidly against one wall of the study and Alan indicated them proudly to Christie. "Built those myself. But your aunt Amelia gave me this when she joined my church," and he tapped a handsome walnut desk in the center of the room. "She couldn't stand the ex-schoolroom desk I was using. Sit down, girls."

Marge and Christie seated themselves on two hard, straight chairs and Christie looked about her wonderingly. Fencing swords were crossed on the wall behind the desk, and there was a silver cup, probably won for some athletic prowess during Alan's school years. On one wall was a single painting of Jesus and the children. Christie noted that the young faces represented many races, and reflected the warmth in their Teacher's eyes.

Piled on the desk was a stack of mimeographed sheets, and Alan set the girls to folding a portion to put into envelopes.

"There are some regulars we mail these out to every week," Alan explained to Christie, turning on a light over the desk. "Church members who have moved away and want to keep in touch, or those who are confined to bed. Most of them are handed out in church Sunday morning."

"And he holds his breath all through Saturday," Marge said, "for fear there'll be a birth or a death that comes at the last minute and doesn't get announced."

Alan glanced around, listening. "There's someone coming," he said, and stepped to the door, his hand outstretched. "Good morning, Father Paul. Come in and join us."

The tall black-garbed Catholic priest came into the study. He was white-haired and lean and impressively dignified, until you caught the twinkle in his eyes that made you suspect a sense of humor and a warm heart. He knew Marge and held out a friendly hand to greet her. Then his keen gaze turned upon Christie, and Alan introduced him as Father Cudahy. There was friendliness in his handclasp as he smiled at her.

"You're the young lady I am especially anxious to thank," he said. "When I saw the light here in Alan's study I came down to express my gratitude for the aid given Aurora Gomez. Now I can express it directly to you. I was most uneasy about having her make the trip home alone, after the way she had run off and frightened her poor mother half to death."

Again Christie found herself embarrassed over being thanked for the little she had done for Aurora.

"I was glad to do it," she told him.

Father Cudahy took the chair Alan brought for him and nodded his approval. "You made a great impression on Aurora, Miss Allard, your manners, your clothes, even your nail polish!"

Christie glanced in astonishment at the light polish on her nails. She recalled Aurora's broken nails with their peeling traces of scarlet.

"I thought she didn't like me at all," Christie said. "She seemed a little resentful most of the trip."

Father Cudahy was understanding. "It's natural that her reaction toward you should be tinged with something of the sort."

"Just having the name of Allard seemed to weigh against me," Christie puzzled. "In fact, that's been either for or against me with nearly everyone I've met in Leola. Why won't people just let me be myself?"

"You can't escape being an Allard in Leola," Alan reminded her. "But you've already done something for the name by being nice to Aurora."

Father Cudahy went on to congratulate Marge on her work in the camp school. Since the nursery school was non-sectarian, all the children attended it, regardless of religious faith, and Father Cudahy had been getting pleased reports from some of the Catholic mothers.

"I'm afraid Mr. Tidings is trying to discourage the whole thing," Marge said. "Only one child appeared for the class this morning."

"Mr. Tidings has been growing increasingly difficult," Father Cudahy admitted. "I am afraid he is barely containing himself until Mr. Macdonald's contract runs out. But it is not just the Allard plant or Mr. Tidings that is the big bad wolf in all this. We have the problem of the whole community to face. A pressure of strong public opinion could force changes and back up John Macdonald's efforts. Yet even this week I've had complaints from my own parishioners."

Alan looked at him quickly. "In what way?"

"As you know, I hold a nine-o'clock mass at the camp

44

on Sunday morning, just as you go out there for your service at ten." He turned to Christie to explain. "The small building where Miss Molloy teaches the children also serves as church, meetinghouse, and recreation hall. So we men of the cloth have to take turns. The objection was made because I go myself, instead of sending a younger priest and celebrating nine-o'clock mass in my own church."

"What was your answer?" Alan asked.

The priest's eyes were bright. "That I would continue to go where I was most needed on God's work—to the camp."

"Father Paul, we have a job to do in this town," Alan said and held out his hand. Father Cudahy shook it warmly. As he rose to go, he had a last word for Christie. "It would be kind and helpful if you could find a way to continue your friendship with Aurora Gomez, Miss Allard."

Christie smiled uncertainly, not knowing what to answer. Her "friendship" with Aurora Gomez was not exactly something to build upon.

More visitors arrived shortly after Father Cudahy left. Rafael Olivera, accompanied by a younger boy, appeared at the door of Alan's study.

"Good morning, Rafael, Lopez," Alan said, and introduced Lopez to Christie.

Lopez Olivera was a younger, heavier edition of his handsome brother. Twelve years old perhaps, or a little younger, and with the same velvety dark eyes and white teeth. But Lopez had an individuality of his own and it was easy to see that he was a less amiable, and more intense person than his brother. At the moment he was tossing a very white, clean baseball in his hand.

Marge Molloy looked up from the folding of bulletins. "Hi, there. boys. Isn't that a new baseball, Lopez?"

Lopez held the ball out to her proudly. "Señor Mac give it to me today. He buy it himself, just for me. A ball like they play with on the big teams."

His pride was so evident that they all went out of their way to admire the ball. Even Fatso woke up and ambled in to see what was so interesting. Lopez noticed the dog

45

at once and knelt to make friends with him, even holding out the ball for him to sniff. Being wary of young people, Fatso greeted these overtures with restraint, but at least he accepted Lopez without the growls he reserved for Christie.

Rafael had brought some borrowed books back to Alan and as he gave them to the minister, Christie noted that the top title was about Mexico.

"Was most good, this one," Rafael said, tapping the bright jacket. "But this time, it is possible, you have a book about the United States?"

"Of course I have," Alan said.

Lopez, finding little to interest him in the small room, gave up trying to make friends with Fatso and went out the study door, tossing the ball in one hand. Books, apparently, were not an interest he shared with his older brother. Alan began taking volumes down from the shelves and the eagerness with which Rafael looked at them was touching.

"By the way," Alan said, as Rafael turned the pages of a book about his own state, Texas, "I know Lopez isn't much of a reader, but I have a book here which might interest him. It's very simply written, a book for younger children, but it's about some of the great baseball players. Perhaps you could help him a bit in reading it."

Rafael's eyes lighted up and he looked around for his brother. Marge, who was nearest the door, stepped into the church to call Lopez. Christie saw her turn with her finger on her lips and beckon delightedly to Alan. Christie tiptoed to the door, too, to see what was happening.

There in the center aisle between the pews stood Lopez Olivera. It was evident that the church had ceased to exist around him, and that he was out on the broad expanse of a baseball diamond. His back was to them as he wound up to a complicated pitch, swinging his arm in a wide arc. Christie stifled a gasp, lest he send the ball straight through the glass doors at the rear of the church, but it never left the boy's fingers. A moment later he leaped high in the air, obviously making a difficult catch, and banged down against the pews as he alighted.

It was his horrified older brother who broke the spell.

"Lopez!" Rafael cried. "In the church is not for baseball!"

Lopez turned, looking sheepish, but still lost in his make-believe. "You see it, the catch I make, Rafael?"

"Don't scold him," Alan said. "He forgot where he was. That was a whopping good catch, Lopez. Only after this, suppose you play outside. In the meantime, I have a book here that you may like."

Alan showed the boy the baseball book and Lopez was at least interested in the photographs of the players.

By the time Rafael had selected the books he wanted to borrow, the bulletin folding was finished. Alan remained behind with the two boys for a few moments as the girls left the study, and Marge nodded knowingly to Christie.

"Alan's making a check about the vandalism last night out on the east side of town. I don't think any of the camp boys had a hand in it, but it's a good idea to let them know they might be suspected. Christie, I get so angry when I look at a boy like Lopez. He lives and breathes and dreams baseball. And how little opportunity he has to play."

"What are his parents like?" Christie asked.

"Mrs. Olivera is an extremely intelligent woman. She has a high-school education and speaks English perfectly. Unfortunately, her husband doesn't speak it well and wants Spanish spoken at home. So the boys get very little practice."

"What does Mr. Olivera thing about Lopez and his urge to play baseball?"

Marge sighed. "I'm afraid he thinks both boys should be out in the fields earning something, and never mind foolish games."

"But Lopez is so young."

"There are those who feel that any child over six can help in the fields," Marge said dryly. "That's one reason it's hard for Mexican-American children of migrants to get an education. Sometimes the income of an entire family will amount to less than five hundred dollars a year."

"How do they live?" Christie gasped.

"I've seen how they live down in the Valley of the Rio

Grande. I've seen the wretched shacks without plumbing or water. Some Texas communities are waking up to their need, but not all, by any means."

"What about Aurora's schooling?" Christie asked. "Will she finish high school?"

They'd reached the stairs to the church entrance and they climbed them slowly, waiting for Alan and the boys and Fatso to catch up.

"High school!" Marge echoed derisively. "She's never graduated from the eighth grade. And now she won't go back to classes with children so much younger."

They stepped into the bright, hot sunlight, but Christie hardly noticed the heat because of her distress.

"Marge, this is America! Doesn't everyone have to go to school?"

There was something sharp in the other girl's voice. "Not necessarily. Not always, when your grandfather came from Mexico."

Christie was silent all the way back to Aunt Amelia's. Somehow the realization that Aurora Gomez, who was just a year younger than herself, had never graduated from grade school touched her more acutely than anything else. In Eve's bright, untroubled, spendthrift world no one thought about the troubles of others. Her mother's cure for the world's ills was to turn off the news commentators, skip the gloomy headlines, refuse to be troubled. Whatever had penetrated to Christie had always seemed unreal and distant, things that happened to people so far away that they had little meaning for her.

But Aurora was right here. So was Lopez Olivera, that intensely eager boy with the yearning to play baseball. And Christie could not put these two out of her mind.

It was lunchtime when they got back to her aunt's, but Christie went first to her own room, wanting a few minutes to herself. Against one of the blue-shaded lamps on the dresser an enlarged snapshot had been propped. Christie picked it up, wondering what Aunt Amelia had left for her to see.

There were three people in the picture, but her first glance was for the tall, unsmiling man in the background. She remembered him with dark hair, but the snapshot showed it gray. In other ways he appeared the same, and looking at her father's face she felt the old twinge of hurt, turning quickly to resentment. The other two in the picture were a woman and a child. The woman was younger than he was and almost as tall. This would be his second wife, of course, and Christie studied her face intently. She looked rather plain and uninteresting, not lively and pretty like Eve. The child was a little girl. She had moved just as the shutter snapped and there was no telling what she looked like. Her hand was trustingly in her father's, and Christie remembered how once she had clung to his hand in just that way.

Christie turned the snapshot over and saw her father's writing on the back: "Myself, Mary, and our Janey on her fifth birthday."

She put the snapshot face down on the dresser. Why had Aunt Amelia left it in her room? Christie had a moment's urge to tear it up and toss the scraps in the wastebasket. Eve would have done so in a moment. But Christie could not. She went over to the bed and flung herself across it.

When Aunt Amelia came upstairs and tapped on her door to summon her for lunch, Christie mumbled that she wasn't hungry and her aunt went away, having the good sense not to urge her. Christie pressed her cheek into her pillow and tried to think herself back into her beautiful little bedroom in the North Shore apartment. Eve would be in the next room dressing. And in a little while the phone would ring in the hall and it would be Phil asking if she'd like to go to a movie tonight. But when she opened her eyes, she saw only the blue forget-me-nots on the walls of this little country bedroom. And if there was any flower Christie did not want for company, it was forget-me-nots.

6

Request from John Macdonald

Sunday morning Christie meant to stay in bed and not go to church with the others. But she had eaten no lunch the day before, and not much dinner last night, so she found herself ravenously hungry and unable to resist the fragrant odor of bacon and pancakes and coffee. She went down to breakfast, but managed to remain remote from all that went on around her. She spoke when she had to, but otherwise behaved as if she were somewhere else.

Alan glanced at her curiously once or twice, but made no comment. Marge put it all down to the humid heat that still enveloped the farm country. It was enough to leave anyone limp. Only Aunt Amelia recognized her mood and explained it to the others as impersonally as if Christie had not been at the table.

"It's what Evelyn, her mother, used to call going off into the solitudes. Lawrence used to do it, too, and it drove everyone crazy. It's a form of defense when one wishes to escape from reality."

Christie gave her aunt a startled look.

"I've been reading a book on psychology," Aunt Amelia said brightly. "I don't always read mysteries."

Alan laughed and Marge nodded in mock solemnity at Christie. "You'd better take warning. Don't become a borderline case."

After that, Christie had less success in holding herself aloof. Life in Leola had a surprising trick of nudging her into its moving tide.

There was to be no escaping church that morning. Aunt Amelia, Marge, Alan, all took it for granted that she would of course attend with her aunt. Alan went off to the camp early to conduct service there and Marge accompanied him in his little second hand car. Since she spoke more Spanish than he did, Alan relied on her to help him.

Aunt Amelia behaved as if everything was quite normal as she and Christie walked to church together. She did not mention her niece's retreat into silence again, nor did she say anything about the snapshot she had put in her room. Christie had slipped the picture under a stack of handkerchiefs in a dresser drawer and said nothing about it.

"I have a great respect for Alan Bennett," Aunt Amelia said as they moved along at a slow Sunday-morning pace. "He is a fine young man with the highest of ideals, but I cannot approve of the way he is trying to stir up a hornet's nest over these migrant workers. If he persists, he may find himself without a congregation."

"It does seem as though something ought to be done," Christie said mildly. "Did you know that Aurora Gomez hasn't even graduated from eighth grade?"

"That is neither my problem nor yours," Aunt Amelia pointed out. "There is no way of educating people who are constantly on the move. Besides, what would you be educating them for? These people are working at the level at which they are needed. They serve an economic purpose."

"But they're still human beings." Christie was a little surprised at her own persistence. "And it doesn't seem as if any human being ought to live in those shacks I saw at the Allard plant."

Aunt Amelia moved more briskly, despite the heat of the morning, and there was impatience in the quickening of her steps. "We must be realistic about these things, my dear. Those living quarters may easily represent luxury to these people. Certainly they are accustomed to nothing better in the Valley where they come from. This town has its own problems, Christie. We can't expect to take on anything so thankless and troublesome as the affairs of these transients."

Christie was silent. After all, she had enough unsolved problems of her own without concerning herself about something she could do nothing about.

51

The church basement was a relief after the soggy heat outside. Christie slipped into the pew beside her aunt, liking the feel of the cool, smooth-worn wood. The congregation was a small one and for the most part elderly, though Christie noted young faces here and there and suspected that it was Alan Bennett's presence which brought the young people. She was aware of curious looks turned in her direction and knew that this small portion of Leola was inspecting the new Allard.

She saw Marge Molloy come in with John Macdonald, that rather distant young man from the plant. Mac, as everyone seemed to call him. He spoke to Aunt Amelia as he took his place across the aisle and gave Christie the same courteous but distant greeting that he'd had for her that day at the station. She wondered again what it was he seemed to have against her.

Aunt Amelia nudged her as he took over his seat. "Your father put him in at the plant. Over Mr. Tidings' head. A foolish move, if ever I saw one."

The organ had begun to play and the young people of the choir were taking their places in rows of camp chairs set below the platform. There could be no choir loft in a basement church.

Alan came out of his study and mounted the platform, and Christie watched him with interest. This was the same red-headed young man whom she had mistaken for Aunt Amelia's gardener that first day in Leola. But there was a difference about him now that was more than a difference in clothes. The informality that made him seem so young had given way to a more serious bearing. As he walked across the platform Christie sensed purpose and determination.

After the first prayer and hymn and a song by the choir, Alan opened the Bible on the lectern. He had chosen two texts for the morning, he announced quietly, and then read them aloud.

The first was from Hebrews 13:2. "Be not forgetful to entertain strangers, for thereby some have entertained angels unaware."

The second was from Isaiah 41:6. "They helped every

one his neighbor; and every one said to his brother, Be of good courage."

Christie sensed her aunt's stiffening, as if she braced herself to resist Alan's words. The rest of the congregation merely regarded their minister with what was probably their usual mild Sunday-morning interest. Only a few in the room knew the direction his words might take.

He began quietly enough in general terms, speaking of the meaning of the texts he had taken. These words were not so remote as they might think, he pointed out. In fact, their advice was applicable to everyday living right here in Leola.

Outside the high windows of the church there was the languorous, humming warmth of a summer day. Behind Alan on the platform stood green plants and several baskets of flowers, gathered perhaps that very morning from Leola gardens. The young people in the black and white of choir gowns listened intently to their minister, and Christie knew by their manner that they liked and respected him.

Slowly Alan built toward the full meaning of his message. These neighbors, these brothers, were here at the very doors of Leola. Indeed, Leola entertained angels in an extremely unaware state, angels upon whom the very life of the town depended, but whom the citizens of the town treated as aliens. In today's world there were no aliens. Every man was your brother.

The normal rustlings and coughings of the congregation ceased as everyone listened attentively. Christie, still feeling herself a spectator whose main concern was interest in the spectacle, stole glances about the room, noting the visible evidence of reaction to Alan's words. John Macdonald looked pleased. Marge was obviously delighted. Aunt Amelia, however, was not affected, though there were others who were. This young minister had the knack of reaching out to his listeners and making them feel. Even Christie forgot that she was only a watcher and was moved by his words more than she had expected to be. He closed with a prayer, and again there was a hymn and the doxology, and the service was over.

53

Christie turned to her aunt. "Wasn't he wonderful?" she said warmly.

Aunt Amelia sniffed. "Yes, indeed. He can be a regular spellbinder, that young man. A dangerous gift if it isn't properly channeled."

"But don't you feel that what he said was right?" Christie asked.

"Not with my mind," her aunt said. "There is more to this question than our redheaded young minister has considered."

Christie glanced at her aunt with a sense of shock. All her life she had respected Aunt Amelia. Miss Amelia Allard, the wise, the capable, the bulwark who could even stand against Eve's emotional, will-o'-the-wisp qualities. Christie could remember when Eve had wanted to shut the door on Aunt Amelia because she was Lawrence's sister and must therefore be included in Eve's feud with her husband. But Amelia Allard had stood for no such nonsense. She'd made it clear that she was Eve's friend as well as Christie's. That she was *family,* and that no quarrel with her brother was going to be stretched to include her. And Eve had given up her attempt to freeze out Aunt Amelia. It was disturbing now to discover so unfeeling an attitude in someone Christie had always looked up to.

As they started down the aisle with the buzzing congregation about them, Marge slipped a hand through Christie's arm and leaned to whisper in her ear:

"Hooray for our side! He did it, Christie! Did you notice the way the women had their handkerchiefs out?"

"Not Aunt Amelia," Christie said.

Marge glanced back at Miss Allard. "The old ramrod! Never mind, we've made a start. In this one little corner we've got people thinking about something they've taken for granted until now."

Christie saw that John Macdonald had fallen into step beside her aunt and was talking to her. When they reached the outer sunlight, he turned to Christie.

"I'd like to include you, too," he said.

She looked at him, puzzled. "I'm sorry. I didn't hear what went before."

He explained as they turned down the sidewalk. "I was telling your aunt that I'd like an opportunity to talk to her for a few minutes in the near future, and she has invited me to stop in now on the way home. I'd like to include you, too, Miss Christine."

"Call her Christie," Marge protested. "She doesn't like Christine any more than I like Marjory. I hope you're going to let Alan and me in on this conference."

"I took that for granted," he told Marge, and then looked at Christie for her answer.

"I'll be there if you want me," she said, wondering uneasily what was coming.

When they reached Aunt Amelia's, Fatso came wriggling to meet them, overcome with delight at being reunited with his adored one.

As usual, Aunt Amelia pushed him away. "Don't slobber on me, Shelley, you foolish old thing," and Fatso wriggled all over with joy.

Christie sat in the wide porch swing and Aunt Amelia motioned John Macdonald to the place beside her niece. Marge jerked off her Sunday hat and ran her fingers through her short hair as she sat down on the top step. She pulled the reluctant bulldog over beside her and he endured her pats stoically, his attention on Aunt Amelia as she seated herself in her favorite straight-backed chair. Her odd hat was still perched atop gray braids and her white-gloved hands were ladylike in her lap.

Since he'd had to stop to talk to members of his congregation, Alan would not be along until later. Aunt Amelia did not wait to unburden herself of the seething that was apparently going on within her.

"I know perfectly well that you all think I am hardhearted," she said. "What other people think has never troubled me, however, and I shan't worry about it now. What I am concerned about is the way you do-gooders are trying to stir up trouble here in Leola."

Marge shook her head reproachfully and drawled her reply in a Texas accent. "When you say that, Miz Allard, ma'am, you better smile. Do-gooder is a fight word where I come from."

Aunt Amelia continued as though Marge had not spoken. "I grew up in this town and I can remember when life was very different here. More gracious and pleasant. Before the war small farmers owned the fields and our own people worked in them. The Allard Company didn't have to be grower as well as packer. And you never saw a brown-skinned face in this town."

Christie leaned against the green cushion in the swing, listening and at the same time aware of the tall young man beside her. He had spoken to her just once and he had not smiled as he took his place in the swing. A sobersides he was, for sure, not an ounce of fun in him.

Marge was answering Aunt Amelia. "Your own people, as you call them, found out that there were pleasanter, better-paying jobs than stoop-work in the fields. You can't blame them for not coming back to the farms when the war was over. That happened everywhere. But just what would the country have done without these men and women who were willing to come all the way up here from Texas to do the hard work? As Alan said this morning, Leola would have folded up without them. Everyone who doesn't have some small business or profession works at the plant in one way or another. Take away the Allard Company and there'd be nothing to keep Leola going. You'd have a ghost town in no time. What have you got against Americans of Mexican descent?"

"It's not their ancestry," Aunt Amelia said testily. "It's the dirt, the smells, the ignorance, the disease. All camped right here on our outskirts, ready to contaminate the town. Even the downtown streets have a changed look at night and on Sundays. You can't tell me trouble isn't brewing when you find eight or ten teen-age Mexican boys hanging around on street corners with nothing to do. And those girls with their flashy colors and loud laughs! These people are paid to do a job. Let them do it and get out quickly. That is all the citizens of Leola ask of them."

That was what the taxi driver had said, Christie remembered. She saw Marge exchange looks with John Macdonald. The man beside her put out one toe and set the swing moving gently.

"If you don't mind," he said, "this isn't what I came

here to talk about. I can understand your point of view, Miss Allard, though I don't agree with it. I think there are answers to these things and I'm interested in working them out, not in talking and arguing. But I don't know how much longer I'll be given a chance. Miss Allard, do you know how I happened to come to Leola?"

Aunt Amelia gave him a direct look. "I have heard, of course. My brother Lawrence put you in over Mr. Tidings's head, and I've always said it was the biggest mistake he ever made."

John Macdonald smiled grimly. "I like directness, Miss Allard, and I mean to be direct myself. Do you remember what the situation was before I came?"

"There was some sort of violence," Miss Allard said. "As you can expect from those people. A knifing, I think. Quite lawless. And I know one of the Mexicans was shot."

John Macdonald nodded. "By a plant official. And after that, word went back to the Valley that workers were treated badly at the Allard plant. So the best workers stopped coming. There was spoilage in the fields and crops weren't properly harvested. The situation got so serious that Mr. Tidings, who usually runs everything to suit himself, went to Mr. Allard for help."

"As a result, you were sent here," Aunt Amelia said.

"That's right. Things were so bad that Mr. Tidings had to take me or maybe close up shop. Your brother said to give me my head for two years and see what I could do with the place. I had some theories I wanted to put into effect. If they didn't work out, I would leave when my time was up. That was the proposition I bought. I also agreed that once here I'd be on my own. I wouldn't go to Mr. Allard for backing. He made it clear that he didn't want to interfere or take any active part. I was to fight my own battles."

"And you've done a good job," Marge said warmly.

"No, I haven't. Two years wasn't long enough. They'll be up in two months and Tidings wants to see me go. All I've had time to do was move the emergency off a little, get the camp a better reputation. You know how hard it was to get workers last year, but this year some of the good ones came back; for which Tidings gives me no credit. Now he feels he can go on without me and he wants to put a full stop to the improvements I've wanted to put through."

Marge hugged Fatso until he grunted an objection. "If you go, the whole effort fails," she moaned. "All the good things you've accomplished for the workers will be lost. And we can't afford losing battles. There's too much to be done with the migrant problem all over the country. With their families, there are some two and a half million migrants, and how few people care, though the country's food depends on them."

Aunt Amelia moved impatiently in her stiff chair. Gloves must have been warm on her hands, but this was Sunday and she was on the front veranda, with church-goers passing on the street. She had an appearance to uphold. In such matters apparently, public opinion count-ed. Now she glanced at the little diamond-studded watch she wore pinned to the front of her dress and turned her attention again upon John Macdonald.

"Mr. Macdonald, you have undoubtedly come here to make some request of me. As you know, except for my concern for the welfare of Leola, I have no connection or interest whatsoever in the Allard plant. Some time ago I offered to buy out my brother's holdings, but he refused."

"And that's a pity," John Macdonald said quietly. "I've always thought it a shame that your father didn't leave you in control, instead of willing the plant to a son who had no liking for the business. I'm afraid I haven't much use for absentee ownership."

"That is neither here nor there," Aunt Amelia said dryly. "What is it that you want of me, young man?"

He stopped the motion of the swing and leaned for-ward, his arms resting on his knees, his apparent attention upon a line of ants crossing the veranda floor. In his pre-occupation, he hardly looked up when Alan Bennett turned down the walk and came toward the steps. Alan, always sensitive, recognized the waiting silence, the atten-tion bent on John Macdonald, and seated himself quietly on the porch railing.

John came directly to the point. "Miss Allard, would

you be willing to come out to the camp and see for your-self what is being done, talk to the workers, get an honest picture, and then present it in a letter to your brother?"

Amelia Allard answered him as directly as he had spo-ken. "I certainly would not. No part of the business was left to me and I made a resolve from the beginning never to meddle with how it was run. It is entirely Lawrence's affair. He has seen fit to leave its management to those my father trusted, particularly Mr. Tidings. The latter has much experience that you lack, young man. I have a feeling that it will be better all around when the matter of personnel is also run as Mr. Tidings sees fit."

Alan spoke for the first time. "But what about the trouble at the plant before Mac came into the picture?"

"That has already been brought up," Aunt Amelia said. "I'm sure that was an isolated incident that will never be repeated, particularly if proper discipline is maintained. It used to be Mr. Tidings's rule to keep these people out of Leola as much as possible. Certainly it is not good that that rule has been changed since your ar-rival, Mr. Macdonald. Perhaps you are unaware of the trouble we are having with vandalism at present? A trouble which undoubtedly stems from the camp?"

"That's not fair!" Marge cried. "You don't know that it stems from the camp. It's wicked to make unfounded accusations!"

"Thank you, Marjory." Amelia Allard nodded stiffly in Marge's direction.

"I don't mean that you——" Marge began, and then changed her words. "Yes, I *do* mean you." She gave Fatso a last pat, got up from the steps, and walked an-grily into the house, closing the screen door not too qui-etly behind her.

Aunt Amelia shook her head. "The young are so uncivilized these days. Well, Mr. Macdonald, is there any-thing else you want to know?"

He left the swing and went down the steps. "Thank you, no," he said. But at the foot of the steps he turned and looked up at Christie. "What about you, Miss Christine Allard?"

"About—me?" Christie echoed in surprise.

"Yes. If your aunt won't write such a letter, what about you doing it? Perhaps your words wouldn't carry the weight of mature judgment your aunt's would, but at the same time a father might be even more willing to listen to his daughter."

She could feel the heat of the flush that swept her fair skin. "Oh, no!" she cried. "I—I couldn't!" She glanced toward her aunt for help and Aunt Amelia confirmed her words briefly.

"It would be quite impossible for Christine to do anything of the kind. Good day, young man."

"Good-by, Miss Allard," he said, but his look was still on Christie and she could not meet the scorn in his eyes. He said good-by to Alan and went off down the sidewalk. Christie watched him go, indignantly. How could he judge her when he knew nothing about the relationship between her and her father?

Aunt Amelia brushed her lap with an air of sweeping John Macdonald out of her life. "I must start Sunday dinner," she said, and went into the house.

Alan's look was sober as he watched her go. "So I failed in my purpose," he said.

He sounded so discouraged that Christie forgot her own irritation. "You didn't fail. Your sermon was wonderful. I'm sure everyone in the church went home with something to think about."

"Except your aunt," Alan said. Then he managed a smile. "Mac has the wrong approach, I'm afraid. We'll never get her to go to the workers, but perhaps we can bring them to her. Do you know, Christie, I've just this minute thought of a most nefarious scheme."

"Good," said Christie. "I'd love to be in on something nefarious if there's any way I can help."

7

Christie Takes Sides

Sunday seemed the longest day Christie had spent in Leola. In the beginning she had welcomed the slowing of time, and the unimportance of the clock. But after the enormous dinner Aunt Amelia had served up she felt heavy and hot and at the same time restless. Her aunt, it seemed, rested on Sunday afternoon. Rested and read her everlasting mystery stories, or listened to radio rograms. Alan was making a sick call and had said nothing more of his plans. Odd jobs which she had no time for during her hard-working week engaged Marge, and besides, she was in a grumpy mood and would talk to no one. Even Aunt Amelia was letting Marge alone.

So Christie got into slacks and a green gingham blouse, despite Aunt Amelia's look which implied a lady did not wear slacks on Sunday, if at all. Then she went out for a walk.

She could remember the long walks she'd so loved along the shore of Lake Michigan, sometimes through Lincoln Park, or perhaps farther north through woodsy sections. Her father had loved to walk, too, and it had made Sunday afternoons something special when they had gone walking together. There had been walks with Phil as well. . . . She put the memory quickly away. There was no one here in Leola to walk with. The prospect was a dull one anyway, but walk she would.

The residential section held little in the way of interest or surprise, she decided, so she followed one of the straight-ruled streets across the tracks and into the more ramshackle outskirts on the way to the Allard plan.

Marge had told her that the social cleavage was very clear in Leola. The old families, the professional people, the doctors, dentists, and lawyers, the store owners, the well-to-do, all lived in the old residential section. Those people who worked at jobs which were less well paid, or "socially" down the scale, lived over where the trees were not so old or the homes so large. But once you'd seen the pattern on this side of town, it was no more interesting than where her aunt lived, and Christie found herself growing hot and tired.

In a nearby vacant lot a group of eleven- and twelve-year-old boys were playing baseball. There was a woodsy section near the lot, overgrown with weeds and disfigured with trash, but at least furnishing shade, and the trunk of a fallen tree to sit upon. Christie rested, yawning, drowsy now in the damp heat, but watching the boys to keep herself awake.

It was the usual boys' game. There was much yelling and running, loud arguments, and missed balls. Once the ball rolled to her feet and she stood up and flung it back to the players, to be rewarded with catcalls and derision over the awkwardness of her throw. She smiled good-naturedly and sat down on the tree trunk again.

She was so quiet there, so well hidden, that the two who came ambling along the walk did not notice her. The boy was Rafael Olivera's brother, Lopez, but Christie did not know the brown-eyed little girl who accompanied him, chattering eagerly in Spanish. Most boys would have been annoyed at having a child of about seven tagging at their heels, but it was plain that Lopez had an affection for the little girl and enjoyed pointing things out to her, explaining in Spanish.

Christie watched them through the green barrier of leaves. Lopez still had his new ball, though its covering was now less brilliantly white. He tossed it in one hand as he talked to the child, and Christie caught a name that sounded like "Tomasa."

But now Lopez had discovered the boys in the lot and he stopped tossing the ball, his gaze focused on the players. The boys paid no attention, absorbed in their game, and Lopez, too, became absorbed. To Christie's amusement he began to go through the motions of each player in turn, while Tomasa watched in delight. He pitched with the pitcher, batted with the batter, caught with the catcher.

It was a shame, Christie thought, that he wasn't out there playing with these town boys. She reached out and parted the shrubbery and beckoned to Lopez. "Come here a minute," she called.

He looked around doubtfully, but he came over, with the little girl following.

"*Buenos días,* señorita," he said politely.

"Hello, Lopez. You want to play baseball, don't you?"

"*Sí,* señorita. Much, much I want to play the baseball."

"Then why don't you ask them to let you play? They're short of boys anyway."

He looked at her as if she had taken leave of her senses. "Those boys, they are Anglos. They no want Mexican-American to play."

He turned back to watch the game, evidently feeling that she had nothing constructive to offer, and Tomasa stared at her solemnly with unblinking brown eyes. The boy at bat hit the ball with a loud crack and the white sphere went sailing off above the pitcher's head. Every boy in the lot began to yell and Lopez yelled right along with them. In the outfield a little wiry fellow, younger than the others, ran like a streak of lightning to make the catch. There was a moment's breathless hush and through it Lopez's voice, shrilling in Spanish, made itself clearly heard. The pitcher, a lanky boy, too thin for his height, with an oily lock of brown hair falling over his eyes, turned around to stare at Lopez.

"Hey there, Mex!" he called. "Where you think you are?"

Lopez cut off his vocal exercises and looked uncertainly at the boy who had spoken.

"Go lose yourself," the pitcher directed. "Go on back to Mexico!"

Lopez stood his ground defiantly. "I am American. I stay here."

"American! Listen to him!" scoffed the pitcher. "Say, look at that ball he's got! Where'd you steal the ball from?"

63

"Aw, lay off, Hank," called the smaller boy who had made the catch. "You don't know he stole it."

"Shut up, Bitsy!" Hank ordered, and started across the field toward Lopez. Tomasa shrank back, frightened by a tone and words she did not understand, but Lopez stayed where he was, boldly waiting for the other boy to reach him. And suddenly the players were all converging on Lopez, shouting insults and mockery as they came.

"It is mine, this ball," Lopez told them, and Christie saw that he was quivering with anger.

Without stopping to think how useless any effort of her own might be, Christie started across the field toward Lopez.

"You let him alone!" she cried to the oncoming boys. "He's just as American as you are. You—you bullies!"

Derisive laughter greeted her words. "Go on home and mind your own business, girlie," the pitcher shouted. "Hey, look! He's got a knife!"

Christie whirled to look at Lopez and saw that he had made a gesture toward his pocket, probably to shove the ball into it and free his hands. But the warning was enough for the boys in the field. Two of them made a tackle that threw Lopez to the ground, and three more dived on top of him. Tomasa began to cry in soft terror and Christie looked helplessly about for aid.

For the first time she saw that there was another observer of the scene. On the back porch of a house on the far side of the lot a man leaned against the railing, watching. Christie shouted to him and waved her arms. He saw her and moved into swift action. Putting his hands on the railing, he vaulted it, landed on the grass, and came running across the lot. Not until he was on his way did Christie recognize him. It was the reporter, Tom Webb.

He looked as if he would enjoy nothing better than a good fracas, and the moment he reached the struggling, squirming heap he began pulling boys roughly off, cuffing them soundly as he pulled. There was no doubt that he meant business and there was a toughness about him that must have roused respect, for the group broke apart.

The Mexican-American boy got shakily to his feet. He

was the only one who still wanted to fight and Tom had to hold him back with a firm grip.

"Easy now, fellow," he said. "The war's over." Then he turned to the sheepish-looking gang. "Pretty brave, aren't you? Jumping on one kid. A fine bunch of Americans. You're going to look silly when your parents read about this in the *Record*."

The sullen pitcher squirmed uncomfortably. "He pulled a knife. We had to stop him."

"What knife? Where?" Tom demanded.

"I have no knife!" Lopez shouted. "But maybe is better I have a knife." He made a sickening, slicing motion in the air.

Tom struck his hand down sharply.

"Don't be a fool. What you want is to play baseball, isn't it?"

Lopez calmed down a little. "Sure. Is all I want—to play the baseball."

"Well, you don't play it with knives. Look you fellows. I've seen this kid pitching out at the camp. He's a lot better than the fumblers you've got. How about letting him into the game?"

They balked at that and objected loudly. All except the younger boy called Bitsy, who had followed Hank's lead half-heartedly. Tom waited until their objections ran out.

"Okay, then. That's just one more item for my piece. Let's see now"—he pointed at the pitcher—"you're Hank Martin, aren't you? And you over there, the fellow who made that swell catch, you're Bitsy Steese. I was talking to your mom at her restaurant yesterday. And you with the red hair, what's your name?"

Christie found herself smiling. This was blackmail, pure and simple. She went back to her tree trunk and sat down because her knees were shaking. Then she tried to coax Tomasa over to her. But the little girl would not come, perhaps regarding her, too, as the enemy.

"Say, mister," Bitsy Steese was pleading now, "if we let him play, will you lay off putting our names in the paper?"

Tom looked solemnly from one earnest face to the next. "What do you think, Lopez?" he asked finally.

"These boys made a pretty bad mistake and they're sorry about it. Aren't you, fellows?"

There was a mumbling of agreement and Tom went on.

"If you want to play with them, Lopez, I'll let them off. I won't write this nasty business up in the paper. What do you want to do?"

The tension had not gone out of Lopez, and Christie suspected that resentment would burn in him for a long time. But now his deep longing to play baseball asserted itself over his hurts.

"Okay," he said shortly. "I play."

"And I'll stay and umpire," Tom said.

Christie applauded. "And I'll be the cheering section."

Hank Martin threw her a disgusted look, but she didn't mind. Tomasa had edged closer to her and she gave the child a reassuring smile. She was eager now to see Lopez Olivera vindicate himself and prove his skill as a player of "the baseball."

One of the boys handed him a mitt and Lopez warmed up with a few throws to the catcher. The Leola boys watched him in silence, neither approving nor disapproving. Just waiting to see.

Then the batter stepped to the plate and Lopez wound up for the pitch. The ball went wild, but there were no catcalls from the players, as there would have been with one of their own number.

"Take it easy," Tom Webb said. "You're good, Lopez, and you know it. So just show 'em."

But the next pitch was worse than the first and the umpire called "ball two." On the third pitch the ball went across the plate and was easily hit by the batter.

Something warm touched Christie's arm and she saw that Tomasa had drawn near for comfort. Christie patted the small hand on her arm and offered a piece of tissue to the child. Tomasa blew her nose and gave Christie a shy smile.

Out on the field Tom went across to talk to Lopez, and Bitsy Steese shouted, "Hey, the ump can't take sides!" Everybody laughed, and the tension was eased except for Lopez himself. By the angry look he threw Bitsy,

Christie knew that he had not understood the good-natured laughter; that he thought they were laughing at him.

His pitching did not improve. He was too anxious to prove himself and still too angry to do himself justice. When he walked the fourth man by hitting him with the ball, Lopez flung the mitt down into the dirt and strode off the field without a word. Tomasa ran after him at once and trotted along at his side.

The boys let him go in silence, but there was a challenge in the way they looked at Tom Webb.

"We gave him a chance," Hank said. "But they're no good, those Mexicans. Just quitters."

For a moment Tom looked as though he might take Hank by the scruff of the neck and shake him till his teeth rattled. Instead, he thrust his hands into his pockets, as if to keep them under control, and strode across the field after Lopez and the little girl.

"All right, fellows," he said over his shoulder. "Go on back to your game. Thanks for trying."

Christie hurried after Tom. She wished futilely that she could think of something comforting to say to Lopez.

Tom caught the boy by the arm. "Don't blame yourself, kid. That was a bum idea of mine. You couldn't play under a strain like that. It's my fault, not yours."

Lopez shook him off and walked on. "Sometime I will pay this town. You will go away now, please, señor." He held out a hand to Tomasa and the child clung to it eagerly.

There was no use arguing in the face of Lopez's shame and anger. Tom let them go without further effort. He did not notice Christie until he turned and found her standing squarely in his path.

"Don't you blame yourself either," she said. "You did everything that could be done. If it hadn't been for you, Lopez might have been hurt."

He looked at her as if he really saw her for the first time since she had waved to him so frantically from across the ball field.

"Well, if it isn't Miss Christie Allard!" he said, as if she had just popped out of the ground. "Don't you know

67

that an Allard mustn't get involved in a mix-up like that? How could I resist the story it would make? *Christine Allard, newly returned to the home of her forefathers, gets teeth knocked out while defending Mexican boy from Allard plant.*"

Christie looked at him steadily, not moving out of his path. "Do you know something? A few minutes ago I almost liked you. I was ready to forgive you for being so poisonous the day you interviewed me. I take it back. You *are* poisonous!"

She turned and started toward the tracks and her own side of town. Tom Webb fell into step at her side. There was laughter in his voice when he spoke.

"You're a long way from home, Christie Allard. So I'll take you back to your Aunt Amelia's. Lest you get into further trouble on the way."

"I'm not lost," said Christie tartly. "And I can take care of myself."

He had a maddening habit of ignoring what she said and going off on side trails of his own.

"I can't blame Lopez for the way he feels. The way he wants to fight, I mean. I suppose you can't fight prejudice with force, but sometimes I still want to fight that way. One of these days maybe I'll blow up and surprise Leola. I'm afraid I wasn't cut out for small-town life anyway."

She said nothing, having no desire to encourage his company. Letting him match his pace to hers if he wanted to keep up with her, she walked briskly on.

"It's a hot day for so much speed," he said cheerfully. "How about cutting across to Main Street for a soda? The drugstore at least is open today. We still haven't compared notes on Chicago."

"No, thank you," said Christie.

She sensed the mocking look he gave her. "Hm. The deep-freeze treatment. But it's been tried with me before. Without success. I'm the insensitive kind. By the way, you're going to like the little piece I wrote about you in the paper. It will appear tomorrow. Three solid columns with pix."

She made no comment and they walked a block in silence. She wished she had her aunt's skill in dismissing unwanted young men, but she had no idea how to get rid of this one. Silence, however, was more uncomfortable than words. And besides, she did not want to stoop to this crude young man's bad manners.

"Those boys should all be severely punished," she said abruptly. "Especially that Hank whatever-his-name-is."

"Oh, I don't know," Tom said. "They're probably not such bad kids. You can't blame them for getting mixed-up notions, when they're not taught any better at home."

"That doesn't help Lopez much," Christie said.

"No, he isn't going to understand such subtleties. When a fellow comes at you swinging, you don't go excusing him for what his parents think. The point is that I don't blame those kids as much as I do the grownups in this town."

"He only wanted to play with them," Christie recalled.

"But he has the quick temper of the Latin, and he's proud, as all his people are. He won't forget this in a hurry. Maybe you'd better tell Alan Bennett about this whole thing. He'll talk to Rafael."

Christie nodded. "I will," she agreed.

They were a block away from Aunt Amelia's now and when Tom slowed his pace, Christie followed his example without thinking.

"That's better," he said. "You know, Christie, I'm glad you've come to this town. There is, I discover, a dearth of suitable girls in Leola."

Quick annoyance went through her. She disliked having this nervy young reporter term her "suitable." But before she could think of a sufficiently cutting answer, he went on, bluntly direct.

"Our Main Street movie palace opens it door twice a week in this town—on Wednesday and Saturday. The pictures are usually terrible, but I'd like to take you to one Wednesday night. How about it?"

She glanced at him in astonishment. Did he actually think she would accept such an invitation?

He grinned ruefully. "Never mind, don't say it. For a little while I forgot that you were the Lady of the Manor."

She didn't like that either. Certainly she wasn't a snob.

But she could just imagine Eve's raised eyebrows if her daughter had ever brought a Tom Webb home with her.

"I—I'm sorry." She tried to soften the refusal. "It's just that lately I haven't——" But her words sounded so feeble that she couldn't finish the sentence.

"That's all right," Tom said without resentment. "I've learned not to get my feelings hurt. Here you are at your auntie's. Now run along in, and after this confine your charitable efforts to playing Lady Bountiful at benefits. Be seeing you, Miss Allard."

He went off, leaving her staring after him, as completely at a loss as she had ever been in her life.

"He's a fast worker, that one!" said a voice from the veranda, and Christie turned to find Marge Molloy watching her interestedly. She was sitting on the steps in the sun, getting browner by the moment and gathering a few dozen more freckles across her snub nose. Beside her, the old bulldog snoozed peacefully.

Christie recovered herself and turned up the walk. "Meeting him was entirely an accident."

"You're pretty when you blush," Marge said. "You're pretty any time, but too pale. Blushing gives you color. A funny thing, I've always wanted to be the fragile type like you. The kind that looks as if she'd break in two in a strong wind and blushes at every third word anybody speaks to her. The protected type. Now me, I haven't blushed since I was six and nobody ever wants to protect me." Her sigh was exaggerated, but her eyes danced as she watched Christie.

"At least you're not grumpy any more," Christie said. Somehow she didn't mind Marge's teasing, even when her implication wasn't flattering.

"Sit down," Marge said, patting the step beyond Fatso. "I've been waiting for you to show up. I have a proposition to make you."

Fatso growled and Christie seated herself as far away from him as possible. Everyone in this town seemed to disapprove of her. Even this silly old bulldog.

"You're a bully, my pet," Marge told Fatso. "You know Christie's afraid of you and you push your advantage. Now behave or I'll smack you good."

Fatso gave her a superior look, perfectly aware that from Marge any such threat was a bluff.

"All right," Christie said without much interest, "what's this proposition you want to make me?"

8

Marge Makes a Wager

Marge scratched the bulldog behind the ears and watched Christie the while. "I expect you'll find it hard to kill time in Leola. There's so little to do."

"I don't mind," Christie said. "All I want is to drift for a while. I didn't come here to *do* anything. I just came to loaf and find out what I want to do."

"Loafing isn't a very good way to find out what you want to do. And it's the worst way possible to forget things you want to forget."

"Don't preach at me," Christie said.

"Sorry. Must be the missionary in me. There are two kinds of people who make me mad. First, the wrong-headed, muddled ones like your Aunt Amelia. I get all the more peeved with her because she has good sense in so many other ways. And she's quite capable of reversing herself if you could ever make her see that she's wrong. Then there are those who waste time when there's so much that needs to be done."

"All right," said Christie calmly, "so Aunt Amelia is a muddlehead and I'm a time-waster. That makes a good diplomatic beginning if there's something you want me to do."

Marge addressed herself to Fatso. "Note what's happening to this young lady, Shelley, my friend. She's getting less protected every minute. Pretty soon she'll stick right up for herself and tell us all off."

Fatso looked unimpressed, and Christie waited with

71

careful indifference, so Marge came to the point. "When the children do show up out at the nursery school, I need help. How about coming with me tomorrow and working for the day?"

Christie shuddered. "I'm no good with small children. I've never been around any. Besides, how do you know they'll come?"

"Mac has his dander up. He says they'll be there, or else. And if you've never been around small children, how do you know what you're like with them? Brown-eyed little Mexican-Americans are fascinated by pretty blond Anglo ladies. Especially when they're nice, the way you are."

"Butter won't help," Christie told her. "It's too late. Small children alarm me and I alarm them." That was a quote from Eve. She didn't really know whether it applied to her or not.

"Do you speak any Spanish?" Marge asked.

"Not a word. I'd be completely helpless."

"That's fine. Then you can teach them some English words. They'll love it. Imagine, Christie, some of these children are third- and fourth-generation Americans and they can't speak English. All their lives the language barrier is the biggest one against them. Even when they learn the language, most of them don't learn it young enough to be able to *think* in English."

"I don't want to go," said Christie. She felt completely impassive to anything Marge might say. This afternoon she had been through an upsetting experience because of one Mexican-American boy. And after refusing John Macdonald's impossible request to write to her father, she had no intention of going within a mile of the Allard plant. Aunt Amelia's attitude was the right one. Keep hands off and nose out. Don't get involved.

Marge sighed again. "Well, it looks like I've lost my wager. But you can't say I didn't try. I really did think you had better stuff in you, Christie, in spite of all your handicaps."

Christie had had enough. She got up, ignoring Fatso's growl, and started toward the front door.

Marge didn't even look up to watch her go. "Now I'll

have to buy lollipops for the whole nursery group," she told the bulldog. "Forty-six lollipops. And I'm already flat broke before the week's begun. Mac can afford it a lot better than I can."

Christie paused with her hand on the screen door. "What has he to do with it?"

"The wager was with him. He said you'd never go out there and help. He said he'd buy lollipops for the whole crowd if you did. And I was foolish enough to say I knew you'd go. And I would treat if you didn't. So I lose."

Christie walked angrily into the house and let the screen door close behind her in the unladylike way Aunt Amelia deplored. She walked resolutely upstairs and went into the sitting room on the way to the haven of her own room. Aunt Amelia sat on the sofa listening to a mystery play on the radio.

When she saw Christie's face, she turned the volume down for a moment. "A dull program. I knew who the murderer was from the start. What's the matter with you?"

"Nothing," Christie said. "I'm hot and tired."

"Did Marjory make you her foolish proposal?"

Christie merely nodded.

"I hope you told her you'd do nothing of the sort. I don't want you going out to that miserable camp. Those children have all sorts of diseases, to say nothing of the runny noses and the dirt. You simply don't fit into that setting, Christine."

"I suppose I'd only do at a charity benefit," Christie said.

"My, my, you do sound upset. Has anything gone wrong?"

All sorts of things had gone wrong, but she couldn't explain them to her aunt. She was angry with Marge and Tom and John Macdonald, and Aunt Amelia, too. Not one of them knew anything about Christie Allard. They just pinned a label on her and expected her to behave in a certain way. And she knew what the label was. It was her last name, and it meant different things to different people.

At the door of her room she turned to face her aunt.

73

"Yes, something *is* wrong. I'm finding out that I don't much like being an Allard. Not in Leola, where everybody looks down on the Allards."

"Looks down!" her aunt gasped. "Now just *who* would look down——"

"I'll tell you who," Christie said. "Marge Molloy, and that John Macdonald, and Tom Webb the reporter, and Aurora Gomez and Lopez Olivera, and maybe even Alan Bennett."

"It's the sun," her aunt said. "You should never take a long walk in the early afternoon."

Christie opened the door of her room. "It's not the sun. I'm tired of being treated as if I were made of glass and had a retarded mentality, and absolutely no—no guts!"

"Christine!" cried Aunt Amelia.

But Christie didn't heed her. She crossed her room and flung up the window over the front porch roof.

"Marge!" she called. "Are you still there?"

"Sure," Marge said. "In case you want to know what time I leave for the camp it will be earlier than usual tomorrow. And we walk all the way."

"That's what I wanted to know," Christie said. "I'll wear low heels."

Then she put the window down to shut out the fierce heat and sat in the rocker beside it. In the other room Aunt Amelia had turned up her program and you could hear the spat-spat of bullets.

I feel wonderful, Christie thought in surprise. *I feel better than I have any time since I was a little girl and Dad taught me how to stop being afraid and stay on a bicycle. I'll show this town about Allards! I'll show Marge and John Macdonald and that awful Tom Webb.*

It felt fine to be determined and fighting mad. She wasn't even afraid of Fatso right now.

In the morning she wasn't quite so mad or quite so elated. Some of the zing had died out and she felt uncertain of her ability to be of any use to Marge. Nevertheless, a quiet sense of determination was still with her. She had managed to turn a deaf ear to Aunt Amelia all through supper last night and Alan Bennett had come persuasively to her aid. What Aunt Amelia finally accepted, Christie was afraid, was the Lady Bountiful aspect of the task. Grandmother Allard had always been one for high-minded good works, it seemed, though not on any such lowly level as this. Grandmother Allard knew the dignity of her name and position. It was a pity, her aunt pointed out, that Christie should waste her time at the Mexican camp, but one taste would probably be enough and she would get over this notion in a hurry.

It was a drizzly morning, but Marge was firm about rejecting Aunt Amelia's offer of a lift in the car. Just because Christie was going didn't mean there were to be special privileges. Christie wouldn't melt in the rain. So they wore slickers and rubbers and carried Marge's big, old-fashioned umbrella between them.

"It belonged to my pop," Marge explained as they started out. "He was a country doctor and this umbrella is like him, solid and dependable and not very modern."

On the way she explained something of her reason for going out to the camp earlier than usual. Her purpose had to do with the "nefarious" scheme Alan had in mind for involving Aunt Amelia with the Mexican-Americans whether she liked it or not. They were, Marge said, going to pay an early morning call on the Gomez family.

"This is a slack time, with the asparagus pack over and corn not quite ready for detasseling, so we'll catch people at home."

They stopped on the way to buy cartons of milk and a box of crackers at a grocery store. Marge explained that she was allowed a small sum for snacks at the camp school, though sometimes she couldn't resist buying extra treats on her own.

"I'm glad to have another pair of arms for carrying today," she said, turning one sack over to Christie.

The drizzle had stopped by the time they reached camp, but it had rained enough during the night to cool the air and to turn parts of the camp grounds into a muddy brown bog. The shacks, the cannery, the office structure had blurred into one wet gray, and above them the water tower stood on spindly legs, the lettered name across the tank satiny black from the rain.

Marge started across the yard and Christie picked her way after her gingerly. If it hadn't been for the dumpings of gravel and cinders, the area would have been deep in mud. Behind them a heavy vehicle rumbled through the gate and Marge turned to watch.

"There's something for you to see," she told Christie.

The truck swung into a cinder-covered parking place and ground to a halt. Packed into the truck body were some forty men, women, and children. A leaking tarpaulin had been pulled over the top, but the sides of the truck were open to the weather. A few huddled on the plank floor, but most of them stood up, either clinging to the sides, or braced against one another.

"A new batch coming up to work in sweet corn," Marge said. "Nearly three days it takes from Texas, riding day and night. Nice way to travel, packed in like that."

The driver of the truck had jumped down from the front seat. He was a Mexican-American like the others and he began shouting at the occupants in Spanish. Stiffly the adults let themselves down out of the truck. Most of the children leaped gleefully to the muddy ground and began to run about wildly, releasing pent-up energy. But those who were limp and weak clung listlessly to their mothers' skirts. One sick little girl was lifted out gently by her father.

Some of the current residents of the camp came to welcome and assist the newcomers. Christie saw John Macdonald hurry across from his office.

"They've probably had no food or drink for hours," Marge said. "Oh, oh—look out!"

She thrust her grocery sack at Christie and ran forward just as a woman with a black reboza over her head crumpled to the ground in a faint. Marge bent over her, calling to the men for help. Two of them carried her into the big barracks-like building indicated by John Macdonald. Christie waited helplessly while Marge spoke to the women and children among the new arrivals, greeting them in Spanish, trying to ease their weariness a little through friendly words.

When she came back to Christie, she looked angry again. "Well, how do you like it? We probably have laws about transporting cattle, but none with any teeth in them for the transporting of human beings."

Christie shivered. "You said they traveled day and night. But how do they sleep?"

"Don't be funny," Marge said curtly. "Who cares whether they sleep or not? It's to the interest of the crew leader to get them delivered as quickly as possible. Anyway, most of them don't have the money it would take if the trip lasted too long. To say nothing of the fact that there are few places where they are welcome to stop along the way. Even restroom facilities are closed to them most places."

"Besides"—John Macdonald had come over to walk with them across the grounds—"as everybody will tell you, they're used to it. They don't know anything better." There was a whip of scorn in his words, but it was not for the migrants.

"Why should being used to it be an excuse?" Christie asked.

"I'd like to have that explained myself," Marge said. "Of course those who get a little money ahead buy secondhand cars and bring their families up themselves. But how much can you get ahead when your earnings are so small for the year? The trucks are the cheapest means of travel. Though of course by the time they get here they owe the crew leaders a good sum per head for every soul he brings up, including the children. And when you think that these people are Americans, just like ourselves——"

"That's not the point," John said. "The real point is that they are human beings." He changed the subject abruptly. "You're here early, aren't you? What's up?"

"We're paying a call on the Gomez family," Marge explained. "Some of Alan Bennett's scheming, as he may have told you yesterday. Incidentally, have you noticed that you owe the nursery school a batch of lollipops?"

John smiled and for once the look he turned upon Christie seemed less disapproving. "I'll be happy to pay my debts. See you later. Have fun."

He went off with a wave of his hand and Marge led the

way to the entrance of the long gray barracks. It was not a beautiful building, but there were screens at the windows and it was new and roomy, and seemed a palace beside the rickety shacks across the yard. Christie noticed, as Marge pulled open the double door, that the screens had been pulled loose and bent outward in both panels. As a protection against flies, the door was of no use at all.

"They lean against the screens," Marge said. "Push them right out. So of course old Tidy is raving about how such luxuries are wasted and the company is out money. All thanks to Mac's harebrained ideas. But what can he expect? During all their generations in this country, no one has gone to the trouble to teach these people about flies and disease carriers. How can they learn American ways if no one shows them anything?"

Marge went through the door and Christie followed her. A long, wide corridor stretched down the center of the building, with wooden partitions sectioning off rooms along both sides. Marge stopped to set down her armload of groceries and umbrella, and Christie followed her example. Rubbers, too, were left near the door as they started down the corridor.

"Won't somebody take those things if we leave them there?" Christie asked.

Marge fairly snapped at her. "Don't *you* talk like that! Do you steal your guests' possessions when somebody comes to visit you? Well, don't forget that we're guests here and these people know a lot more about hospitality and good manners than we've ever managed to learn. Maybe we can teach them sanitation, but they can teach us a lot, too."

Her voice had evidently been heard, for here and there along the corridor doors opened and young faces looked out at them. Then with welcoming cries of "Mees! Mees!" some two dozen small children scurried out to surround Marge. Those who were quick enough caught her by the hands and one very small toddler, who was comfortably minus panties, caught her skirt at the back and held on stoutly. Marge talked to them in Spanish while they all chattered back. Christie recognized one little girl with velvety dark eyes and an enormous smile. She was the child who had been with Lopez the day before.

"Hello, Tomasa," Christie said, and the little girl gave her a shy look of recognition, while the other children stared solemnly. Christie was a curiosity and they were not ready to give her the eager friendship they gave "Mees."

"You know Tomasa?" Marge asked, surprised.

"I saw Lopez Olivera yesterday," Christie said, "and she was with him. Is she his sister?"

They started down the corridor with their Pied Piper following and Marge explained.

"No, Tomasa is Aurora's little sister. But there are no girls in the Olivera family and Lopez seems to have adopted Tomasa."

Marge sent the children scurrying back to their rooms, with admonitions about being on time for school. Only Tomasa and the littlest one who clung to her skirt stayed with them. Marge picked up the baby and held out a hand to the little girl.

"We are coming to visit your house, Tomasa," Marge said.

Tomasa wore a clean, well-pressed dress in a bright Mexican print and there were huaraches upon her bare feet. Her hair, which had tumbled free over her shoulders yesterday, had been neatly combed into two short pigtails and tied at the ends with scraggly ribbon. It was her smile that won your heart, though, Christie thought, shy, offering friendship without being sure you would return it. When Tomasa slipped her other hand gently into Christie's, Christie knew she had been accepted. The small sun-browned hand was as soft and warm in hers as a flower that had grown in the sun and Christie smiled down at her. This sort of "talk" needed no words.

Tomasa's "house" was a room off the middle of the corridor. Before she tapped on the door, Marge pointed to a small sign on which a name was neatly printed: PEDRO GOMEZ.

"That's an idea of Mac's," she whispered to Christie. "It gives every family a sense of ownership, of identity. It makes the people who live in this building feel of some importance, instead of just being pushed around the way they are in some camps. It's not like this out in those shacks, of course. This is deluxe housing, believe me, and again Mac's doing. If the money were allowed him, he'd turn the whole camp into something like this."

Tomasa did not wait for Marge to tap on the door. She ran to push it open, announcing the arrival of guests to those inside.

Immediately, the door was flung wide and Mrs. Gomez eagerly welcomed them in. She recognized Christie and greeted her with pleasure. Marge spoke to her in English and Mrs. Gomez answered in kind, out of courtesy to Christie.

Her husband, she explained, had gone to town for groceries, since there was no work in the fields today. That Aurora, the lazy one, would not get up at all, but lay there like a do-nothing. They would excuse it, please.

The square room was fairly large, Christie saw, but three beds and the everyday living possessions of a family of four crowded it. On one of the beds lay Aurora, face down beneath a sheet, only the dark, tangled mass of her hair showing above the cover. She did not turn over or give any sign of hearing her mother's words.

Mrs. Gomez had been pressing a dress and at sight of the ironing board Marge nudged Christie. "Electricity. Tidings won't put it out in the shacks."

Mrs. Gomez hastened to dust off the one wooden chair that already looked spotless and offered it to Christie, who sat down with Tomasa close beside her. Marge, as an old friend of the family, sat on a corner of Aurora's bed, bouncing the baby on her knee. Overhead a naked electric bulb hung down from the ceiling, lighting the room against the gray of the lowering day outside. The single window had been curtained with bright yellow material in an effort to give the room something of the appearance of a home. There was a colored picture of the Blessed Mother on one wall, and in a place of honor in the corner a crucifix with a blade of dry palm, probably from the last Palm Sunday, twisted around it. Before each burned a vigil light.

Marge shifted the baby, now contentedly sucking its

thumb, and reached out to pat Aurora on the mound beneath the covers. "Good morning, Aurora Gomez. I haven't seen you since you got back to Leola. How was Chicago?"

Aurora swished the mound and said nothing, and her mother spoke to her severely in Spanish, shaking her head apologetically at her guests.

"Nothing can I do with her. Always she has the sickness in the head, or the sickness in the stomach. She does not go to the fields when the work begins, though her papa scolds every night."

"Leave me alone!" cried Aurora, and pounded her fists into the mattress.

"We'll do that," Marge said cheerfully. "Mrs. Gomez, you know the very nice minister of Glenview Church, Mr. Bennett?"

Mrs. Gomez nodded. "The one with the so red hair? *Sí*. He gives the mass here at the camp for your church when Father Cudahy has finished."

Marge let the reference to mass go uncorrected. "That's the one. Well, next week the ladies' club of his church is giving a dinner to raise money for poor people. And we wondered if you would come and cook the dinner for us. Real Mexican dishes. I have never tasted enchiladas better than yours, or better tamales or frijoles. Would you be so kind as to come and give us a real Mexican dinner?"

Mrs. Gomez looked pleased, though she made little deprecating movements with her plump hands. Her cooking was nothing. It was unworthy. But if she was needed ... and she would make tacos also. The so wonderful tacos with the meat juicy inside the crust. Perhaps Mrs. Olivera, too, would come and help her.

Marge jumped up from the bed and hugged Mrs. Gomez in delight. "Then we have your promise. I'll be out again to get the list of foods you will need and you can let me know about pots and pans."

Mrs. Gomez nodded. "I will make the list. And Aurora also will come to help with the cooking."

"No, I will not!" said Aurora from under the sheet.

"Nobody invited you," Marge told her. "We are doing

81

all this in order to show the Anglos in our church what fine people you Mexican-Americans are. But if you come over and scowl at us, that won't help much."

Aurora flopped over in the bed and stared with angry eyes at Marge Molloy. She ignored Christie completely. "My mother is American. If she has sense she will not go to your church and make the Mexican cooking. Me—I want to forget about enchiladas and tortillas and all the rest. Ugh!"

"You do not say *ugh* when I give them to you for dinner last night," said her mother. "You are the foolish one to pretend there is no Mexico. To pretend you are Anglo."

Marge glanced at her watch and stood up. It was nearly time for the nursery school to start. Mrs. Gomez bowed her guests courteously to the door. On the way out Christie threw an uncertain look at Aurora. The other girl had not glanced at her once and there had been no opportunity to speak to her. Now she lay on her stomach again, ignoring their departure, and Christie hesitated to risk a rebuff by telling her good-by.

Mrs. Gomez, like all mothers, admonished Tomasa to be a good girl, and the child came with them, putting her hand again trustfully into Christie's.

"You've made a conquest," Marge said as they picked up paper sacks, umbrella, and rubbers at the door. Christie found one barefooted little boy parading the corridor in her much-too-large rubbers, but his mother came out and reproved him and returned them with apologies. Now children poured out of shacks and barracks from all directions and Marge greeted them by name, allowed them to cling to her hands and skirt. She was really wonderful with these children, Christie thought in admiration.

The school building was the distance of a couple of blocks across the puddle-dotted yard and Marge pointed it out before they reached it.

"Mac had an awful time getting it built. Tidy felt it was a foolish idea. But now it serves so many needs— church, school, meetinghouse."

It was a low, one-story, rectangular frame building, painted gray on the outside and gray on the inside, for practical purposes, rather than beauty. Again there was a screen door and screens at the windows, but as Marge proudly pointed out, these were intact.

"Our education on flies begins with the children and the church. But there are the listless ones who attend nothing and we still have to reach them."

Christie regarded the swarm of children uneasily. No public school she knew of would take so many children into so small a space. She wondered how on earth Marge ever managed to control them. It wasn't just the little ones who crowded about them. Their older brothers and sisters were there, too, wide-eyed, mischievous, gay, chattery.

As Marge opened the small padlock on the front door, she spoke over her shoulder to Christie.

"I hope you're still feeling brave, my girl. This is where you take on your first duties."

9

Mr. Tidings Interferes

Apparently the entire army of children meant to squeeze themselves through on Marge's heels. She promptly selected two of the older ones to help her and motioned Christie ahead of her.

"You stay right here at the door," she directed Christie, "and put 'em through a sieve. Only the little ones can come inside." Then in Spanish she directed the two children she had honored as helpers to start the sieving work outside the door.

The children were good-natured but determined. Despite Christie's frantic efforts and her shouted English directions, several of the larger boys wormed themselves past her through the entrance. The toddler who had clung to Marge was handed over the heads of several smaller children, still minus panties and howling lustily. Christie grasped the small, squirming body and set the baby in a safe area on the floor. There was no time now for the quenching of tears. At length, in some helter-skelter fashion, the sheep were separated from the goats, the littlest were inside, the biggest outside, and the screen door securely hooked. Through it all Marge remained unruffled and in full command. Christie was dripping with perspiration and felt as grimy and gritty as the floor under her feet, where the children had tracked in gravel, cinders, and mud from the yard.

"It's not usually quite this bad," Marge explained calmly. "On a sunny day, with work in the fields, a lot of them would be out there, working or getting in the way. In the afternoon I'll put the little ones outside and take the big ones in for their turn. Then you'll hear the howling that goes up from the ones who are put out."

Christie stood by the door, unhooking it cautiously when a child appeared who was small enough to belong to the nursery group and blocking the attempt of older boys who tried good-naturedly to force their way in. Those who managed to sneak in were finally ejected by Marge, and the school was ready for the business of the morning. It was apparently all a wonderful game for these children who had so little amusement in their lives.

The group of small ones inside were surprisingly docile and well-behaved. Tomasa released her grip on Christie's hand and took her place on one of the long green benches beside the other children. But now she whispered and nudged and pointed to Christie, claiming friendship.

First, with Marge leading, they all sang a few lively songs with simple hand motions, and even the toddler without panties fluttered her tiny hands in the air like birds flying. Tomasa sang louder than anyone else and in a remarkably tuneful, clear little voice. Before them on a camp chair sat Marge, with her "desk" in her lap. The desk was a battered checker board on which she rested a sheet of paper as she drew crayon pictures for the children. She would dip into the cigar box of crayon scraps at her feet and draw some simple object for the children to identify.

Someone rattled the screen door vigorously and Christie turned to shake her head at the ten-year-old boy who stood there, importantly demanding admission. But he would not accept her refusal and put up a cry of "Mees, Mees!" The other boys and girls outside joined their voices to his. Here, apparently, was someone who all felt should be admitted.

Marge came to Christie's help as the uproar increased. "It's all right," she called. "Pablo is the messenger of propriety. Let him in."

So Christie opened the door a crack and let the privileged Pablo slip through. Then she saw why he had come. In his hands he held a pair of freshly ironed white panties into which he now pushed his wriggling baby sister. Then, having proudly completed his mission, he went obediently out the door and about his own business.

Every now and then the children outside, particularly the boys, popped their heads up at a window behind Marge's back and shouted lustily, then ducked out of sight. Now and then they kicked the sides of the frame building, or pounded on it with their fists. But neither the rows of children on the green benches, nor the imperturbable teacher, troubled to notice them. Only Christie suffered from the continual din and her admiration for Marge increased by the moment. She was glad when she was given another chore besides that of watching the door.

"They've given up now," Marge said. "They always do. So you can start pouring milk into those plastic cups on the picnic table."

The only other piece of furniture in the room was a long wooden picnic table, with benches attached. Turned upside down in a cardboard box on the table were several dozen brightly colored plastic cups. Now Christie poured milk into the cups, glad to be useful to Marge. The children, who had been circling the room in a singing game, settled themselves to wait eagerly for milk and crackers to be brought them. No one snatched, or pushed, or crowded out of turn. Tomasa would not take her cup from Marge, but waited for Christie, the big smile lighting her face.

"*Gracias,* Mees," said Tomasa, and Christie was touched. These were such young children to have such nice manners. Outside, their older brothers and sisters might raise an uproar, but Christie suspected that when their turn came to be inside, they, too, would be courteous and well-behaved.

Most of the children had been dressed for school in the best their mothers could manage. Only a few were dirty, with tangled, uncombed locks. Christie had just handed a cup of milk to a little five-year-old in pink hair ribbons which matched her pink dress when she saw Marge turn and look uneasily toward the door.

"Here comes trouble," Marge warned.

Christie glanced out the door and saw a man coming toward them across the yard. He was small and slight, with thinning gray hair and a tight, thin mouth. She had no need for Marge to tell her who he was. This was Mr. Tidings, the general manager of the Allard plant. Christie went back to the doling out of milk and crackers. After all, Mr. Tidings was Marge's problem, not hers.

He came in with an air of authority, and some forty-odd pairs of velvet-brown eyes stared at him in apprehension. Tomasa wiggled out of line and came to stand close beside her friend Christie. Outside, the voices of the older children died away and suddenly there was not a child in sight anywhere in the yard.

"Good morning, Miss Molloy," Mr. Tidings said with a forced joviality. "I see you're at your little hobby again."

Marge did not stop pouring milk. "That's right, Mr. Tidings. Nothing else to do with my time."

"If you mission people would only be more realistic," the manager said impatiently. "You don't seem to realize how much you interfere with the lives of these people."

Marge said nothing and Mr. Tidings turned away from her.

"But that is not what I am here for. Miss Molloy, will you be kind enough to present me to your guest?"

Christie looked around in surprise. Mr. Tidings did not wait for Marge to swallow her irritation, but came straight to Christie and held out his hand.

86

"I know you're Miss Christine Allard," he said. "I am Mr. Tidings, and I want to welcome you to Leola. No one told me and I did not realize until I saw the paper today that you had come to our town." He flashed a look of reproach at Marge and patted Christie's hand with his own clammy-damp one.

"How do you do," Christie managed and got her hand back as quickly as possible. Beyond acknowledging his greeting, there seemed to be nothing to say. She felt a further twinge of uneasiness over knowing that Tom Webb's piece had appeared in the paper.

"Perhaps you don't fully understand," Mr. Tidings went on, "what a—well, if I may use the term—what an historic occasion this is."

Christie stared at him, disliking his thin smile and the steel-colored eyes that belied the smile.

His mild laugh was rusty, as if from long disuse. "I'm afraid you don't understand. But we at the Allard plant feel highly honored to have you visit us. I knew your grandfather and grandmother very well. Your grandfather taught me the business, you know. And I have run it to your father's satisfaction all these years. To have John Allard's granddaughter here on our grounds—as I say, it is an honor."

"She came to work in the nursery school," Marge said shortly.

"So I see." Mr. Tidings sniffed at the children heated from their games, and then put his handkerchief delicately to his nose. "You should, of course, have brought her directly to my office. Come along, my dear, we must get out of this at once. I want to show you the plant buildings, the cannery. I shall conduct you on a tour of inspection myself."

Christie handed the last cup of milk to a little boy who had looked crestfallen, thinking she had forgotten him. She did not care for Mr. Tidings and she did not at all like people who told her what she must do. But before she could announce her intention of staying right where she was, Marge spoke quietly.

"I can manage now. Thanks for your help, Christie. Mr. Tidings is right, of course. Your name is Allard and you should certainly have a look at the things he wants to show you."

Christie hesitated a moment longer, torn between her own distaste for this man and her realization that Marge had put a note of entreaty into her voice. It made her all the more indignant to think that Marge Molloy, who was doing so much single-handed to help these children, should have to bow to the power vested in Mr. Tidings. But she gave in to Marge's plea, said *"Adiós"* to the now friendly children, and allowed Mr. Tidings to open the screen door for her.

"I'll see you at home, Christie," Marge called after her. "There won't be time for you to come back here before lunch."

"All right," said Christie and walked beside Mr. Tidings across the muddy yard. At least, she thought, if he was going to run out a red carpet as if she were someone important, she might as well behave as if it really counted to be an Allard. Perhaps she could express herself frankly, where Marge dared not.

"Marge Molloy is certainly doing wonderful work with those children," she said, hoping she sounded confident and casual.

Mr. Tidings made a little gesture of dismissal. "You mustn't be so easily impressed, Miss Allard. These mission people can be troublemakers. They stir up the workers, get them to want ridiculous luxuries. They make them dissatisfied and hard to work with. And I'm afraid these people have been innoculating you already. As your father's daughter, you must not let yourself be so easily deceived by sentimentality. After all, I have been running this plant for a good many years. And Allard Canned Vegetables have not done so badly in that time."

Christie decided that nothing would be gained by arguing with Mr. Tidings at this moment.

"I'm sure they've done very well," she agreed.

He looked gratified. "A fine man, your grandfather. Never have I known anyone I respected more. If I may say so, you bear a considerable resemblance to him."

This was news to Christie and she was not sure she was flattered. She remembered the framed photograph of her grandfather in Aunt Amelia's upstairs sitting room. He had looked like rather a forbidding and strong-minded old gentleman. She would have considered him the last person on earth to whom she bore any resemblance.

"I suppose it is a matter of expression more than anything else," Mr. Tidings hastened to explain. "Something you do with your mouth, something about the jaw line. In a much more feminine way, of course. Ah, here we are. The more modern executive offices are in the cannery building, but I have kept the old office here."

He opened the door with something of a flourish and stepped aside to allow her to enter. She went up two low steps and entered a bare waiting room with plain wooden chairs lined up about the walls and an uncarpeted floor. Beyond the partition a woman worked at a typewriter without looking up. On one of the waiting-room chairs sat a worker whom Christie had noticed on the truck that morning.

Mr. Tidings gestured apologetically. "We seldom have visitors like yourself, Miss Allard. Usually this room is filled with Mexicans waiting to see our personnel man."

Christie glanced toward the open door of a room beyond. There was a low murmur of voices and she recognized John Macdonald's tones. But Mr. Tidings motioned her toward a second room on the left.

"This was once your grandfather's office, my dear. That is why I keep it for myself. In his day we had our Allards working right in the plant. I have changed it very little."

Somehow Christie's irritation slipped away as she crossed the threshold of the spacious office and looked wonderingly about the room. Except for the massive mahogany desk, it was not impressive in its worn furnishings. The rug was a dull brown, the wine-colored draperies faded and limp. A comfortable green leather armchair stood in one corner, but there were cracks here and there on its once-shining surface. Windows ran along one side, looking out upon the cannery, which made for a more inspiring view than if it had opened upon the drab yard that housed the workers. There were framed pictures of the plant on the walls. But Christie's attention was caught by the bookshelves which rose solidly along one wall. Each section was individually glassed in and the volumes seemed to cover a wide field of subjects.

Mr. Tidings noted her interest. "Your grandfather was a great reader, and a poor sleeper. Many a night he would stay here when everything had shut down. He'd sit in that old leather chair and read until two or three o'clock in the morning. Then he'd walk through the town when nobody else was stirring and snatch a few hours' sleep at home before he turned up here in the morning, earlier than anyone else."

Christie went over to the shelves to read a few titles. There were heavy tomes of history and scientific subjects, but there was fiction, too. Dickens and Scott and Thackeray, those old-timers no one read any more. Her grandfather must have had a taste for romance and adventure. For the first time he began to seem faintly real to her.

"Sit down, please," Mr. Tidings said. "I'll rest just a moment and then we'll go over to the cannery."

She glanced at him again as she seated herself in a straight chair beside the desk and saw that he looked a little gray. "Is anything wrong?" she asked.

"No—it's nothing." He waved a reassuring hand. "I've been having a little trouble and I'm afraid there's an operation ahead. Nothing serious. I postpone it because I can't afford the time. But when an upsetting morning like this one comes along, I find that I am more disturbed than I should be. Things were much simpler in your grandfather's day."

She wondered what had disturbed him. The arrival of that new truckload of workers? Marge's school? But she said nothing, and after a moment he spoke again.

"There was little of this migrant labor in your grandfather's time. We worked with our own people. Their problems were easily dealt with. In a sense, we were a family. A Leola family. Now this foreign group has come in and the labor problem is tremendous. I know your father trusts me to cope with all this, but if I may say so, there are times when I wish he himself took a little more interest in the business. I liked the old ways better. Proof, I suppose, that I am getting old."

Strangely, considering her first disliking for the man, Christie felt a little sorry for him. He was getting old and he had lost the ability to keep up with the changes about him. Now, in this unguarded moment, perhaps because she was Josh Allard's granddaughter, he had revealed something of his own uncertainty and defeat.

"I could have retired," he said. "But what is there to retire for? This place is my life. In the old days, when your grandmother was living, I was made welcome in her house. It was like a second home to me. I am glad she isn't here to see the type of people now working in the plant, overrunning the town."

"They seem very pleasant, friendly people," Christie ventured.

The look Mr. Tidings gave her was disquieting and for the first time she remembered Alan's talk about his twisted notions. He recovered himself with an effort.

"I have a feeling everything will run more smoothly around here in another two months," he said.

"What's going to happen in two months?" Christie asked. Mr. Tidings pointed a bony forefinger toward the opposite office and there was a suddenly vindictive note in his voice. "In two months the time will be up for that personnel man whom your father put in during one of his rare moments of remembering us out here."

"Mr. Macdonald?" Christie said. "But I thought he was supposed to be doing a very good job."

The grayness had left Mr. Tidings's face, to be replaced by an angry flush. "I suppose those mission people have been filling your head with nonsense. If that young man had his way much longer, the Allard plant would be operated as a social-service center for migrant workers. The mere matter of running a business and making a profit would have been forgotten entirely. In a sense, young lady, it might serve your father right if that very thing happened. When Lawrence was a boy, he couldn't wait till he shook the dust of this town from his shoes. It might have been better if he had also released his interest in the Allard plant. Miss Amelia Allard would, I am sure, have seen eye to eye with me on the matter of migrant labor."

"Do you suppose we could see the cannery now?" Christie asked abruptly.

Tidings stared at her for a moment. There was no telling by his cold, unflickering look what he might be thinking. He rose from behind the desk, picking up a newspaper as he did so. "Perhaps you'd like this copy of the *Record* which carries the piece about you?"

She thanked him and took the paper, but she did not glance at it then. Whatever Tom Webb had written, she preferred to be alone when she read it.

As they went into the outer room, John Macdonald came to the door of his own office to summon the man who waited to see him. Christie saw him look at her and then at the plant manager and there was a speculation in his eyes that annoyed her. She knew what he thought. The boss's daughter was being shown about ceremoniously by Mr. Tidings. And it was true, of course, but it wasn't anything she could help.

"I don't know about those lollipops," John Macdonald said, half teasing. "You don't seem to be on the job, Miss Allard. I think I'll have to take the matter up again with Marge Molloy."

"Never mind," Christie told him. "I'll buy them for her myself."

"Much the easiest way out," he said, and went back into his office.

"What was that all about?" Mr. Tidings asked suspiciously as they left the building. Christie shook her head, dismissing the matter without explanation.

Her escorted tour of the plant proved more interesting than she had expected. The efficiency of modern machinery, shining clean rows of cans, all made an impressive picture of industry in action. In answer to a question she asked, Mr. Tidings shook his head emphatically. No, of course not, no migrants worked here. These jobs went only to Leola residents. Or, when the plant was short-handed, men and women came in from nearby towns. The Mexicans were fit only for field work.

"Why?" Christie asked.

"Because they're not trained for anything else," Mr. Tidings said curtly. "That's all they know how to do."

"Why aren't they trained for anything else?" she persisted.

"They're inferior workers, that's why," Mr. Tidings said. "Anyway, no one would employ them for better jobs. They're too unreliable. Do you know, my dear, you remind me more and more of your grandfather. He was a great one for asking questions straight out point blank."

"I'm glad to hear it," said Christie warmly. She was beginning to like this remote grandfather better by the minute. She wished she could have his office to herself for a few hours and get at those shelves of books.

She had no chance to read Tom's piece in the paper until her tour of the plant was over. It was eleven-forty by that time and, as Marge said, there seemed no purpose in returning to the school just before it closed for the morning. Besides, Christie had a need to be alone for a little while, a need to digest the new impressions she had gathered that morning.

She left Mr. Tidings and the plant without again seeing John Macdonald, and started the long, hot walk back across town. The sun was out again, the sky cloudless blue, and heat beat down upon her head and up from the sidewalk. Hot little gusts of wind stirred the dust of the dirt road and again she had a feeling of griminess and grit that made her long for a shower.

Now, as she walked along, she could unfold the paper and glance at the three columns Tom Webb had written.

Her own picture looked gravely out from the first page and the caption under it made her prickle with embarrassment.

FUTURE HEIRESS TO ALLARD PLANT?

A future heiress was certainly the last thing in the world she was likely to be, or wanted to be. The more quickly she could be completely independent of her father, the better she would like it. The very nickels and dimes in her purse were from checks he had sent when her mother had died, and which she had accepted because she had no choice. But very soon now she would think about a job, some way to earn money that would free her entirely from any obligation to him.

The picture itself was as mildly horrible as news pictures usually were. There she sat in her aunt's living room, with her chin thrust out, due to Tom's heckling. Why hadn't he used the smiling pose? But for all her solemnity, she looked ridiculously young.

She glanced down the page and scanned the article. Then, with a glance at the sidewalk now and then so as not to stumble, she went back and read the whole thing word for word as she walked along.

So! She was the Dresden-doll type, was she? A bright little girl, just out of high school, and entirely unfitted to face the world. He didn't actually say so, but the implication was clear. She was a typical rich man's daughter, fragile, protected, secure in her own corner, and believing it was the world. It was all there, not in so many words, but with the meaning clearly between the lines. This was what that fresh young reporter had thought of her! On the surface the piece seemed to flatter and praise. What credit he gave her for leaving her "gay city life" to bury herself in quiet little Leola! An Allard had come home. And so forth.

She would like, Christie thought, to wring his neck. With her own hands. He had made a complete fool of her. Everyone in Leola would be laughing at her before the day was out.

She stepped off a curb without looking and stumbled. The sudden clanging of a bell warned her that she had reached a crossing and the black-and-white striped gates clanged down almost under her nose. But the train was still well down the track, so she ducked under the gate and ran across, to find that she had taken the wrong turning and reached Main Street, instead of following the more direct route to her aunt's. Now she looked where she was going and consequently noticed when she came face to face with a sign above the sidewalk ahead of her. A large sign, black-lettered:

For a moment she stopped and stared at the words. Then she folded the paper with a decisive gesture, tucked it under her arm, and walked determinedly toward the sign. Old Josh Allard's granddaughter had a bone to pick with a certain young reporter.

10

Christie Talks to Tom

Christie jerked open the door of the Leola *Record* with a grip that nearly pulled off the knob, and stepped into a little anteroom with the inevitable wooden bench. Beyond was a waist-high partition, and beyond that a large room in which worked the small staff of the newspaper. In the middle of the room she saw Tom in shirt sleeves, at his typewriter.

There was a swinging wooden door in the partition and Christie pushed it open and walked straight to Tom's desk, ignoring the curious looks of those she passed. As the others in the room fell silent, Tom Webb glanced up from the page in his machine.

"Oh, oh," he said. "Lightning is about to strike."

"I want to talk to you," Christie told him grimly.

Tom teetered back in his chair and grinned at her. "Yes, ma'am, Miss Allard, ma'am. Would you like to tell me off here in public, thus rejoicing the hearts of my confreres, or do you want to talk to me more private-like?"

"Stop clowning," Christie said. "I'd prefer to talk to you alone." For the first time she became aware of the delighted attention of the others in the room.

Tom left his desk with alacrity and reached toward a clothes tree for his coat. Then he led the way back to the swinging gate, pushed it open for her, and followed her into the street.

"You've just caused a great deal of suffering back there," Tom said. "Everybody's been hoping someone would eventually turn up and give me what is known as a tongue-lashing. You've let them down."

"This isn't funny," Christie said.

"I was afraid you wouldn't think it was." He sighed. "In that case, don't you think the very least I owe you is a lunch? Mrs. Steese's restaurant down the street isn't half bad."

"This isn't a special occasion," Christie told him. "I just want five minutes of your time."

"You *are* peeved, aren't you?" Tom said. "Peeved and hurt. I don't mind making you mad. But I didn't think you'd get your feelings hurt. The trouble is, of course, that I interviewed the wrong girl that first day. And that's your fault."

"What are you talking about?" Christie asked. Somehow, in spite of herself, she was walking along at his side in the direction of the restaurant.

His grin returned. "There! A good reporter always hooks the interest. But it will take a little time to explain my full meaning. So you'd better make it lunch."

"Aunt Amelia expects me home," Christie said primly.

He stopped before the restaurant door, pulled it open. "We have telephones in Leola. In fact, there's a booth right over there."

Now the diners in the restaurant were staring. She couldn't stand here and argue. So she walked over to the phone booth, while Tom, still grinning, took his place in one of the empty booths to wait for her.

When she returned from a talk with her somewhat mystified aunt, he was studying the menu. He handed it to her after she sat down opposite him. She wasn't in the least hungry, but she ordered a fruit salad and iced tea and then looked about her, trying to sort out in her mind exactly the things she wanted to say to Tom Webb.

The restaurant followed the pattern of the average city eating place, and there was a terrifying monster of a lighted juke box at the rear, from which a popular singer's wailing tones were issuing.

"At least we have privacy," Tom said. "Nobody can possibly hear a word anyone else says over that cater-wauling. Or am I speaking of your favorite artist?"

Christie drew a deep breath and opened her mouth. But Tom Webb was too quick for her.

"The thing I want you to understand is that if I'd come to interview you after I saw you jump into that bunch of kids yesterday, I'd have presented a different picture. You're a lot less fragile than you look, Miss Christie Allard."

She didn't mean to be placated so easily. "That was a perfectly ridiculous piece you wrote about me. You've made me look a fool to everyone in Leola. It just isn't excusable."

The waitress set a bowl of soup down before Tom with a cheerful thump that sent the contents slopping over the rim.

"Have a soda cracker," Tom said, passing the plate to Christie.

"No, thank you. The thing I don't understand is how the editor of your paper is willing to keep you on as a reporter when you make fools out of the people you interview."

"He really is a pretty good guy." Tom took a spoonful of steaming hot soup. "And ahead of this town in his policies."

"He still has to sell his paper. And I don't think you can be making it very popular."

"You'll be surprised to hear that I am. Our local residents have taken to reading my little pieces with a good deal of relish. You do have to remember that my piece about you will be taken at face value. You'll be the only one who thinks it pokes fun at you, or teases a little. You and maybe the writer."

Suddenly, she didn't want to talk about it any more. She no longer even wanted to put this young man in his place. She felt limp and listless and confused. There was so much in Leola that she was beginning to dislike. She wished now that she hadn't gone out to the camp with

Marge at all this morning, that she had not seen that miserable truckload of migrants, or looked in on the Gomez family, or watched Marge trying to handle more children than any one girl should ever have to face in so small a room. If she hadn't seen any of those things, then they wouldn't be painting ugly pictures in her mind. She didn't *want* to think about them. There was nothing she could do and being upset didn't help.

Her fruit salad came and it was made of canned fruit, instead of the fresh segments that might have tempted her appetite. She poked without interest at a cube of pineapple and knew she couldn't swallow a bite. The juke box switched to a tune that had been popular last year when she was still in high school. She and Phil had danced to that number more than once at school affairs. In another moment she'd be getting tearful.

She swallowed quickly and stared at her plate, so that Tom couldn't see that her eyes were suddenly swimming. But this reporter was not one to be easily fooled.

"Go ahead and bawl if you want to," he said. "I don't think I'm the only cause of your being mad. Come on and tell ol' Uncle Tom what Leola has been doing to you."

She looked at him then, indignant in spite of her tears. "And find it all in print by the day after tomorrow?"

"By tomorrow," he said calmly. "Anyway, blow your nose. I hate women who sniffle."

So she blew and was angry enough to stop feeling weepy and sorry for herself. In order to reach safer ground, she tried a new direction.

"I wonder what my grandfather was like," she said.

Tom finished his soup and began buttering a piece of rye bread. He didn't seem surprised by this sudden switch of subjects.

"I'm afraid he was considerably before my time," he admitted. "But I think he still haunts this town. He must have been a pretty forceful, vigorous old guy."

Christie nodded. "Today, when I was in what used to be his office at the Allard plant, I couldn't help wondering how he would have dealt with this migrant problem."

"He'd probably have been a lot tougher than Tidings,"

Tom said, "considering that your Aunt Amelia is his daughter and that she's as prejudiced as they come."

"I don't know," Christie found herself wondering out loud, almost forgetting the man across the table. "Lots of times children aren't at all like their parents. I'm not like either of mine." That was true enough. She could resemble no one less than she'd resembled Eve. And she could never have behaved in the way her own father had behaved. So why couldn't her grandfather have been different from either Amelia or Lawrence?

"If you really want to know about him," Tom said, "why don't you stop in at the town museum sometime? That was the old Allard mansion, you know. There's still a lot of him to be found in that place."

"Thanks," Christie said. "Maybe I will."

After that she made an attempt to eat her salad, and sipped her iced tea gratefully.

"Feeling better, aren't you?" Tom asked. The waitress had brought his steak and he was eating with a hearty appetite.

Christie smiled. "I haven't forgiven you, if that's what you mean."

"But you will," he said, and for once there was no mockery in the grin he gave her.

It was odd how easily they slipped into talk about Chicago after that, comparing notes on favorite pictures at the Art Institute, on out-of-the-way bookshops, Grant Park concerts, and windy days on Michigan Boulevard. For the first time Christie found she could think of Chicago without wincing away in pain. There were friends she had not written to, she thought with a start, and little pullings of affection here and there that she had been too numb to recognize.

"Do you think you'll ever go back?" she asked Tom.

He looked surprised. "Of course. Chicago's my town. I'm only down here to earn something ahead on a good job. Won't you go back?"

"I don't know," she said. "I don't really know."

When Tom paid the check and they were out on Main Street again, Christie told him she was going straight home. He returned to the office and she went off down a cross street by herself, trying again to sort out the events of the morning. One thing she knew—she couldn't return to the camp again that afternoon. Everything in her rejected the prospect.

When she reached home, Marge was just getting ready to leave, and Christie begged off from going back. She knew her excuses sounded lame and that Marge didn't approve of her change of heart, but she couldn't help that. She tried vainly to explain how she felt.

"Those people in the truck, and the way Mr. Tidings acts about the workers, and those children who haven't even been taught to speak English. Marge, I can't help feeling sick over it all. My head hurts and——"

"I understand," Marge said coolly. "The ostrich cure. It's very effective for some people, I believe. Well, have a nice afternoon. So long."

Aunt Amelia wanted to question her about the morning, but Christie managed to evade her and go up to her own room. As she crossed the sitting room, she paused in front of the photograph of her grandfather. He looked very important and competent. In his own way he had probably been one of the early captains of industry in this part of the country. But the picture gave her only the surface look of him. She couldn't tell what he might have been like underneath.

She turned away and went into the room with the blue forget-me-nots on the walls. When she'd closed the door, she went straight to the mirror above the dresser. Its oval surface gave back the reflection of a girl who looked hot and tired and whose face was slightly dirty. She had picture-book pretty blue eyes and fair hair that was soft and fine as a baby's and hung now in blown wisps about her face. Her mouth was soft, too, and youngish, with the lipstick somewhat smudged. But below it was a firm, strong jaw line that indicated a certain ability to resist, or perhaps to persist. There was definitely a resemblance to the man in the portrait—old Josh Allard. But right now his granddaughter did not want to persist about anything at all. Inwardly she was tied into a knot of resistance. Resistance against Leola and all the converging elements

100

that seemed to be pushing her in a direction in which she did not want to go.

The ostrich cure, Marge had said. Well, it was her own business if she found she was much more comfortable with her head in the sand.

11

Encounter

For the next week or so Christie kept strictly away from all that was troublesome. Except for helping her aunt around the house, she worked at nothing. She wrote a few letters to long-neglected friends in Chicago. She went to the library and brought home an armload of books. Always before she had found it comforting to lose herself in the experiences of storybook people. But now her choice seemed to be inevitably poor. The characters in every book seemed to be either dredging the depths of futility, or else busily and courageously engaged in solving oversized problems. The first was depressing, the second irritating.

She avoided the camp altogether. She did not see either Tom or John Macdonald. And she was grateful for the fact that Marge treated her impersonally and let her alone. Even Alan Bennett seemed to understand her need of withdrawal and offered kindly sympathy but no advice. She didn't even trouble to tell him about what had happened Sunday with Lopez and the town boys. It no longer seemed to matter. Aunt Amelia was openly pleased. Christie, she said, had come to Leola to be quiet and think things out. And she was very glad to see her doing just that. She was especially glad that she had come to her senses and was staying away from that filthy camp.

Plans were going ahead for the church supper and Marge and Alan were busily publicizing the fact that real

Mexican food was to be served. Aunt Amelia had objected strongly at first. She didn't want one of those camp women cooking anything that *she* ate, and she didn't care about foreign foods anyway. But the young people at the church thought it would be fun, and they coaxed their elders into accepting the plans. In the end Alan and Marge persuaded Miss Amelia Allard to give the experiment a chance at least.

The supper was scheduled for a Sunday night. On Wednesday of that week the postman brought two letters for Christie. Both were from New York. She recognized the handwriting on each and took them up to the seclusion of her room to be read. The first was from Agnes O'Regan, a long, sometimes cheerful, sometimes tearful letter. Agnes had climbed the Statue of Liberty, and taken a boat up the Hudson. She had gone to Radio City and seen the lights of Broadway, and she'd had the time of her life every minute. But just the same, her love and longing for her "darlin' " Eve showed through the lines, and her worry about Christie, who was now out of her sight and keeping. In some ways it was a painful letter to read and made Christie feel all the more guilty about the one short note she had written to Agnes. It had been hard to write because she could not possibly have told her about the real Leola.

The second envelope she dreaded opening. The writing was in a strong, clear hand which she remembered from her childhood, and had often seen since on envelopes that brought checks to Eve. Her heart thumped queerly as she slit the flap and took out a single white sheet of paper with a few lines across it. Folded within was a check for one hundred dollars.

The written words said merely that though she had not written to that effect, she must be in need of spending money by now. Perhaps this was something which would help. And would she reconsider and write him about her college plans when she had had time to think the matter over.

College! How little interest she took in the idea. How little interest she took in anything, for that matter. All the hurtful things she had fled from Chicago to put behind her had come right along with her. There was nowhere she could go, she was beginning to suspect, where she could get away from her own thoughts and heartache. There was nothing which would make the hurting stop, which would make her forget. People talked about time. But time passed so slowly.

With several quick jerks she tore her father's note across and across and across and dropped the confetti in her wastebasket. The gesture reminded her painfully of that morning in the station when she had torn up Phil's letter. The check she folded and put away in the hiding place beneath her handkerchiefs, where she had put the snapshot of her father. She would decide what to do with it later. She didn't want his money. Not a penny of it. She didn't want anything from him ever again. Not college and certainly not support. But she couldn't just stay here letting her aunt take care of her, as if she had been a child.

She took out her navy-blue handbag and opened her billfold. There was a five-dollar bill in it and four singles. She had a little change besides. That was her entire fortune. As quickly as possible she would have to get a job. And that would take some thinking about. She had no desire to consult her aunt. Aunt Amelia would only protest that she didn't need to work yet and try to press money upon her. This was something she had to figure out herself.

Several times her aunt had offered her the use of the car if she wanted to drive around a bit, but until now she had been indifferent. Perhaps today was the time.

After lunch Christie got into the car and Alan gave her a bit of instruction. Then she drove off in the direction of downtown. It felt good to have a wheel beneath her hands again. Eve had often let her drive on week-end trips and she enjoyed it and was a good driver. In a little while she would turn out toward the highway, perhaps drive into the country. But first she had an errand to do downtown. Marge had said that John had paid for his wager with an armload of lollipops for the children, but Christie wanted to do the same thing herself. As a rule, crackers were all Marge could manage from the meager funds given her, and those children needed the treat of sweet things once in a while.

As the few blocks slipped by, she thought about the job she would look for. It might not be easy in a town like Leola. She was no saleswoman and wanted to avoid a store job except as a last resort. She wasn't sure she would make much of a stenographer, either, but at least she'd had shorthand and typing in school, and though she didn't feel particularly efficient, she could brush up at home and see if Leola was in need of her services.

She had reached Main Street now, and she turned in toward the curb and dropped a coin in the parking meter. Then she crossed the sidewalk and entered the dime store. When she had bought a sack of brilliant green and red suckers, she turned to the stationery counter and purchased some long yellow pencils and a stenographer's notebook. Just making the purchases made her feel more purposeful, more capable of solving her problem.

Then, as she started back toward the door, she saw something which made her stop at the cosmetic counter, half hidden by a sign. The jewelry section was just an aisle away and before the bright array stood Aurora Gomez. She was dangling a pair of shiny red earrings admiringly in the air, comparing them with some equally bright ones of blue glass. Behind the counter a sour-faced elderly woman watched with open disapproval.

Christie hesitated, uncertain of how Aurora might greet her if she spoke. She had no wish to be rebuffed again, but somehow she didn't want to leave the store without speaking to the girl. She took a step toward the other counter and at that moment Aurora pulled off her own green earrings and started to screw one of the red ones to the lobes of her ear.

The clerk spoke to her sharply. "Don't you go trying those on! Do you think other folks want to come in here and buy something you Mexicans have been pawing over with your dirty hands?"

Aurora flung the earrings down on the tray, but before she could walk out of the store, Christie flew across the aisle and stopped beside her.

"I heard what you said," she told the clerk. "If you'll

104

take the trouble to look, you'll see that the hands of this young lady are probably cleaner than your own."

Aurora stood where she was in astonishment, while the clerk gaped.

"I have never heard of any store, least of all a dime store," Christie went on, "where customers were not permitted to try on earrings if they chose. That's why you have that mirror there."

The clerk recovered her voice. "It ain't for the likes of her."

"I wish," said Christie firmly, "to speak to the manager of this store."

"No," Aurora said bleakly, "please, no!"

"He ain't here today," the clerk told her. "And anyways you won't get nowhere with him. We have our orders. We're supposed to wait on them camp people and get 'em out of the store quick's we can. Let 'em spend their money and git!"

"Well!" said Christie haughtily. "I shall come back another time and talk to him. I'm sure there is no excuse at all for treating Miss Gomez like this."

She slipped one hand through Aurora's unresisting arm and walked her firmly to the door and out into the familiar Leola heat.

Aurora would have drawn her arm away and gone off down the block, stiff with wounded dignity, if Christie had let her. But Christie tightened her hold because she herself had a need to cling to someone.

"My goodness!" she said shakily. "I've never in my whole life talked to anyone like that before. I wouldn't have thought I had the nerve. I just got spitting mad all in a flash. And now I feel trembly. Don't go away, Aurora."

The other girl hesitated, and Christie drew her toward the curb.

"Look, I've got Aunt Amelia's car here. Come for a ride with me. Let's go out on the highway some place and get ourselves some slathering big dishes of ice cream. It's my treat."

Again Aurora tried to slip out of her grasp, but Christie pulled open the car door and gave the girl a little push. Helplessly Aurora got into the front seat and plumped herself down in it. Christie slammed the door shut and ran around to her own side before Aurora could escape. A few moments later the car was purring along through the outskirts of town.

Christie threw her unwilling companion a sidewise glance and saw that her hands were folded tensely in her lap and that her eyes were fixed unseeingly on the road ahead.

Christie rambled along, talking a little breathlessly to cover Aurora's silence. "*I am* glad I ran into you. I still don't know any girls my own age in this town. This afternoon I was lonesome, wishing I had somebody to talk to."

Aurora seemed not to hear her. She sat in strained silence while the car turned onto the long, straight highway.

"You mustn't be hurt by anyone like that clerk back in the store," Christie said gently. "I was angry, too, but what she says doesn't matter."

It mattered to Aurora, however. "Tomorrow it is finished," she said. "Tomorrow my father will not scold me. My mother will not cry. I will go back to the fields. It is finished."

Christie knew what she meant. That all Aurora's stormy rebellion was over. That her struggle to escape, to find somehow a better life than her parents and her companions knew, was ended, done with. Aurora Gomez would go back to the fields, to the roving from camp to camp, to the poverty-stricken days; to the life where too many people were crowded into the confines of a small, boxlike room.

"There must be some way out," Christie said helplessly.

"*Qué voy a hacer?*" Aurora said, slipping into the tongue she knew better than English. "What am I to do? My mama, my papa, they want me in the fields."

"They shouldn't want you there," Christie said. "It's all wrong."

Aurora laughed. "It is easy for you to talk like that. Your mama and papa, they give you what you like. You can go to school if you want. Go to any work you like. For you, America, it is a free place."

106

Ahead on the highway there was a gas station, and beside it a roadside diner with a gaudy sign advertising ice cream and hot dogs. Christie took her foot off the gas pedal and the car slowed. She did not answer Aurora until she had turned off the road and parked the car in the cleared space beside the diner.

Then she spoke shortly. "I don't suppose it has anything to do with the case, but I might as well tell you that I don't have either a mother or a father."

Aurora uttered a little gasp of distress. "Ah, *pobrecita!* Your mama, I did not know. But the papa you have, the Señor Allard, yes?"

"I haven't seen the Señor Allard since I was nine years old," Christie said. "My parents were divorced."

Again Aurora made a sound of distress and astonishment. "But divorce, it is a bad thing, no?"

"I think so," Christie said. "Well, let's go in and get some ice cream."

For the first time Aurora looked around and saw where they were. Then she shrank back in the seat, shaking her head. "No, please."

Christie opened the door on her side. "Oh, come along. It will make us both feel better."

"It is not that," Aurora said. Her fingers had twined themselves together in her lap again.

"Then why?"

"I will tell you why," said Aurora, facing her suddenly. "Maybe I go in there with you, and maybe the man at the counter he say, 'No Mexicans here.' Many times it is like that."

Christie got out of the car grimly. "You stay here," she said. She crossed the gravel-strewn parking lot and went into the diner. There was no man behind the counter, but a large, middle-aged blond woman with a rough-and-ready manner.

"I just want to know one thing," Christie said. "Do you have any objection to serving Mexicans? I have a Mexican-American friend in the car and we're not coming in if——"

"Whoa there, kid," the woman broke in cheerfully on her words. "You sound like you're getting all set for a fight and there ain't gonna be no fight. I don't hold with none of this no-Mexicans business. You bring your little friend right along in."

Christie found that she had indeed been holding every muscle tense, as if for a struggle. She relaxed and smiled back at the woman behind the counter.

"Thank you. I'll go get her."

Aurora came in a little timidly, but the woman's warm smile was for her, too, and Aurora took a stool at the counter beside Christie. They ordered huge dishes of ice cream, with nuts and chocolate sauce, and their hostess generously piled mounds of whipped cream on top of everything else, until Aurora's eyes grew round with pleasure.

"*Es verdad*—is nice to be rich. Is true," she murmured in wonder. Christie did not explain that the bill she pushed across the counter was one of her last. That might have surprised Aurora.

It was a slow time of day and their hostess was lonesome and ready for company and conversation.

"You know something?" she said. "I been all around America. My first husband, God rest his soul, liked to change the scenery a couple of times a year. I guess he was looking for something he never did find. But I didn't care, I went along. And you know what, every place you go there's somebody looks down on somebody else. Maybe it's the fellow with brown skin, or maybe yellow skin. Or maybe it's the fellow whose nose is made different from yours, or one you fought in a war a hundred years ago. Honest, I used to get all mixed up sometimes about who I was supposed to think wasn't as good as me."

Her laughter was hearty and warming. Even Aurora found herself smiling.

"It does sound silly when you put it like that," Christie said.

"It's so silly," the blond woman told them, "that I gave up looking down on anybody fast as I could. Me—I guess I just like human beings."

"And I guess they just like you," Christie said, and felt

suddenly sorry for that gray creature back in the dime store who was probably liked by no one.

A couple of truck drivers came in then and the blond woman went to wait on them. Aurora spoke softly to Christie.

"I am sorry about your mama, your papa. If I could—what you call it—loan you a little of mine, that would be nice. Is true, my papa gets mad sometimes, and my mama cries. And is true also it is I who make them like that. But we have much love with us. My papa likes to sing, to play the guitar. And my mama likes to laugh, and the small Tomasa also. I wish I could give you some of this."

"Thank you, Aurora," Christie said. "I think that's about the nicest thing anyone has ever said to me." And surprisingly enough, she felt it to be true. Here was a generosity of heart that was new in her experience. They finished their fast-melting ice cream, told the woman behind the counter good-by, and went back to the car, which waited sweltering in the sun.

"I'll drive you back to camp," Christie said. "Can we take a different road back?"

Aurora pointed to a crossroad on ahead. "Turn there. We cross to the other road back to town." She gave Christie a quick, speculative look as they bumped out of the driveway and back onto the pavement. "Maybe you like to see the fields, yes?"

"The fields?" Christie did not grasp her meaning at once.

"Where the corn grows for the Allard plant. Where I will work tomorrow. But not today."

Christie hesitated. She didn't in the least want to see the fields, but since it might please Aurora she nodded her assent.

"Is good for you to see," Aurora assured her, and Christie wondered what she meant.

12

Cornfield

Row upon long green row the cornfields stretched, a vast green ocean across which rippling motion spread at every touch of the breeze. In the fields nearest the road, workers made separate moving rows of their own, their straw hats, like giant mushrooms, shielding them from the hot sun.

As Christie slowed the car, Aurora explained. "This field is hybrid seed corn. It is the detasseling now. The fields are planted at different times so that all will not be ready at once. Now the tassels must be pulled out of the plants. Not one must be missed because the pollen must not spread. Stop here and we will get out."

Christie turned the car onto the grassy shoulder of the road and braked to a stop. Aurora hopped out quickly and Christie followed her down the embankment at the side of the road.

She could see the workers more clearly now. Some of the women had footless cotton stockings pulled over their arms for protection from sun and insects and sharp corn leaves. Some were barefoot, while others wore rough men's shoes. Both men and women wore bandanas knotted about their necks to protect them from the fierce sun. Some of the workers walked between the rows, reaching skillfully, swiftly in among green leaves to pull out the tassels. Others stood on platforms drawn by tractors moving between the rows.

"Walking I like best," Aurora said. "When you stand on the platform, you must work very quick or the tractor has pulled you past."

A few looked up as the two girls crossed the ditch at the side of the road and walked into the cornfields. There was disapproval in their gaze as it rested on this lazy one, Aurora; curiosity as they glanced toward Christie. But there was work to be done; their hands never ceased their busy reaching and no one stared for long.

One of the men—Aurora whispered that he was a crew leader—spoke to her sharply in Spanish, but she only shrugged and answered him in an impudent tone.

"I tell him I come tomorrow," she explained to Christie. "Señor Tidings does not like when José bring the lazy worker like me up from the Valley."

Suddenly a little girl ran across in front of a parked truck and came toward them, a wide smile on her face, her small hands grubby with earth. It was Tomasa Gomez and Aurora caught her up in a wide swing that landed her at Christie's feet. The child held out her hands to her new friend and Christie took the grubby little paws into hers. Once she would have drawn back from this contact, but now it was more important not to hurt Tomasa's feelings.

The three walked along together and as Christie looked down the rows more closely, she saw there were other children scattered about the field.

"Why aren't they in the nursery school?" she asked Aurora.

"They can help here in small ways," Aurora said carelessly. "Every family needs the earning ones. And the mamas like to have them near."

"But aren't there laws?" Christie asked. "About child labor, I mean?"

Aurora shrugged. "You watch. When a car comes by on the road, all the children stand up. To show they don't work."

"Is that allowed at all these camps?" Christie asked.

"Some camps, no," Aurora said. "Allard camp, yes, though Señor Mac try to stop it. Is more money for family if children work. Is more work gets done and Señor Tidings like that."

Looking down one row, Christie saw a child of about two staked to the ground with a rope around its waist. There was enough length to the rope to permit some movement, but Christie found her indignation growing when she thought of Tidings's opposition to the nursery school.

Rafael waved to them from across several rows and then wiped a dust-streaked hand across his sweating face. For once Aurora smiled at him in friendly greeting. Lopez was there, too, following along the row behind his brother, and Christie called "Hello" to them both, but only Rafael answered. Lopez probably remembered her in connection with his own humiliation and did not care to recognize her.

As they moved on, Christie fanned herself in the breathless air and slapped at a swarm of midges.

"How can they work like this in the blazing sun all day long?"

Again Aurora shrugged. "Many people do. Is better than when it is raining. Then the ground is thick mud and clothes get wet and cold."

"You mean you work out here in the rain, too?"

Aurora laughed at her ignorance. "What do you think? That the crops stop growing because it rains?" Then she added abruptly, "Now we go back. That José, he likes to make me work." She glanced almost pleadingly at Christie. "But not today, yes?"

"Not today," Christie said, understanding. Tomorrow Aurora would go back to this work she hated, but every moment of today's freedom was something to cling to.

As they climbed the embankment, Tomasa scampered back between the rows to walk beside Lopez. The boy smiled at her affectionately and teased her in Spanish.

On the way home Aurora told Christie more about the work in the fields. How, during the harvesting, everyone worked Saturdays and Sundays, too, though later, of course, on Sunday, because of church. Weekday mornings the workers came out to the fields at dawn, while dew was still on the corn leaves, making them soft to the hands. Later, when the sun dried out the rows, those same leaves could slice a hand like a razor. Working could be painful then. But no matter what, when the corn was ready it must be jerked. Later would come the gay time of the Leola Corn Festival. And then the Texas workers would go back to their homes in the Valley, some of them stopping off to pick cotton through the fall in Texas. After that no work till the crops were ready again next year.

Christie let Aurora out at the camp gate and the girl stood for a moment beside the car.

"Muchas gracias," she said in her soft Spanish tongue, and the words sounded more gracious than if she had spoken them in English.

"I've had fun," Christie told her. "Aurora, will you promise me something?" The other girl looked uneasy, and Christie hurried on.

"It's nothing very terrible. Will you come with your mother to the church supper Sunday night?"

"To be Mexican cook?" Aurora demanded, ready to spark again.

"I'll be there helping, too," said Christie, though this was news to herself. "And afterward I'd like you to sit beside me at the table. I don't know many people in Leola. I'd like a friend there."

Aurora's look softened. Perhaps she was remembering the *pobrecita* Christie who had no papa and mama in her home.

"Maybe I come," she said, and darted away, running across the yard as if she had been a child of ten.

Christie backed the car from the gate, glad to escape without seeing either Mr. Tidings or John Macdonald. Either, she was sure, would regard her presence with disapproval.

As she drove back across the town she realized for the first time that the purpose she had driven out for—the solving of her own problem of where to apply for a job— had not been realized at all. In fact, she hadn't thought of her own troubles once since that moment when she had seen Aurora in the dime store. Yet she felt more cheerful than at any other time since she had come to Leola. Her troubles hadn't changed by a hair, but she had managed to forget them and for a little while the hurting had stopped. Oddly enough, she didn't feel like brooding about herself just now. Brooding would seem ridiculous in the face of what she had just seen in the cornfields. And anyway, she had settled her problem. Next week she would get a job. In the meantime, she would brush up on her shorthand. And that was that. Probably there would be ads in the *Record*. She'd watch for them. Something would turn up.

When she parked the car at the curb in front of Aunt Amelia's, she heard someone talking in the back yard. She left the car and went around the house by way of the driveway. There a tableau met her eyes.

Alan Bennett, again in overalls, was exercising his green thumb, and at the same time declaiming dramatically to a fascinated audience of one. His listener was Fatso, and the dog's bleary old eyes never left Alan's face. Somehow he managed to look wise and comprehending over the burst of oratory.

Just to make sure he kept Christie in her place, however, he growled deep in his throat at her appearance and Alan broke off in the middle of a word to grin sheepishly.

"I thought I had the place to myself," he confessed. "I like to practice a sermon on my friend here. If he goes to sleep, I know the congregation will, too."

Christie seated herself on the back porch steps. "He seems to approve of this one. Sorry I interrupted. How are the plans coming for the supper Sunday night?"

"The plans are all right." Alan went back to his garden work, a lock of red hair falling over his forehead. "But the responses are mixed. I can't say your Aunt Amelia, much as I respect her, is of any great help. Our big hope is, of course, that once she and the other ladies meet Mrs. Gomez and Mrs. Olivera and talk to them, the ice will be broken. Marge and I put in our propaganda every chance we get, but so far I'm afraid we haven't cracked the surface. At least John Macdonald will be there to help us that night. He has promised to bring Mrs. Gomez and Mrs. Olivera over in his car and stay for the supper. And Tom Webb will be there long enough to cover the affair for the *Record*."

This was not news Christie could regard with delight. But here was her chance to tell Alan about the scene in the vacant lot last Sunday, when Lopez had been in a fight with town boys.

Alan listened gravely. "I know some of those kids. Hank Martin's something of a bully, I'm afraid. But Bitsy

114

Steese would be all right if we could get him away from Hank's influence. Too bad Lopez couldn't show them what he can really do with a baseball."

Not until dinner that night, when Aunt Amelia asked where she had gone, did Christie say anything about her drive with Aurora. Then she launched into an account in some detail and found herself growing indignant again as she talked. There was the incident of the dime store, and Aurora's hesitation about going into the diner, and later the sight of children working in the fields with the very little ones running about underfoot, unwatched, or perhaps tied to a stake.

"I don't think I'll ever be able to eat another mouthful of Allard vegetables without choking," she said. "When I think what lies behind the food we serve on our tables——"

Her aunt broke in with some asperity. "Nonsense! You can't be sentimental about such things. Everything we use, our clothes, all our possessions, come out of someone's labor, labor that is necessary to keep the country going. Some people fit one niche, some another. You don't go around being sentimental about garbage collectors because they have to collect garbage. Society needs them and pays them for what they do. If they don't like the job, they can do something else."

Marge took up the argument quickly. "That's all true. But most workers have unions to protect their interests. They're well paid and they're not exploited. Not any more. And as you say they can change jobs if they don't like what they're doing. But prejudice works against the Mexican-American. His education is so poor and his opportunity so limited that he is forced into certain lines of work. Not all the migrants who work the crops are Mexicans, of course. Some are Negroes, some whites who have had to leave worn-out land, or who have become disgusted with share-cropping, or lost other jobs. But there's no one to speak for them and some of the conditions they work under, live under, are pretty awful. I have a guilty conscience, if you don't, Miss Allard. And I want to see Leola do something about the problem right here within reach."

"Bravo!" cried Alan applauding.

Aunt Amelia rolled her eyes upward. "This missionary zeal!"

"Go right ahead; I can take it," Marge said. "I'm not ashamed of my work. Pretty soon we'll open with some really big guns. I had a little chat with Mr. Bigelow yesterday."

"Ed Bigelow who owns the dry-goods store?" Aunt Amelia asked.

"That's right. He's coming to the supper Sunday night, even though it isn't his church."

"I'll talk to Ed," said Aunt Amelia. "He's on the school board with me."

Marge wrinkled her nose impudently into a ridge of freckles. "I've talked to him first. And you know my irresistible charm. If only we could get to old Tidy out at the plant. But I'm afraid poison is the only treatment for him."

Christie took a second helping of Aunt Amelia's fluffy mashed potatoes. This was the hungriest she'd been since coming to Leola. "You know," she said, "I felt a little sorry for Mr. Tidings when I talked to him last week. He seemed sort of—oh, mixed up and sick and bewildered."

"Spencer Tidings is a very good man," said Aunt Amelia. "I respect him highly."

"Then you don't know him very well," said Marge shortly.

Spencer! Christie thought. He would be named something like that.

Aunt Amelia gave Marge a straight look. "I went to school with Spencer. We were in the same class. And my mother thought highly of him and always made him welcome at our house. In fact, he proposed to me once when I was in my twenties."

All three young people stared at her. Marge, with her mouth full, stopped chewing. Alan's fork paused on the way to its destination. Christie clicked her glass of milk against her teeth.

Miss Amelia Allard regarded them with some vexation. "I can see that it astonishes you to realize that I have been as young as you three are now."

They all burst into words at once, trying to make up for their momentary lapse, and after that the conversation did not return to dangerous topics.

Marge and Christie did the dishes and afterward Marge asked Christie up to her room to see something she was making. It was the first time she had invited Christie in. Her big, airy room looked out through the green boughs of old trees in the back garden. There were yellow curtains at the windows and the walls were papered in mossy green.

"Oh, I like this!" Christie cried. "An outdoor room."

Somehow it suited Marge. Again there was an old-fashioned rocking chair beside a window, and at Marge's invitation Christie dropped into it. Marge began to rummage in a closet.

"Spencer!" Christie echoed softly. "And he proposed to Aunt Amelia. I can't get over it."

"Me either," Marge said from the depths of the closet. "I'll have to take another look at the old boy. I wonder what she said to him?"

Christie giggled. "At least it was the right answer. Imagine having to call him Uncle Spencer!"

"Here we are." Marge came out of the closet with a large rectangle of white cardboard in her hands. Christie caught a glimpse of black ink on the glossy surface before Marge turned the picture side away from her. "Now then, let's see how good an artist I am. It's not finished yet, but tell me what you think it is. Just one guess."

She turned the cardboard around and Christie gave a mock shudder at the ferocious monster sketched in pencil and partially filled in with India ink. The creature had bulging eyes on each side of its head and its ugly, sprawling legs were covered with tiny hairs. Thin veins ran along its opened wings.

"It could be prehistoric, of course," Christie said, "but I'd guess that it's a blown-up version of a housefly. Your version."

"Hooray!" Marge cried triumphtly. "But what do you mean, my version? This is a slight exaggeration of a picture in one of Aunt Amelia's old schoolbooks. Do you think it will make an impression?"

117

"On the children in the nursery school, you mean? I should think so. They'll probably have nightmares and screaming meemies."

Marge took another admiring look at her handiwork. "I hope they do. Then maybe they'll get the idea of closing doors and keeping their hands off screens and chasing flies." She sighed. "There's so much they need to learn. And we have them for such a short time. But at least we're not working alone. There are communities waking up to the migrant problem all over the country."

When Marge had put away the fly picture, Christie spoke of her own problem. Somehow she could talk to Marge tonight.

"I want to get a job next week," Christie said.

Marge plumped up the pillows on the bed, kicked off her shoes, and stretched herself out comfortably.

"Good for you. I don't suppose I can talk you into helping with the camp school?"

"It has to be a job with pay," Christie said. "I'm spending my last ten dollars right now."

Marge's eyes widened.

"I know it sounds queer, considering Aunt Amelia, and my father, and all. But I don't have a penny of my own and I've just got to earn my own way. I do want to be independent, Marge."

"A noble ambition," said Marge. "What are you going to try for?"

"I'm not sure. I took typing and shorthand in school, but I'll probably be the world's worst stenographer."

"Why don't you try the plant?" Marge asked.

It was Christie's turn to stare. "The—the Allard plant? Oh, no, I couldn't."

"Why not? This town isn't exactly crying for stenographers. You'd have the best chance out there. Besides, they'd hardly dare turn you down."

"But that's just it," Christie said. "I don't want anybody to hand me anything. I want——"

"All very fine. But in this case foolish. It would be up to you to earn your pay. Besides, Miss Christie *Allard*, the plant is where you belong. Where you might do some good."

118

"How?" said Christie. "I'm a zero out there. John Macdonald has no use for me, and Mr. Tidings treats me as if I were seven years old."

"That's all right. You'd be a zero with eyes and ears."

"But how would I go about it? I mean applying and all that?"

"Mac is the personnel man. You'd see him, of course."

"Oh, no!" Christie said. "I wouldn't ask him for a job." She got up quickly before Marge could argue her into anything. "I think I'll look around other places first. There must be some sort of job in Leola that I can do."

She went off to her own room and tried to start a letter. "Dear Agnes," she wrote, and sat for a long while with her pen poised above the paper.

She could just imagine the way John Macdonald would look down his nose if she came to apply for a job. No, indeed, the last place in the world where she could apply was in her father's own company.

13

Mrs. Olivera Scores a Point

On the night of the church supper Christie's intention was to go over early with Marge in order to be there when Aurora arrived. But Marge drew her out of her aunt's hearing and whispered instructions.

"You stay with Auntie and don't let her out of your sight. She's feeling a bit restive and skittish tonight and there's no telling which way she might jump. Alan and I are trusting you to get her there if you have to drag her by her topknot."

Christie shook her head. "The topknot comes off. I'll do better than that."

Marge hurried away and Christie roamed aimlessly around the house, keeping an eye on Aunt Amelia, who postponed dressing until Christie began to get nervous. Alan wasn't there; a very old lady in his parish was desperately ill and wanted him at her bedside.

Despite Christie's anxiety, however, Aunt Amelia was ready to leave a good half-hour before the affair was to start.

"We might as well go over and see if there is any last-minute help we can give," she said, and Christie agreed with relief.

When they reached the church, Christie had her first look at the other rooms which opened away from the church proper. There was a good-sized meeting room for Sunday-school classes, a cloakroom, and an old-fashioned kitchen. From the kitchen were emanating wonderful, spicy odors which made Christie sniff hungrily.

"What heathenish smells," Aunt Amelia said. "I don't know why I'm here tonight. I shan't be able to eat a bite."

"But you'd die of curiosity if you stayed away," Christie teased.

Aunt Amelia said "Humph!" and stalked down the hall past the kitchen without so much as looking in. In the meeting room long boards had been set up over wooden trestles to make the banquet tables, and there the crowd was gathering.

When her aunt had joined the group in the dining room, Christie stepped into the steamy kitchen, where Mrs. Gomez stirred an immense potful of red beans with a wooden spoon. Mrs. Olivera, who was as thin and tall as Mrs. Gomez was short and fat, busied herself with a second concoction on the stove. Marge was taking dishes from a cupboard. The two women from the camp greeted Christie in a friendly fashion, but there was no Aurora in sight.

Marge handed Christie a stack of paper napkins for the dining room and shooed her toward it.

"Did you get Auntie here all right?" she whispered.

Christie nodded. "She's here. But what about Aurora?"

"In the other room," Marge said. "See if you can get your aunt back here to meet Mrs. Gomez and Mrs. Olivera."

The front meeting room, Christie discovered, was already buzzing with guests. John Macdonald's tall figure loomed head and shoulders above the others as he moved about, having cheerfully volunteered to help Aurora set tables. Following close on John's heels wherever he went was Tomasa Gomez. The little girl produced her usual big smile for Christie, but it was apparent that John Macdonald held first place in her affections. He spoke to her in Spanish as she trotted after him, and found little ways in which she could help.

Christie went quickly to Aurora to explain that she had been delayed and the girl greeted her in a more pleasant manner than had been her custom.

Aunt Amelia was talking to a cheerful-looking fat man, whom she introduced as Mr. Bigelow. Christie regarded him with interest, recalling that he was the drygoods store owner whom Marge had mentioned a few days before as being on their side.

"Marge would like you to come out to the kitchen for a moment," Christie told her aunt.

Aunt Amelia thrust in one of the silver hairpins that held her braids in place. "You may tell Marjorie for me that the odor out there is quite dreadful. I'm sure she can come here more comfortably than I can go to her."

Mr. Bigelow smiled sympathetically at Christie and she found herself liking this plump, pink-faced little man.

"Marge wants you to meet Mrs. Gomez and Mrs. Olivera," Christie persisted. "They're too busy to come out here. It's a matter of courtesy."

Aunt Amelia sighed. "I suppose one must observe the amenities. At least it sets these people a good example. You'll excuse me, please."

Feeling like a fisherman who had netted but not yet subdued his catch, Christie led the way back to the kitchen where Marge promptly took over the introductions. Wiping one hand hastily on her green apron, Mrs. Gomez extended it to Miss Allard with a warm smile and a friendly *"Buenas noches."*

There was just a hint of hesitation before Aunt Amelia took the small plump hand in her own and said "Good evening" stiffly.

121

Mrs. Olivera was too busy at the stove to extend her hand. Nor did she smile in the friendly fashion of her neighbor. Rafael's mother carried herself in the erect, proud-headed manner characteristic of her people, and her dark features had the high cheekbones of possible Indian ancestry.

"Good evening, Miss Allard," Mrs. Olivera said with a dignity that matched Aunt Amelia's. Her dark eyes met the other woman's directly and there was nothing of subservience in her manner. Christie sensed a moment of challenge between the two. Then Mrs. Olivera turned again to the stove and Aunt Amelia left the kitchen hastily.

"Well, I never!" she said as she and Christie stepped into the hall. "Did you see that woman look me over?"

"She was probably wondering whether you were worth knowing," Christie said slyly.

The set of her aunt's shoulders answered her as Aunt Amelia turned quickly to the other room. Christie would have followed, but someone hissed her name from the nearby stairs, and she looked around to see Tom Webb, camera in hand, beckoning to her with an air of secrecy.

"Hello," she said, mystified. "What are you doing a cloak-and-dagger act for?"

"I forgot my press card," he whispered. "Do you suppose you can sneak me in?"

"Idiot!" she said, and felt almost glad to see him. At least Tom could be counted on for laughs.

At that moment Aurora came out of the dining room, all grace and color in her bright skirt and white blouse, her hair a thick black cloud on her shoulders, green earrings tapping her cheeks.

Tom whistled appreciatively and Aurora, flouncing past, gave him a sidelong look. She went on toward the kitchen and Tom put his camera unceremoniously into Christie's hands.

"Here, hold this, little girl. I have to mail a letter." And off he went in Aurora's wake.

Christie didn't know whether to laugh or to feel annoyed. But before she could decide, Tom was back forlornly, to take his property out of her hands.

"Wow! Why didn't you tell me her mama was out in the kitchen? They're dragons for sure, these Mexican mamas!"

"And probably a good idea," said Christie tartly, and started once more for the dining room.

Tom came along without invitation. "Never mind, I still like blondes. But it does make for complications when I also like redheads and brunettes. Keeps me in quite a whirl. Well, Miss Christie, ma'am, how is the shindig going?"

She stopped him at the door. "Do you suppose you could possibly get it through your head that this is a church? That this is a church supper, not a shindig? And that making like a wolf is out entirely?"

He gave her a lugubrious look that made her giggle and walked solemnly into the dining room. Thereafter he gave himself over to the business for which he had come. Christie lost track of him for a while, except for an occasional bulb flash as he caught candid shots of the gathering. Once she saw him posing Aurora and Tomasa together.

"That should make a good picture," someone said behind her and she looked around at John Macdonald. "How does your aunt feel about this supper tonight?" he went on.

For once he didn't seem superior or coolly disapproving, but Christie still felt uncomfortable with him. "I'm afraid she doesn't approve," she said, and found a quick excuse to move away from him as Alan Bennett came into the room.

It seemed that the old lady whom he had attended had decided to rally, so there had been no sad occasion and he had been able to get away in time for the supper.

Shortly afterward Marge began to urge the guests toward the long tables. Tom Webb waved an elaborate farewell at Christie and disappeared with his camera. Everyone started to find seats. Marge seated Aunt Amelia in a place of honor, and before that lady knew what was happening, Mrs. Gomez had been put on one side of her and Mrs. Olivera right across the table. Christie could tell by her aunt's look that it was a distinct shock to discover that the cooks were also to eat as honored guests.

Christie glanced about for Aurora and found her hesitating uncertainly.

"You're sitting next to me, remember?" Christie said. "I haven't had a minute with you this evening."

She hurried Aurora toward a place between herself and Marge, with Mrs. Olivera on Christie's other side. John Macdonald was at another table, the small Tomasa on his right. Several girls from the church's Youth Group had agreed to act as waitresses and their presence added to the fun of the occasion.

When everyone's plate had been heaped with hot, flavorful Mexican food and the diners were eating with evident enjoyment, Marge leaned toward Christie.

"Will you look at your aunt? *There* is a lady who has been trapped, if ever I saw one."

Christie glanced across the table and saw that Aunt Amelia was really in a spot. Despite protestations, her plate was piled with frijoles and the tacos Mrs. Gomez had promised, to say nothing of other delicacies. And at her side an anxious and eager Mrs. Gomez watched every mouthful she lifted on her fork. Apparently not even Aunt Amelia had the heart to tell Mrs. Gomez that she was prepared to dislike Mexican cooking. Christie saw that her aunt was chewing and swallowing resolutely. Her face grew red and her eyes bright, but she carried on nobly.

On Christie's left Mrs. Olivera sat in silence and Christie decided she had better try to draw her into some sort of talk.

"How are your sons, Mrs. Olivera?" she asked.

"Very well, thank you." Mrs. Olivera spoke clearly and without the slightest Spanish accent.

"I've been wondering if Lopez managed to get interested in the baseball book that Mr. Bennett loaned him," Christie went on.

"He doesn't care for reading, as Rafael does," his mother said. "But Mr. Bennett made a good choice. When I have a chance I read to him out of the book. He likes to listen, but he wouldn't touch it himself until I

124

came to a piece about Jackie Robinson. Then he couldn't leave the book alone. He has been trying to make out the words himself."

Of course Lopez would find comfort and encouragement in the Negro player's story, Christie thought. But had even Jackie Robinson had as hard a road as faced Lopez?

Mrs. Olivera went on earnestly without waiting for a further question from Christie.

"I want a good education for my sons. Rafael will be all right. He will find his way. But Lopez—I worry about him. I was able to finish high school, and Rafael will finish, even though he is behind. Lopez hates school."

"Lopez may surprise you. He seems to have a lot of determination," Christie pointed out, anxious to keep the conversation going. "I've noticed, by the way, that neither he nor Rafael has your accent. You speak more like other Texans I've heard."

"I grew up in Texas," Mrs. Olivera said. "My mother was in domestic service with a very fine family in San Antonio. We lived in their house for many years and I went to school with the daughter. I wanted to become a teacher, perhaps to help my own people."

Christie wondered what had happened to change her purpose. She seemed the sort of person who would hold to any plan she might make.

Mrs. Olivera sighed. "It is possible to be very foolish when one is young."

She said nothing more, but Christie could imagine what might have happened to a spirited, intelligent girl if a gay, swaggering young man had come along. A young man who was, perhaps, neither so intelligent nor so ambitious as the girl. What steps had led through the years to the migrant camps there was no telling, but Christie felt a surge of sympathy for the woman next to her. She wished her aunt could get to know Mrs. Olivera and have her eyes opened to a few things. A plan began to stir in Christie's mind.

When the meal was finally at an end, with everyone agreeing that the food had been wonderful, Christie found a moment in which to draw her aunt into the hallway.

125

"Let's invite Mrs. Gomez and Mrs. Olivera over to the house some evening, Aunt Amelia. I think you'd especially enjoy talking to Mrs. Olivera. And it would mean a lot to her."

Aunt Amelia stared at her niece aghast. "Christine, my dear, I think you and I are going to have to sit down and have this matter out sooner or later. There are certain things which are not fitting for an Allard to do. If you insist upon fraternizing with these Mexicans, giving them notions they shouldn't be getting, I am going to have to send you back to Chicago."

Christie must have looked her astonishment for Aunt Amelia softened her manner.

"This isn't the time to talk about these things. All this dreadful food has upset me. Goodness knows what dirt and germs I have eaten by now. I'm sure we can talk this matter out agreeably at a more opportune moment."

"I'm not sure we can," Christie said quietly. She had never expected this threat of being sent back to Chicago. "I do think that Mrs. Olivera and Mrs. Gomez, too, could teach us quite a few things we don't know."

Aunt Amelia was accustomed to dealing with rebels. She patted Christie a little sharply on the cheek. "Nonsense, child. Please use some judgment. Under no circumstances will I permit one of those camp people to set foot in my house. Under no circumstances——" She stopped abruptly, and Christie turned to find that Mrs. Olivera had come out of the kitchen and had undoubtedly heard her aunt's last words.

Mrs. Olivera stood where she was for just a moment with her head held high. Her dark eyes flashed at the insult and she walked proudly toward them, as straight-backed as Aunt Amelia herself. When she spoke it was with restraint and dignity.

"This has been a fine effort tonight on the part of your church, Miss Allard. I know how hard you must have worked to help make it a success. Now I would like to ask you—it would do my house great honor if you and your niece would visit us some evening next week. On Wednesday, perhaps?"

Aunt Amelia seemed suddenly out of breath. "I—

126

ah———" she stammered, and then collected herself. "I am afraid that I can't possibly make it that night. Ah—thank you just the same."

Mrs. Olivera bowed graciously. "Another time, perhaps." She smiled a slow, grave smile and went past them to the dining room.

"I feel faint," Aunt Amelia said. "I'm going home at once. No, don't bother to come with me. The fresh air and a little walk will revive me. And, Christine, don't you dare repeat a word of this offensive invitation to anyone. Not to anyone at all."

She turned and walked toward the stairs. Watching her, Christie hardly knew whether to laugh or to cry. Mrs. Olivera had won this bout in a way that had rocked Miss Amelia Allard back on her heels.

Christie felt the need for a breath of fresh air herself and a chance to think things through. Before anyone else could come out and find her, she would catch a few moments alone. Outside. She ran up the stairs toward the entrance, but before she went out the main door, she stopped beside a second door that she had not noticed before. There was only emptiness out there and no room which it could open upon, so she turned the knob curiously. It was not locked so she pulled the door open and slipped quietly through it, to find herself on the wide, flat roof of the basement church.

The night was star-spun, with a thin crescent moon balancing a diamond near its tip. Here, away from city lights, the stars seemed very bright and close. A faint breeze stirred, lifting the fine threads of Christie's blond hair, cooling her hot forehead. In the distance there was a flash of heat lightning that made the darkness all the more complete when it had vanished.

Christie went lightly across the roof and sat down at its edge, where she could swing her legs into space. Aunt Amelia's threat to pack her off to Chicago had both astonished and disturbed her. And it had brought home something she had not realized until this very minute. *She didn't want to go back to Chicago.* She wanted to stay right here in Leola and see what might happen between two factions which seemed to be gathering their forces for possible battle. She could remember thinking that life with Eve had been lively and exciting, but she recognized that excitement now as the thrill of make-believe. What was happening in Leola was real. Perhaps there was even something she might do to help. Somehow she no longer wanted to be a mere spectator. Somewhere along the way her own feelings had become involved and she was ready to take sides. If she got a job, Aunt Amelia couldn't send her back to Chicago, even if she wanted to.

So lost was she in her thoughts, that she was startled when a voice spoke to her from the bushes below.

"Moon-gazing, Christie Allard?" It was John Macdonald and he stepped out of the shadows and onto the grass at her feet.

For the first time she did not try to snub him or run away. She had more important things to think about.

"What do you know about Mrs. Olivera?" she asked abruptly.

He hesitated, surprised by the sudden question. "Why, that she's one of the most wasted people I know. That is, unless she can do something for those boys of hers. And she is handicapped in trying to do the right thing for Lopez."

"I've just realized something," Christie said wonderingly. "She and my Aunt Amelia are a lot alike." She clasped her hands about her knees and looked up at the spangled sky. "My, but it's a beautiful night!"

"The setting is wrong," John Macdonald said. "On a night like this there ought to be a ridge of mountains cutting off the horizon. It's too flat around here. Flat as that roof you're sitting on. It's been two years since I've seen mountains, and I guess I'm homesick for them."

"Any special mountains?" Christie asked.

"Very special ones. The Rockies. I grew up in Denver, and they were always there along the skyline, all those vast miles of them. Weekends and summers we could get up into them. Flat ground's not for me."

"But you came here," said Christie.

"Because I had a job to do. And I suppose I think people are even more important than mountains."

128

"How did my father happen to pick you to come here?" she asked curiously.

"In a way, I suppose I picked him," John said. "He was out in Denver to see one of his firm's authors. We had a mutual friend and the friend told me about the problem which had developed in Lawrence Allard's plant in Leola. When he mentioned Mexican-American migrants, I started finding out all I could about what was wrong."

"Why?" said Christie in the blunt way that had reminded Mr. Tidings of her grandfather.

"I suppose because I grew up with Mexican-American boys and girls in Denver schools. My dad is principal of a high school and sometimes we used to have the kids we liked best home for dinner. Then, too, Colorado has its own migrant problem and I'd done a lot of research on the subject for my college thesis. I speak Spanish and I wanted to work with these people if I could. So when this matter came up, I got an introduction to your father through my friend. I guess I sold him the idea that I was the boy to mend the situation. So that was that; my first job."

He moved restlessly and looked up at her.

"That was quite a piece Tom Webb did about you for the *Record*. Quite penetrating, I thought."

"Penetrating?" said Christie, unclasping her hands from about her knees and sitting up straight.

"You sound as if you don't agree. I thought it was a very good piece."

"He called me a Dresden doll!" Christie cried. "Something fragile and breakable."

"Well, aren't you?" John asked, and there was a hint of laughter in his voice.

She had almost begun to like him when he had talked about his coming here, but now she was angry again.

"I'm tired of this little-rich-girl role," she said.

"But it's one you can't escape," John told her. "Not in Leola. Not when you're Lawrence Allard's daughter."

She wriggled back from the edge of the roof and stood up. "You might as well catch up on some of my family history, Mr. Macdonald. I haven't seen my father since I

129

was nine years old. I don't have anything at all to do with him. We aren't even friends, and I don't have a dime."

She did not wait for an answer, but turned and walked across the roof toward the door. Thanks to John Macdonald she had just made up her mind about something. She was going to take Marge's advice the first thing tomorrow morning. She was going straight out to the Allard plant. But she wasn't going to ask Mr. Personnel Manager Macdonald for a job. She was going right to her grandfather's friend, Mr. Spencer Tidings.

If things were coming to a head in this town she wanted to be right in the middle of the fight. That, she suspected, was where her grandfather would have been, and tonight she liked the idea of resembling him.

14

Accident in the Fields

When Christie walked into the old office building at the Allard plant Monday morning, only Mr. Tidings's secretary was in sight. The girl looked up from dusting her desk and smiled an uncertain welcome.

"Good morning," Christie said. "I would like to see Mr. Tidings, please," and wished her tone didn't sound so much like the boss's daughter.

The girl at the desk put her dustcloth down and went to the door of Mr. Tidings's office. "Won't you sit down, Miss Allard? I'll tell him you're here. He isn't feeling very well this morning."

Christie remained beside the partition that walled off the bare little waiting room. She wanted to be ready to walk straight in the moment she was summoned, before she could weaken in her resolve.

She had taken special care with her appearance this morning. Her navy-blue summer suit, tailored white blouse, and neat blue suède shoes had seemed suitable and businesslike. Aunt Amelia had looked puzzled over her early appearance all dressed up, and Christie had announced that she was going to look for a job.

Immediately her aunt had been full of suggestions, but Christie told her quietly that she knew where she wanted to go first. She had not, however, revealed her destination.

Now she felt increasingly uneasy. What if Mr. Tidings pooh-poohed the whole idea? Or, what if there really wasn't anything she could do here? Mr. Tidings's secretary came back from his office and Christie looked at her anxiously.

"Go right in," the girl said, returning to her typewriter.

Christie drew a deep breath and went through the door into her grandfather's office. Mr. Tidings came from behind his desk to greet her and she saw that he really looked dreadfully ill.

She took the same chair beside his desk where she had sat last time and stated her purpose at once.

"Mr. Tidings, I'm looking for a job. Do you suppose there would be something in the stenographic line that I could do here at the plant?"

Her request must have surprised him, but he leaned back in his chair and put his fingertips together, regarding her thoughtfully.

She hurried on, feeling that she had to answer his possible objections before he spoke them. "This would be my first job and I know I'm not very quick with shorthand. But I can practice at home and I would try very hard."

"I don't question that, my dear," he said gently. "And I'm sure working here would be an admirable idea. You would have an opportunity to learn something of the business from the ground up, so to speak. Admirable, admirable."

She tried quickly to correct his misconception. "It isn't that. I just happen to need a job, and I thought—well ——" Her words died out feebly. It wasn't possible to get this man to look at her as if she were not Lawrence Allard's daughter.

He tapped his fingertips together once or twice and then reached toward the bell on his desk. "I believe we

131

have just the spot for you. Miss Webster, will you ask **Mr.** Macdonald to come in, please?"

She had hoped this might be managed without consulting John Macdonald, but that apparently was not to be the case.

A moment later John stepped into the office. He said "Good morning" to Christie and waited to learn why he had been summoned.

The plant manager made a little gesture toward Christie and she sensed that he was enjoying himself.

"Your new secretary, John," he said smoothly. "Subject, of course, to your approval."

John stared at Christie in surprise and for once seemed at a loss for words.

It was Christie who tried to explain, but Mr. Tidings stopped her. "Of course it would be difficult if you decided not to take her, John. Difficult to explain to her father."

"My father has nothing to do with this!" Christie wailed. "Why won't anybody believe that I'm here on my own? I need a job. I thought this might be a logical place to come. But I don't want to be pushed in where I'm not needed just because my last name is Allard."

"Oh, but you're very much needed," John Macdonald told her, and there was a sudden light in his eyes she didn't quite like. "Mr. Tidings knows I've been in need of assistance since the last girl left. When can you start work, Miss Allard?"

Being John Macdonald's secretary was not a choice she would have made of her own free will. Any sort of first job must be hard for the beginner, but to find herself in the position of working for a man who was unreasonably prejudiced against her——

He noted her hesitation. "I might as well warn you that I can be a slave driver, Miss Allard. It's probably wise of you to think twice before you accept the position."

She made her decision and stood up. "I can go to work right now, Mr. Macdonald. And thank you, Mr. Tidings."

"Come along then," said her new employer.

For the first time in a great many years the name of Allard was again on the working roster of the plant.

It was a busy morning. John explained that he had long been wanting to gather a more complete file of information about the workers. He took her back into his smaller office and gave her the details of his purpose carefully. Her name might have been Smith, to judge by his manner, and she was relieved by that.

"Ever since I took this job," he explained, "I have been trying to build up the reputation of the Allard plant so that it would attract the best type of worker we could get. In any group of people there are always loafers and incompetents. That was the only sort of help Mr. Tidings could get after the trouble here a few years ago. It seems elementary to recognize that high-grade workers do high-grade work and that good work reflects to the great advantage of the company and pays out in the end. But to get good workers and improve standards of work you have to recognize human needs."

She listened eagerly, wanting to understand.

"That's why I'd like this file," he went on. "I want a record that includes the human element. If Ramón Garcia's wife is a slattern, then that is a mark against hiring Ramón. If there are so many children in the Mendoza family that they will be too crowded in the quarters we can supply, then that is a reason for not hiring Mendoza."

For the first time Christie ventured a question. "But isn't that awfully hard on the Mendozas?"

"Perhaps. But I have to solve the problem with the buildings we have. If I stay here, I'd like to put in larger living quarters for those with big families. At present we aren't in a position to accommodate them. Mr. Tidings accuses me of running a social-service center for migrant workers and forgetting the good of the company. But it seems obvious to me that the well-being of a worker *is* the good of the company. Just as the success of the company is for the good of the worker. Now, if you'll bring your notebook and come along——"

She ought to know the camp inside out if she was going to be useful to him, he said, and he took on her education himself. She trudged about in the hot sun, scuffing through dust and cinders, as she followed him from one building to another. This was a very different tour from

133

the one on which Mr. Tidings had taken her. He showed her the old carriage house, now being turned into a building which would hold showers and better washroom facilities.

"You can't blame a town for objecting to migrant camps," John said, "when there are outhouses around drawing flies, breeding disease. Of course, instead of criticizing the workers, the town ought to force the plant to do something about such conditions."

They stood for a few minutes watching workmen hammering up partitions, repairing the roof.

"I should think this would have been done long ago," Christie said.

"The policy," John told her dryly, "has been to give these people nothing better than they've been accustomed to in the past. I had to fight like blazes for the money to do this job." He turned away. "Come along, there's more to see."

As they went by the school, Christie saw Marge at the door and waved at her cockily. Marge saluted her smartly behind John Macdonald's back. Then she looked past them toward a truck that had just driven through the gate and her expression changed to one of alarm. At the same instant John wheeled and started toward the truck.

"Christie, come here!" Marge shouted, and Christie, hearing the urgency in her voice, ran across the dusty yard. "Stay here with the children," Marge ordered. "Don't let them out. That's a truck from the fields. Something's happened."

Inside, the children were noisily enjoying their playtime and Christie took her place on the step, with her back to the screen door so that no one could wriggle out. She watched, bewildered, as Marge ran across the yard after John. The truck ground to a halt with a squealing of brakes and Aurora jumped to the ground plainly frightened and excited.

For a moment Christie thought Aurora herself had been hurt. Then John reached into the back of the truck and gently lifted out the small body of Tomasa Gomez. The little girl screamed as he raised her and Christie saw that her right leg hung limp, the foot a bloody pulp. She

134

leaned against the door, fighting the sickness that rose in her. Behind her, children shouted and played and she could only hope that none of them would realize what was happening outside.

Aurora ran into the barracks building and came out a moment later with her frantic mother, while John and Marge vanished into the office. The next moments seemed like hours to Christie as she waited anxiously until Marge came out of the building and ran toward the school.

"Mac wants you, Christie," Marge called. "I'll stay with the children."

Christie asked no questions. She flew across the yard and ran up the steps and into John's office. There the scene was chaotic. Mrs. Gomez wept and wailed and prayed aloud, while Aurora tried to hush her. Mr. Tidings seemed to be engaged in a furious argument with John Macdonald and was looking sicker than ever. Bandages had been wrapped about Tomasa's foot and the child moaned in John's arms, clinging to him.

He saw Christie and broke off his argument with Tidings. "You can drive a car?"

Christie nodded, her throat dry.

"I'm taking Tomasa to the hospital. But she won't let anyone else hold her. You can drive us in the plant station wagon. Aurora, make your mother stop yelling and get her back to her room. There's nothing she can do and we can't have her disrupting things at the hospital. Where's your father?"

"My papa was in other field," Aurora said. "We do not wait to call him." She turned to her mother firmly, as if she were the adult, her mother the child. "Mamacita, come. Señor Mac will arrange all." She managed to lead her anguished mother out of the building and off toward their living quarters.

Mr. Tidings made himself heard again. "This is all highly irregular. I must insist that the child remain here until the company doctor can be summoned."

"Your company doctor happens to be the worst in town," John told him, already carrying Tomasa toward the door. "This child is going to have hospital attention at once."

Mr. Tidings blocked his path. "Just who is going to pay the hospital bills?"

"The Allard Company," said John, and pushed past him.

As Christie hurried after them she could hear Mr. Tidings's choked objections, but John paid no attention.

"Over here," John Macdonald directed curtly, and Christie flew ahead to open the car door. She tried vainly to assist as he got Tomasa into the back seat and slipped in himself to hold her in his lap, her dark little head, with one hair ribbon lost, against his wide shoulder.

Christie got into the front seat. Her hands were shaking as she put the car into gear. From across the yard she heard Aurora calling to them.

"Wait for her," John said.

Aurora got into the back seat carefully, so that she wouldn't disturb Tomasa, and held her little sister's hand.

Christie drove the car over the bumpy dirt road toward the gate, while John gave directions.

"Straight ahead to the paved road. Cross the tracks and go straight again until you come to the route marker. Then left about six blocks to the hospital."

Clinging to the wheel steadied her a little. She had only one purpose in the world, to hold this wheel, to keep her foot on the gas pedal, to keep to the road and not run into anything. She could hear them talking behind her in the car, hear Aurora telling John what had happened.

"My papa says is better Tomasa come to the fields this morning. Everybody say you will go from this place soon, Señor Mac, and that Mr. Tidings, he is boss. Mr. Tidings does not like nursery school." She hesitated, almost apologetically, then went on. "You know this small one, she runs like the little flea. She hops and jumps so you don't know where she is next. The truckman, it is not his fault. He look to back up and there is nothing behind. So he run the truck back and Tomasa is there." She choked and broke off and Christie could hear her crying softly. But it was the moaning of Tomasa that cut Christie clear through.

136

"You've missed the turn!" John said sharply. "Go back around the next block. We can't afford delay."

The anger in his voice steadied her and she did not miss the turn on the way back. Ahead of them on the road the new hospital rose in its clean pink brick. Christie swung the car to the curb and got out with the others.

15

"Make a Phone Call, Miss Allard"

The antiseptic smell of the hospital, with its lingering traces of disinfectants and ether, met them in the hallway. There was a wide, curved desk making a little bay into the main corridor. John strode toward it, Tomasa whimpering against his shoulder, now as much frightened as in pain.

"Emergency," he told the woman behind the desk.

She was quite obviously made of starch and cardboard. She moved one hand toward a buzzer and then withdrew her finger from the button. Appraising eyes that were accustomed to pain regarded Tomasa and Aurora with distaste.

"Mexican? We can't take the camp people here, you know."

"You'll take her," John said.

The starched lady included him in her look of disapproval. "I'm sorry, but you know these people have no residence. The relief agencies won't take care of them. They are not the responsibility of the town."

John Macdonald turned from the desk without answering her. He went toward the elevator and Aurora and Christie hurried after him. Behind them Christie could hear the indignant footsteps of the woman at the desk as she came in pursuit.

As they reached the elevator, the gates opened and a

man in the white coat of a doctor on duty stepped out. He recognized John Macdonald and noted the little girl in his arms.

"Dr. Hunter," John said, "I have an injured child here who needs immediate attention. Your dragon back there doesn't like her ancestry. Will you take care of her?"

Dr. Hunter was a large, dark-haired young man with a manner of moving quickly and surely. He did not look like one to be easily ruffled. "I will take the responsibility," he told the dragon, and she returned haughtily to her desk.

"Come along," he said to John, and stepped back into the elevator. "Tell me what happened."

The girls got into the car, too, and John explained on the way up, while Dr. Hunter listened gravely. A nurse hurried to help them as they stepped out of the car, and she motioned Aurora and Christie toward a small waiting room. At the moment the room was empty and Aurora sank dazedly into a chair. Christie touched her arm gently.

"Don't worry. She's in good hands now."

Aurora shuddered. "You did not see her foot. And she was such a one for running and laughing. The *pobrecita!*"

Christie reached wordlessly for Aurora's thin, rough hand and held it tightly. She remembered that morning on the train when she had wondered at the roughness of the skin, the broken nails. She understood now—the work in the fields.

In a few moments John Macdonald came into the waiting room and saw them sitting there. There was a streak of blood on his gray slacks and sweat-dampened patches on his shirt. He stood beside Aurora, and Christie had not known he could be so gentle, so kind.

"Dr. Hunter is a very good doctor. I've been trying to get him for the plant for some time. She'll have the best possible care, Aurora. There is nothing to do now but wait."

Aurora nodded dully. She wore no earrings today and her hair hung matted upon her shoulders after a morning in the fields.

"I will work for the money to pay," she said. "I will go

138

again to Chicago. In Chicago maybe there is work for Mexican-American girl."

John touched her shoulder gently. "You'll stay right here. Don't worry about the money. The Allard Company will take the responsibility for this if it's the last thing I accomplish. Aurora, I have to go back to the plant now and I'll talk to your mother. Will you stay here until your sister comes out of the operating room?"

Aurora nodded. "I stay. Señor Mac, from my heart I thank you."

John turned to Christie and his manner was less kind. "Suppose you stay, too. See that Tomasa Gomez has everything she needs. When you've seen her settled, come back to the plant and report to me. Do you suppose you can manage?"

His implication seemed to be that she was helpless and half-witted. She could only nod humbly.

He went off then, and Christie and Aurora tried to settle down to their anxious wait. There were others in the waiting room now, with worry in their eyes. The waiting ones made a brotherhood in this world of pain.

"What did that woman downstairs mean when she spoke of residence?" Christie asked Aurora.

The other girl answered vaguely. "It is something about how long you live in a place. You stay long enough, they take care of you if there is no money. But how can we stay long when the crops grow all over? So with us, if we starve, we starve; if we die, we die. It was like so when the baby twins, my small brothers, die. In Florida. There was no Señor Mac to help us there."

Christie could feel tears sting her eyelids, and she blinked them back angrily.

Someone crossed the room and a kindly voice spoke Aurora's name. They looked up to see Father Paul Cudahy, and Aurora greeted him with a little gasp of relief.

"Miss Molloy telephoned me from the camp," he said. "I came right over."

Christie slipped away to leave the two alone and he prayed softly with Aurora. Christie stood in the doorway, watching the nurses go by with their trays and bottles.

The waiting seemed endless. She poked a toe idly at a worn place in the carpet and glanced down to see what she was poking. For the first time since that morning she noticed her shoes. The blue suède was cut and smudged and dust-covered. The discovery made her smile wryly. It seemed a long while back to the day when she had taken Aurora to the camp in a taxi and had not wanted to submit her new shoes to the cinders of the plant yard. A pair of shoes had seemed so much more important then than they did now.

A stretcher was rolled out of the operating room and Christie looked at it anxiously. Tomasa's eyes were closed, her body quiet beneath a blanket. The nurse who pushed the stretcher looked so businesslike that Christie did not dare speak to her. She went to tell Aurora that her sister had come out of the operating room and Father Cudahy rose at once.

"I will see what I can learn," he said. "Dr. Hunter is a friend of mine."

Aurora twisted a fold of her flowered skirt nervously as she waited for him to return, and Christie wished she could leave this little box of a room and pace the long corridor. But she managed to wait, as others in the room were doing.

Father Cudahy was back before long, his eyes grave. "You must have courage, my child," he told Aurora. "There will be more waiting before they know. The doctor hopes to save the foot. In a few moments the nurse will come to get you and you will be able to stay with your sister for a while."

Aurora nodded, her eyes swimming with tears.

"Is there anything I can do?" Christie asked. "Mr. Macdonald told me to see if there was anything Tomasa needed."

"Everything has been taken care of," Father Cudahy said. "There is nothing more to do."

He left shortly afterward and Christie waited until a nurse came to summon Aurora to Tomasa's bedside. Then she went downstairs in the elevator. There was a sense of unreality about everything. The little girl who lay unconscious upstairs couldn't be real. The reality was Tomasa running up to slip her hand into Christie's, trotting around adoringly after Lopez Olivera. The reality couldn't be that woman at the desk telling them the hospital would not take camp people because they couldn't pay their bills. As she left the elevator she glanced toward the desk, wishing she might speak her feelings. But the dragon was well occupied. Leaning on the counter before her, smiling engagingly, was Tom Webb.

"Oh, come now," he chided her, "you can't let me down like this. My spies tell me there was some sort of accident out at the plant. I beseech you——"

Christie stopped beside him. "Don't waste any time beseeching. I can tell you all about it. Tomasa Gomez, Aurora's sister, was hurt in the fields, where she never should have been. And this hospital would have refused to take her in just because she's from the camp."

"Is that so?" said Tom. "Very interesting."

"*I* can give you a story, if that's what you want," Christie said.

The woman behind the desk broke in hurriedly. "Now just a moment! You'd better talk to the proper hospital authorities, young man, before you go putting anything in your paper. Every hospital has certain rules and——"

"Whatever the rules are, your Dr. Hunter broke them," Christie said. "Come along, Tom, I'll tell you all about it."

He drove her back to the camp in the *Record* car and on the way she gave him the story, including the news that she was working at the Allard plant. He listened soberly, put in a question now and then, and whistled his surprise over her new job.

"I don't know yet whether I'll stay," she confessed. "I know Mr. Macdonald doesn't want me there. He only took me because Mr. Tidings pushed me at him. If all I do is irritate him, then it won't seem sensible to go on with the job."

"Stick it out, baby," Tom said. "Never mind what Mac thinks. If you do your job, he'll swallow his feelings about your last name. I expect that's the only thing that ails him. Your father put him in there, but he hasn't exactly stood by him. You're not too repulsive, you know."

"I didn't mean it the way it sounded," she said quickly. "If I'm helping Mr. Macdonald do what he's trying to do, I'll stay. If I'm adding to his troubles, I'll leave."

He gave her a quick look as they turned off Main Street toward the plant. "Sounds like you're growing up, Christie Allard. Anyway, thanks to you, I have some ammunition now. I'm going to do a story about this that will have the town wringing out its handkerchiefs. I can pull out all the stops—seven-year-old in fields. Accident. Severe injury. Hospital refuses admission. And so forth."

His flip tone troubled her. They'd reached the plant and she put her hand on the door handle. "This isn't just a *story,* you know. Tomasa is a real little girl. Did you see her last night at the supper?"

Tom nodded. "I saw her. Don't worry. This story won't be my usual corn. But if I didn't wisecrack once in a while, I might start smashing things. I'm tempted that way sometimes."

She left him and ran across the grounds toward the office building. Above shacks and barracks and cannery towered the familiar water tank with the name of Allard across it, and Christie was uncomfortably conscious of it as she went inside. The moment she stepped into the office she knew that something had happened. Marge was there, leaning against the partition, her eyes bright with excitement. Miss Webster, Tidings's secretary, sat at her desk, white-faced and close to tears, while John Macdonald paced the square of waiting-room floor, apparently outlining some plan of action.

He broke off when Christie appeared in the doorway. "You're back quickly. How is she?"

"They're not sure if they can save her foot," Christie said.

Marge thumped one fist angrily into the palm of the other hand. She looked as if she wanted to smash things, too.

"Father Cudahy got there," Christie went on. "He talked to Dr. Hunter. Aurora is with her sister now. There wasn't anything else for me to do." She glanced around, wondering where Mr. Tidings was.

Marge saw her look. "Mr. Tidings has collapsed and

has been taken to the hospital himself. I don't wish him any ill luck, but this couldn't have happened at a better time."

Behind her, Miss Webster sniffed audibly and blew her nose. John stopped his pacing and looked at Marge.

"I'm all for that meeting of yours. Get it together for tonight if you can, and count me in."

"Tom Webb's going to run a story about Tomasa and the hospital and tell the whole thing," Christie put in. "If there's anything more he needs to know, you'd better call him."

"Good," John said. "You see to Tom, Marge. But tell him to keep this meeting quiet. It's off the record for the moment. And, Marge, before you get started on the telephone, will you talk to Mrs. Gomez?"

"Of course," Marge agreed, and hurried out.

John Macdonald looked at Christie speculatively. "That's right," he said, "I do have a new secretary. Will you make a phone call, Miss Allard? Put through a long-distance call to New York City. Right away."

"New York City?" Christie echoed.

"Yes," said John quietly. "A call to the publishing house of Sage and Thorpe. Get me Mr. Lawrence Allard on the wire."

16

Meeting at Mr. Bigelow's

The local operator said she would ring the plant as soon as the New York call was completed, and Christie put the phone down with a hand that shook a little. She had been half afraid that she might get her father on the wire at once and the thought filled her with dismay. Of course he wouldn't know who she was, or connect her in any way with the Allard plant. She had only to say that she was

Mr. Macdonald's secretary. But she was relieved to have the moment postponed for a little while.

When the operator finally rang, however, it was not Lawrence Allard on the telephone, but his secretary. She said Mr. Allard was out of town that day and would not be back till tomorrow. Was there anything she could do?

In relief Christie gave the telephone to John. It was apparent that he disliked the delay, but he talked to the secretary at some length. The situation was urgent, he explained, and told her about Mr. Tidings's collapse. There was much that he could accomplish here in the two months' time before his contract ran out, but first he must have the proper authority to act. Would Mr. Allard wire him to that effect as soon as possible? It was left at that, and Christie somehow felt that she had escaped an ordeal.

There was one more disturbing incident to come during the afternoon, however. Christie, running across the grounds on an errand for John, saw Lopez Olivera come through the gate. His shirt and pants were sweat-stained, dirty with soil from the fields. Apparently he had not worked out his day, but had quit and walked all the way back to the camp. He looked intent on some grim purpose of his own and would have walked past without seeing her if she had not spoken to him.

"Hello, Lopez," she said. "You're back early."

His quick, dark eyes recognized her and he paused in his course toward the barracks which housed the Gomez family.

"Where is Tomasa?" he demanded. "To where they take her?"

Christie remembered the boy's fondness for the little girl on past occasions, the way he had played something of the big brother, having no little sister of his own.

"She's been taken to the hospital, Lopez," Christie told him gently. "They're taking good care of her there."

"Is no good for small ones to be in fields," Lopez said bitterly He waited for no answer, but hurried into the barracks.

Christie looked after him, worried. The boy seemed as angry as he had been that day when he had wanted to play baseball. It was probably a good thing that there was no single person whom he could blame for Tomasa's accident.

John proved surprisingly patient during the rest of Christie's working day. She tried out her shorthand when he dictated letters, and he slowed his pace, repeating when necessary, making corrections when she read the dictation back to him. She was glad, nevertheless, when the long day was ended and she could get away.

When she reached home and told Aunt Amelia about her job, she couldn't be sure whether her aunt approved or disapproved. Probably her reactions were mixed. It was possible that she found a certain satisfaction in having an Allard back in the company, even in so humble a position. But she obviously did not approve of Christie's interest in the Mexican-American workers. The threat she had made to send Christie back to Chicago still hung between them.

At dinner, however, Christie's job faded into the background beside more important matters. Marge was full of plans for the meeting that evening. What had happened to Tomasa gave the whole thing impetus. Now was the time to rouse the interest and sympathy of the townspeople.

"We're going to hold our meeting at Mr. Bigelow's house tonight," Marge told Alan. "I've reached Father Cudahy and Dr. Hunter and they'll both be there. And of course John Macdonald and you. You, too, Christie, if you want to come."

She had not included Aunt Amelia in her invitation and that lady did not overlook the fact.

"May I ask just what sort of meeting this is to be?" Miss Allard inquired.

"I shouldn't tell you," Marge said directly, "since you'll probably join the enemy. But as a matter of fact we'd like to have you if you're willing to come. This is to be a strategy meeting of a few of us who want to get behind John Macdonald out at the plant and help with this problem of the Mexican-American worker. It's not just the plant's affair. What has happened to Tomasa makes it of concern to the whole community. Leola can't stand by and allow such things to happen. Of course, since Mac is closest to the plant, we have to be guided by his experience and advice. But there is plenty this town can do if we can once wake it up."

"Just what do you think you're going to accomplish?" Aunt Amelia asked.

"Between us," said Marge, "we ought to be able to work out some sort of campaign. Figure out how to start some good old propaganda work right here in town. Propaganda of a positive sort, based on facts. Somehow, somehow we've got to get Mexican-American and Anglo-Americans together so they can both find out the other fellow isn't so bad. Some of the Mexican-Americans don't have much use for us and I can't say I blame them. Prejudice needs to be broken down on both sides."

Alan had listened quietly, letting Marge do most of the talking, but now he had a suggestion of his own. "Don't you think we ought to invite one or two of the camp people tonight? We could use their advice."

"How about Aurora?" Christie put in.

"All right," Marge said. "Aurora and Rafael, and Mrs. Olivera, if she will come."

"I shall attend this meeting," Aunt Amelia announced, "if for no other reason than to furnish weight on the side of sanity. I have had the interests of Leola at heart for a good many years. I have no intention now of giving up the fight."

It was evident enough, Christie thought, on which side Miss Amelia Allard meant to lend her weight.

But as Marge pointed out that evening as they walked to Mr. Bigelow's, they could listen to Aunt Amelia's views with profit since she would be speaking for those in the town who felt as she did. Unless they knew the arguments the opposition would bring up, they could not be ready to refute them.

Mr. Bigelow belonged to one of the town's oldest families and his home was not far from Aunt Amelia's. It was a big, old-fashioned house with an enormous living room that made a good place for a meeting. His wife, plump and bright-eyed, was evidently as interested as her husband in what was astir in Leola.

Christie, Marge, and Aunt Amelia were the second group to arrive that night. John Macdonald, Dr. Hunter, and Father Cudahy were already there. Alan had driven out to the plant to bring back Mrs. Olivera, Aurora, and Rafael, and had not yet appeared. Tom, of course, would not be there, since Alan felt that some of those who came would hesitate to speak frankly with a reporter present.

Mr. Bigelow, who had taken a liking to Christie, found a chair beside her near the front windows.

"Your grandfather was one of my father's best friends," he told her. "I remember him very well, though I was only a boy in those days."

Then Aunt Amelia asked Dr. Hunter about the little Mexican girl at the hospital and Christie turned to listen.

"She's making a brave fight," Dr. Hunter said. "We have some hope of saving her foot."

Aunt Amelia nodded. "I thought the accounts I'd heard were exaggerated."

"They were not exaggerated," Dr. Hunter told her quietly. "The child might have lost her life."

There was talk about Mr. Tidings, too. He was gravely ill and an operation would be performed shortly.

A few moments later Alan's car pulled up in front of the house and he came in with his three guests from the camp. He deliberately seated Mrs. Olivera next to Aunt Amelia. Christie had saved a place for Aurora and beckoned her into it. Rafael sat next to Marge. Mrs. Olivera held herself as erect as Aunt Amelia and wore a guard of reserve as if she did not altogether trust the apparent friendliness of these Anglo-Americans. Aurora, too, was on guard, watchful, as she had been the day Christie had first met her.

Marge asked Alan to lead the discussion and he began by outlining the ultimate goals he felt they should all keep in mind. It was important to move slowly and do nothing drastic in the beginning. Eventually the public schools must be opened to the children from the camp. At present no Mexican-American children were accepted in a Leola school, even when they arrived while the schools were still in session. But more than that, some arrangement ought to be made for summer classes. Every community should recognize its responsibility to help with the education of

147

these children who had an equal right with other American children to the benefits of education.

Aunt Amelia broke in the moment he stopped for breath. "There must be a great deal of sickness and disease out at the camp. I'm sure the citizens of this town do not want these children brought into contact with our own. And I speak as a member of the school board."

It was Father Cudahy who reproved her gravely. "Tonight I think we must forget that we are school board members, or clergymen, or doctors. We are here to solve a common human problem which concerns us all as human beings."

Alan thanked him with a glance and went on as if there had been no interruption. "We want to get rid of the segregation which has been creeping into the town. Those signs, *White Trade Only*, in downtown windows, the limiting of Mexican-Americans to balcony seats in the movie house, and any other discrimination that comes to our attention. You agree, Mr. Bigelow?"

The little man nodded heartily. "Indeed I do. One selling point of this whole plan is the fact that people like Mrs. Olivera and her friends must shop for their families. I have known of instances when they avoided Leola stores and went out on the highway, or even to other towns, to make purchases. Those among us who are interested in the economic angle will realize that this is a loss of good business for Leola. It gives us a talking point with those who may not be reached in other ways."

Marge was taking notes for the meeting and she looked up to smile at Mr. Bigelow as she wrote down his words.

"A health clinic is another matter of importance," Alan went on. "Dr. Hunter can help us on that. If, as Miss Allard says, there is a higher incidence of disease among the camp people, then we of the communities where they live, both here and in Texas, are at fault. Marge, would you like to add some words for your own pet projects?"

Marge put down her pencil. "We need adult classes at the camp, too."

Aunt Amelia smiled benevolently. "I am in agreement there. The Mexican people have great artistic talent. An arts and crafts group would help to keep them busy and

148

happy. After all, they do have their own culture which should be preserved."

Mrs. Olivera had been sitting quietly, looking down at her hands in her lap. Now she glanced up and caught Alan's eye.

"Yes, Mrs. Olivera?" he asked.

"Sometimes we are too tired coming in from the fields to play pleasant games. But if you will permit me to speak for my people, the culture of Mexico is good. We do not want our children to forget it. But my boys, Lopez, Rafael, and the other children also, are Americans and must live as Americans. You expect them to act like Americans, but you do not teach them how. So they grow up confused and do not always know what they are, or how to be Americans."

She spoke in a low voice and Christie saw her aunt watching in some surprise, as if one of the chairs had begun to speak excellent English.

John Macdonald joined the discussion for the first time. "I hope you all realize what an important point Mrs. Olivera has just made. The younger generation doesn't want to be thought of as Mexican. But how little we go out of our way to help these young people to *be* the Americans they actually are."

"Is true," Aurora said gravely, and then looked uncomfortable at having spoken.

"Not everything American is worth learning." Aunt Amelia sounded testy.

"That is also true," John agreed. "Unfortunately, the newcomer is apt to pick up some of our most unattractive qualities to copy. But it's better to risk that and try for greater assimilation."

There was a pause and Alan glanced around the room. "Any more suggestions? Father Paul?"

"One of the things most needed," the priest said, "is a mothers' club. Simple instruction in baby care, in child care. I think you'll find these women wonderfully eager to learn, if only we'll take the trouble to teach them. Isn't that so, Mrs. Olivera?"

Rafael's mother nodded.

"That would be a step toward better health, too," Dr.

Hunter said. "I believe I can get some of the nurses from the hospital to take turns in coming out to give just such instruction."

Mrs. Olivera relaxed her stiffness a little. "This will be good," she said eagerly. "I will speak with the other women. They will come. But, please, the classes are one thing, but if there is a clinic, then a small charge should be made. We like to pay for what is given us. We do not ask anything for nothing."

Everyone seemed to want to talk at the same time after that, and Alan made no further effort to hold the meeting to order. Now Mrs. Olivera, Aurora, and Rafael were being pulled into the discussion by the others, and the semblance of a formal meeting broke into a social evening.

Christie went to help Mrs. Bigelow bring in refreshments. As she carried around plates of ice cream and cake she saw that Aunt Amelia had entered into a spirited argument with John Macdonald. An imp possessed Christie, and as she bent to hand Mrs. Olivera her serving, she spoke quite clearly into a pause, so that Aunt Amelia could not miss her words.

"You invited us to come to see you," she said. "We couldn't make it for the evening you suggested, but we are looking forward to a visit at another time."

For once her guarded poise forsook Mrs. Olivera. She looked down at the plate of ice cream in her hands, not meeting Christie's eyes. Apparently she had repented her proud invitation the night of the church supper. But she could not leave Christie's words unanswered and she could not withdraw her invitation.

"My house is yours," she said in a low tone. "Perhaps you could come next Monday evening?"

Christie looked at her aunt. "That would be fine for me. What about you, Aunt Amelia?"

The moment she spoke the words, she was frightened. What if her aunt chose to exhibit her prejudice before Mrs. Olivera? But Miss Amelia Allard's vaunted good breeding did not fail her now.

Her eyes might be icy cool with indignation, but it was for Christie. She turned to Mrs. Olivera with her most lady-of-the-manor air and said, "That will be delightful. My niece and I will accept your kind invitation for Monday evening."

Mrs. Olivera bowed, but this time she lifted her eyes to meet Aunt Amelia's and again Christie had the feeling that here were two women who matched each other in strength of character.

"Then it's settled," said Christie breezily, and dashed off for another plate of ice cream.

Before the group left that evening some definite plans were laid. Among them was the gentle campaign each person meant to start wherever he went in town. The ministers and leaders of other churches were to be drawn in. Whenever possible each one here tonight would make an effort to say a good word about the people at the camp. When there was a response, the listener could perhaps be added to the little group of word-spreaders.

Mac indicated that he had definite plans of his own in mind which would answer some of the very objections Miss Allard had raised; though their success, of course, would depend on first receiving the necessary authority from Lawrence Allard.

Alan and Marge went home feeling particularly encouraged and neither of them paid much attention to Aunt Amelia's disapproval. They were on their way and a bit jaunty and spirited about it. Nothing Miss Allard could do or say could stop them now.

"When we're ready, perhaps in a few weeks," Alan said, "we'll hold an open meeting. We'll get things settled right out in public. If there's going to be a fight, then we'll be ready. And as Joe Louis said one time, 'We're on God's side.' "

It was the following day that the wire from Lawrence Allard was laid on John Macdonald's desk.

17

Vandals!

Christie was in John's office when the wire came. Since he was busy on the telephone he motioned her to open it. She picked it up, not knowing who it was from until she had unfolded it and read the words pasted to the yellow form. The message was direct and minced no words. Lawrence Allard would not interfere in plant affairs. Mr. Tidings or his assistant manager was still in full charge of all policy-making moves and could veto changes. The very fact that he had wired, instead of telephoning, indicated his own intention not to become involved.

When John hung up the telephone, Christie handed him the wire wordlessly. He read it through twice, then crumpled it into a ball and threw it angrily into the wastebasket.

"So that's that," he said. "My hands are tied completely."

He got up from his desk and walked out of the building and Christie saw that the usual briskness was gone from his step. Mentally she made one more black mark on the list against her father. It wasn't fair that he should keep the ownership of the plant, when he lived so far away and had no interest in it except for the income he took out of it. The only time he had ever worried about it was when that income had been threatened. What did he care if a child like Tomasa was crippled in the fields, or if Lopez Olivera might never have the opportunity to realize his dreams? It wasn't fair that everything John Macdonald wanted to do had to depend on Lawrence Allard.

She heard Miss Webster's typewriter clattering in the outer office and went out to speak to her.

"Have you heard how Mr. Tidings is?" she asked.

Miss Webster fiddled nervously with the roller in her machine. "He was operated on this morning. I guess he's getting along as well as can be expected. But goodness knows when he'll be back. I don't know what will become of things while he's gone."

"What about the assistant manager?" Christie asked. She had spoken to the man only once or twice, since he had his office in the cannery building where she seldom went.

"Oh, him!" Miss Webster was scornful. "He hasn't an ounce of get-up-and-go. And the production manager won't care what goes on, so long as the lines keep moving. Well, if you'll excuse me, I still have some letters to get off."

Christie went thoughtfully back to her own typewriter to finish work which John wanted her to get off today. When he returned to his desk, she quoted Miss Webster's words casually. Under the circumstances, she asked, did he really need a higher authority than his own?

He grinned at her wryly. "Now if only *you* were my boss. No, Christie, I'm afraid that's not the way a business is managed. A maverick down the line can't just take over and start running things his own way. Well, maybe it won't matter too much, what with the plans that were made last night. Maybe you can all get things going around here without my help."

The prospect began to look more promising when Tom's story appeared in the paper. Marge came running in with a copy of the *Record* almost as soon as it was out.

"See if you can read this without crying," she said, unfolding it to the front page and spreading it on John's desk.

Christie leaned beside him and they read it together. Tom had done as he had promised. He had pulled out all the stops, but he had managed it without being sentimental or maudlin. By the time the reader finished the last word there would certainly be tears in his eyes, even if he had never seen Tomasa Gomez running and laughing and then screaming in pain.

Tom made you see vividly, in your mind's eye, what had happened. He reached deep into your feelings and

153

twisted. The hospital story was there, but the hospital was not wholly blamed. Those in the town who had never heard of "residence" would hear about it from Tom's piece. Heading the column was the picture he had taken of Aurora and Tomasa the night of the church supper. Aurora had been smiling for once and she looked lovely, but it was the small face of Tomasa Gomez, with its wide smile and bright dark eyes, that made your heart turn over.

"At least," Marge said, "this will open the whole thing up with a bang. Maybe a few people will be ready to take some interest now."

Christie felt an odd flash of pride over Tom. He was good! Any city paper would be proud to run a human-interest story as movingly written as this one.

During the afternoon telephone calls began to come in, and John set Christie to answering the telephone. She found herself telling ladies with tears in their voices that there was no definite word yet about the little Mexican-American girl at the hospital. No, they didn't know if her foot could be saved. Yes, she would undoubtedly love flowers, candy. Of course children were not supposed to work in the fields, and Mr. Macdonald had given strict orders . . . and so on, and on. Christie loved it. John was less impressed.

"All this emotional hoopla won't last," he said. "It doesn't mean that the town is taking the migrants to its great, big, generous heart."

But Christie felt encouraged anyway. Not even Aunt Amelia's wet-blanketing at dinner that night could deflate her. Apparently Aunt Amelia had not been moved in the least by the account in the paper. She said she knew Tom Webb too well to swallow such a story lock, stock, and barrel. You'd think to read this, she sniffed, that children were being run over in the fields by the dozen. Accidents could happen anywhere. No one carried on to such an extent when a town child chased a ball into the street and got hit by a car.

That night, when Christie went to bed, she had trouble getting to sleep. So much had happened in the last two days that she couldn't stop thinking. It was after midnight when she fell asleep, only to waken at three and again at four. She slept very little after that. Her mind was too stirred up, her thoughts too active.

If she'd had any idea of giving up her job at the plant because John Macdonald disliked her, the notion had evaporated. She knew now that she was in this to stay. Personalities, one's own sensitivities, just didn't matter any more. She could hear Tom's words echoing in her memory, "Stick it out, baby," and she meant to do just that.

When daylight was bright outside her window, Christie raised herself on one elbow to look at the clock on the bedside table. Nearly seven at last. In a little while she would get up. Her pillow was crumpled and damp. No air stirred through the room. It was going to be another scorching day.

How quiet a small town seemed in these early morning hours. No footsteps clicked along the sidewalks. There was no sound of cars and taxis and trucks astir as there would have been in the city. Only the birds woke to greet the day uproariously with their calls. She could hear a single car coming from blocks away. It sounded as though it was traveling fast; no reason why it shouldn't in these empty streets. Then she realized in surprise that it was stopping in front of the house. At the same moment Fatso began to bark.

Christie slipped out of bed and ran to the front window. It was the *Record* car and Tom was getting out, slamming the door behind him, running down the walk toward the steps. She put on a blue silk negligee that had been Eve's, pushed her hair back from her eyes, and hurried downstairs. The bell rang just before she reached the door. Tom blinked his surprise when she pulled open the door, and Fatso growled indignantly.

"Well! That's the kind of service I like. Hush yourself, pooch." But he wasted no further time on flippancy. "I've got to see Alan right away, Christie. May I go up to his room?"

But there was no need, for Alan, too, had heard the car. He appeared on the stairs, his red hair touseled as a small boy's, hastily pulling a dressing gown over surprising plaid pajamas.

" 'Morning, Tom; Christie. What's happened?"

"The Marquette Grade School," Tom said, still out of breath. "Somebody broke in last night. Quite a gang, I'd say, by the damage done. A milkman saw some broken windows and raised the alarm."

"The police are there?" Alan asked.

"Right. And since they think kids are mixed up in this I decided to come for you."

"Thanks," Alan said. "I'll go back with you. Just give me five minutes."

"I'll come, too," said Marge from the stairway, looking rumpled and half awake.

Christie tore back upstairs and flung herself into some clothes, thrust her bare feet into loafers, not bothering with socks. A quick flick of a washrag and she was ready. Never mind the lipstick or a hair-do. She wasn't going to be left behind.

Aunt Amelia slept soundly, but all this traffic wakened her, and she put her head out of the door of her room, looking surprisingly frowsy without her braids, just as the three hurried downstairs.

"What is it? What's going on?"

Alan called back to her. "Somebody's broken into the Marquette School building during the night. We're going over to have a look. We'll be back before long. Don't worry."

Christie heard her aunt's voice calling after them. "Those Mexicans! I know it's the Mexicans!"

If the others heard, they said nothing. Marge and Alan got into the back seat of Tom's car and Christie took her place in front. The school was only a few blocks away and they were there as quickly as Tom could make it. The main door of the old brick school stood open and a police car waited out in front. A policeman stopped them as they came up the steps, but let them go in when he recognized Tom and Alan.

The door opened directly upon the school's main hallway and the moment Christie stepped inside she saw the first evidence of destruction. A big canvas mural covered

156

the wall facing the door, depicting a scene from history—explorers and Indians. At least she gathered these had made the picture's subject. Now the painting was scarred across and across by slashes from a sharp knife. Down the hall more destruction was visible. Glass from broken doors and smashed pictures powdered the corridor. Students' art work which had been displayed on a bulletin board had been wantonly ripped down, strewn around the hall.

"You're right," Alan said to Tom. "No one boy did all this."

He returned to the front door to talk to a police officer and Marge went with him. Tom, looking grimmer than Christie had ever seen him, spotted the school janitor and began to ask questions. Left to herself, Christie climbed halfway up a flight of stairs and sat down on the steps. There was nothing she could do except keep out of the way. From where she sat she could see the slashed mural, and the look of it made her feel a little sick. How could anyone want to mutilate like that? What fun or satisfaction could there be in wasteful destruction?

"I don't understand it," she murmured, hardly knowing that she spoke aloud.

Tom had left the janitor and come to the foot of the stairs. He heard her and leaned against the banister.

"It's not hard to understand," he said. "If a fellow learns how to get the things he wants from life in the right way, he's okay. I mean the things we all want—love and respect and a chance to feel worth while. But sometimes conditions in a boy's home, or some injustice done him, can set him off on a mistaken course. Then maybe he finds there are bigger rewards for misbehaving than he can get through good behavior."

"But how could there be? What rewards?"

"Respect of the boys in his gang. Being part of a group. Things society hasn't given him in other ways. Excitement and danger, too—something to break dull monotony. Some boys have a bigger share of primitive yearnings than others, maybe."

Christie looked at him wonderingly. "You sound as though you'd done some work with delinquent boys."

"I have." His voice was sharp-edged. "But not in the way you mean. I was hauled into juvenile court more than once when I was a kid."

Christie stared, and he looked up at her mockingly.

"Oh, I was a most unsavory character. I was up for stealing and for vandalism. That's why this sort of waste of property and human beings makes me sick. It might not happen so much if parents knew more about being parents, and if a community took a more responsible interest in its young people."

Christie listened in surprise. Tom glanced down the hall at the slashed picture and went on, as if he were talking to himself:

"Discipline alone isn't the answer. There has to be rewards. In some queer sort of way the kids who did this were getting a bigger reward than decent behavior has brought them."

A fear, an uneasiness had been tugging at the back of Christie's mind. She could not entirely dismiss her aunt's parting words.

"Tom, you don't think any of the boys out at the camp would——"

"I'm not doing any guessing," he said shortly. "It's much more likely to be a town gang, though the authorities probably won't want to accept that. They'd much rather pin something on the transients. More comfortable all around."

Christie thought of Lopez, humiliated and angry that day when he'd wanted to play ball in the vacant lot. Then again yesterday, broken up over Tomasa's injury. There was certainly a pattern of no rewards there. But she put the nagging fear out of her mind. Lopez wouldn't have been running with a gang of town boys.

"How did you—I mean, when you grew up——" Christie found it hard to phrase the question she wanted to ask.

He grinned at her. "You mean how did I happen to reform? Well, there was a redheaded Irish copper put on our beat in Chicago. He liked kids and he had a way of getting it across to you that he thought you were really pretty swell. After the way my teachers hated me—not that I blame them—and my Pop . . . Well, this came as a surprise. Somehow, when a fellow you respect thinks you're okay, you begin to want to prove that he's right. But he didn't stop there. He dug up some excitement for us, kept us busy at games, took us on what he called exploring expeditions. It was surprising how much we didn't know about Chicago. He knew about rewards, too. He knew that sometimes you have to give them for pretty small things before a fellow is ready to earn them for bigger things. And he could deal out punishment, too. No nonsense, or you couldn't be one of *his* gang."

"He sounds like a wonderful person," Christie said softly. "Are you still in touch with him?"

Tom looked away. "He was killed a few years ago. Shot down by a nineteen-year-old boy he'd tried to help. Some of them we can't help. We don't know enough yet, or we don't get to them in time. Well, I can't stand here. I'm supposed to be a reporter on the job."

He went off abruptly, as if he felt he'd talked too much, and she stood up wondering if she'd be in the way if she joined the group at the door. Marge seemed to be arguing furiously with the officer in charge and as she walked toward them Christie caught the word "Mexican" once or twice from the policeman. So they *were* trying to blame the camp people. Alan drew Marge away and they said good-by to Tom. As Christie walked back to Aunt Amelia's with them Marge was still sputtering. Alan tried to reassure her. "There's no evidence against the camp people," he pointed out. "No conclusive way in which this can be turned against them. You can't condemn a man without proof." .

"Some people can," Marge said hotly.

It began to appear that she was right during breakfast. When Aunt Amelia heard what had happened at the school, she made a flat pronouncement.

"It doesn't matter whether there's actual proof or not," she said. "Everyone in this town who has any sense will know where to place the blame. And no one will hesitate to place it. I'm afraid your little plans for brotherly love are mistaken under the circumstances."

Alan spoke again quickly before Marge could make an

angry answer. "Not everyone in town feels as you do, Miss Allard. Don't forget the interest and sympathy that were shown yesterday for Tomasa."

"The same people aren't going to stand for this sort of destruction," Aunt Amelia said. "I think you'll find Leola much less sentimental today."

After breakfast, when Christie and Marge started off together for the plant, Christie knew she had never seen Marge so discouraged.

"To have this happen right when our hopes were so high and our plans under way!" Marge wailed. "What are we going to do?"

"I can't believe the rest of the town will jump to conclusions the way Aunt Amelia has," Christie said.

"Not everyone will. But while we're fighting to get the camp people accepted by the town, those who feel the way your aunt does will use this to shut them out. Now that your father has refused to back Mac in the things he might do to help—well, I can't say the prospect looks rosy."

They went out of their way that morning to stop at the hospital and inquire about Tomasa. They couldn't see her, since visiting hours were strictly enforced in the wards. But they were told that her condition was "satisfactory," whatever that meant.

On the walk from the hospital to the plant Christie found herself talking about Tom Webb. Marge apparently knew quite a lot about him. His mother had died when he was two years old and he had lived in a tough section of Chicago's west side with a bartender father to look after him. Nevertheless, he'd grown up with plenty of ambition and he'd been going to night school, working for a college degree before he came down here. But apparently Tom had told Christie more that morning than even Marge had learned about him, and Christie did not betray his confidence.

When she reached the plant office, she found Mr. Tidings's secretary already at her typewriter, with no one else in sight. Miss Webster gave Christie a gloomy "Good morning" and said Mr. Macdonald was out in the workers' quarters. Something terrible had happened over in town and a police officer was here.

"I know," Christie said. "Marquette School was broken into last night and quite a bit of damage was done. I suppose the police will check up everywhere. Did Mr. Macdonald mention what he wanted me to do?"

"He didn't mention you at all," Miss Webster said, and turned back to her work.

Christie looked into John's office to see if there was anything she could find to do. She glanced out the window across the dusty grounds and saw the parked police car, with a few children standing around looking at it. Whatever investigation was going on must be indoors, for neither John nor the officer was visible.

She went back to the outer office, too restless to sit down, and moved about idly until her attention was caught by Mr. Tidings's closed door. She spoke to Miss Webster again.

"Do you suppose I could go in there for a little while?"

The secretary raised her hands from the typewriter keys. "Well, I don't know, Miss Allard. I——"

"I won't disturb Mr. Tidings's things," Christie said quickly. "It was my grandfather's office, you know. And I've been wanting to look at his books."

Miss Webster hesitated a moment longer just to emphasize her loyalty to her employer. Then she went to the door and opened it for Christie. "I expect it will be all right."

"Thank you," Christie said, and stepped into the dim quiet of the big office.

18

Lopez Plays Ball

Christie turned on a lamp near the bookshelves and began to scan the titles curiously. She slid open the glass doors which protected one section and took down a volume of Dickens—*The Chimes*. When she opened the book and fanned through the pages, a smell of dust tickled her nose. The pages were yellowed around the edges from the years. She saw at once that Grandfather Josh Allard had been a margin-marker. In a clear hand, cramped a little to fit the narrow space, he had written comments along the way as he read. Sometimes the words were in agreement with a passage, sometimes in criticism of it. Opposite one paragraph of the book in her hands were written the words, "Let us remember this," and she read Dickens's passage through:

> *Give us, in mercy, better homes when we're a-lying in our cradles; give us better food when we're a-working for our lives; give us kinder laws to bring back when we're a-going wrong; and don't set Jail, Jail, Jail afore us, everywhere we turn.*

Farther down the same page some more writing had been cramped into the margins:

> *I do not believe that any man has a right to happiness. I believe he must earn it. I do not believe a man has a right to a job, but that he does have a right to equal opportunity to get himself a job.*

That was something to think about. It might be possible to learn quite a lot about her grandfather from these penciled words, Christie thought as she put the book back. Her hands moved slowly along the green and maroon and gilt-lettered backs of the rows of volumes. They hesitated over a book by Thomas Paine and she pulled it out curiously. So Grandfather Allard had been interested in the writings of that ahead-of-his-age gentleman.

With the book in her hands, she went over to the seedy leather chair where her grandfather had sat reading for long hours on those nights when he could not sleep. The cracked leather was slippery and uncomfortable until she kicked off her shoes and curled herself into the chair's depths. Then she opened the pages and settled down to read. Not just Tom Paine, she'd had him in school, but the things her grandfather had written about the words of Tom Paine.

The book she had chosen was the famous *Rights of Man*. As she turned the pages she found a marked passage that she read over twice with growing pleasure.

> *The world is my country,*
> *All mankind are my brethren,*
> *To do good is my religion,*
> *I believe in one God and no more.*

Opposite it in the margin her grandfather had written, "A creed to live by." She laid the open book face down in her lap and sat there dreaming. If only she could have known him, the old man who had read these books and thought so earnestly about the writings of great minds. She was startled when a voice spoke to her from the doorway and she looked up to find Mr. Bigelow watching her gravely.

"Hello, Christie," he said. "Looks like you were a long way off. I just heard about what happened at Marquette. Somebody said camp boys were in on it. So I came out to see whether I could help."

"It wasn't camp boys!" Christie cried. "Anyway, no one knows yet who it was."

"I thought as much. Is John around?"

"He's out in the workers' quarters with the police of-

163

ficer." Christie started to uncurl herself from the chair, but Mr. Bigelow gestured her back.

"Stay where you are. I think I'll just sit down and wait for John. What do you know about this business?"

Christie told him about going over to the school building that morning and of the heartbreaking wreckage. Mr. Bigelow sat in Mr. Tidings's chair and listened soberly.

"Marge thinks it's going to set back all our plans," Christie finished. "She thinks the town will blame the migrants and be against everything we want to do. Do you think that's so?"

"I hope not," Mr. Bigelow said, but he looked worried.

Christie tapped the book in her lap. "I wish Grandfather Josh was alive. I've just been reading comments he made here and there in the margins of his books. Even though he was wealthy and important, I don't think he forgot about—well, about human beings. I don't think he'd have sided with Aunt Amelia on this at all."

"I don't know but what you're right," Mr. Bigelow said.

"I've been wondering about him a lot the last few days," Christie went on. "It seems odd that he left the Allard plant to my father who was only interested in getting away from Leola. Why do you suppose he did?"

Mr. Bigelow pondered the question for a moment, playing with a paper knife on the desk. "Your grandfather was a great believer in American small-town life. He said cities might take over for a while, but in the long run men would turn back to the land, to the friendliness of the small town."

"What did he know about city life?"

"Enough to dislike it. He was a well-traveled man until he married and settled down in this town where he was born. This was where his roots were, and he believed that the plant could do a lot for all this country roundabout Leola."

"Then why, when Aunt Amelia felt about Leola the way he did, why didn't he leave the plant to her?"

Laugh crinkles formed about Mr. Bigelow's eyes. "You're quite a one for direct questions, aren't you?

Haven't you learned that direct questions are frightening in polite society?"

"But I want to know," said Christie. "I'm an Allard, too."

"Good for you. I'll tell you what I think, though I may not be right. For one thing, you have to take into consideration the fact that the plant is not a woman's job. Also that in your grandfather's time women's jobs were much more limited than they are now. But there was another thing—his disappointment in your father."

"Lots of people have been disappointed in him," Christie said, resentment creeping into her tone.

"I knew him as a boy," Mr. Bigelow said. "I always liked him."

An unexpected wave of hurt flashed through Christie. *So did I,* she thought bitterly, *so did I!*

Quietly Mr. Bigelow went on: "You can't force the other fellow into your own pattern. And perhaps your grandfather made a mistake to try with your father. Toward everyone else he seemed far more tolerant and understanding. They had a rousing good fight when your dad pulled out. When it came to drawing up his will, Josh Allard must have thought he'd leave his son a good load of responsibility. Something that might, after young Larry had had his fill of cities, pull him back to Leola. Of course it didn't work out like that. Your father simply put everything in Spencer Tidings's hands and never came back at all. While Spencer is a good man and one who takes his responsibilities seriously, he isn't the man your grandfather was. Which, perhaps, is part of his trouble. He is forever trying to prove to your aunt, and perhaps to himself, that he is Josh Allard's equal."

"There's another thing," Christie said. "Considering the sort of man my grandfather must have been, how could Aunt Amelia grow up with ideas so very different from his?"

"Well, there was your grandmother's influence to be reckoned with, too."

"No one ever seems to say much about her. It's always Josh they talk about."

"Maybe because most folks loved Josh, but while they

respected your grandmother, I think they were a bit afraid of her. Money meant a lot to her. And position. There were those who said she thought she was better than anybody else, and maybe a little of that rubbed off on your Aunt Amelia. Though she's got her father in her, too, and she can surprise you sometimes. I don't think old Josh was much of a family man, really. The plant was his child and the way it gave work to a whole community was the important thing in his life. He let his wife have whatever she wanted, providing she didn't bother him. And he pretty much left the raising of the kids to her."

"I'm beginning to see the picture," Christie said.

"You're a throwback." Mr. Bigelow's eyes twinkled. "Has anybody told you how much you sometimes resemble your grandfather?"

"I'd like to resemble him," Christie said softly. "I wish I could have known him. Mr. Bigelow, how do you think he would have felt about these migrants from Texas?"

Mr. Bigelow shook his head. "I don't know for sure. I think he'd have regretted the way people have moved away from the land. But if I can make a guess, I think he'd have jumped in and done everything he possibly could to help the migrants and understand their problems. I think he'd have recognized their importance in the picture, and he'd have recognized their importance as individuals, too."

"That's what I'd like to think," Christie said.

She heard the screen door open just then and heard John's step as he came into his office.

"There's John now!" she cried. "Maybe he has some news."

She flew out of the chair without stopping to pull on her shoes, the book still clasped in her hands, and ran to the door of John's office. Mr. Bigelow followed more slowly.

John stood at the window beyond his desk, watching the police car pull away. Discouragement was stamped in the slump of his shoulders.

"What happened?" Christie asked. "Did that policeman find out anything? It wasn't the camp boys, was it?"

John did not look around. "He couldn't get anything out

of those who are home today, so now he's going out to the fields to talk to more of the workers. But I don't think it'll do any good."

"Because there's nothing to get," Christie said firmly.

He did not answer and she knew how worried he was.

"Why did something like this have to happen now?" he said. "No matter who's to blame it will raise a lot of ugly suspicions. It makes the job all the harder. A fine time to be as helpless as I am now."

Mr. Bigelow spoke from behind Christie. "Just how are you helpless? I thought you had some plans in mind?"

John turned to smile wryly at the older man. "Hello, Ed. I had plans all right, but there's a fellow named Allard who owns this plant. He refuses to give me the authority to go ahead."

Christie glanced at the book in her hands and a sudden rebellious thought began to grow in her mind. "I'm not so sure you don't already have the authority," she said.

John really looked at her then. At her stockinged feet and the book in her hands. Again the wry smile quirked his lips.

"Do you always come to work without your shoes?"

"I was reading," she said, as if that explained everything.

John seemed to forget them both, looking out the window again, speaking his thoughts aloud. "If only there was some way to get a go-ahead sign from Allard. If I start changes, only to be stopped in a week or two, it might be worse than not trying."

Christie padded across the bare boards of the floor and laid the book open on the desk. "That's what I'm trying to tell you. There's your authority."

He stared at her, not understanding, and she pointed a finger to the words of Tom Paine. John read them, and, still puzzled, read the notation in the margin.

"Josh Allard made those pencil marks," Christie said. "My grandfather. He said this was a creed to live by. It seems to me it takes in all the things you want to do here, and I guess there's never been anybody whose word counted for more around here than Josh Allard."

Mr. Bigelow's chuckle was heartening. "You know, John, maybe Christie's got something at that."

Christie hurried on, excitement prickling through her. "After all, Mr. Tidings can't interfere from a hospital bed, and I've heard his assistant isn't very forceful. My father doesn't really care. He just doesn't want to be bothered. So who is there to stop you?"

John looked at her and then at Mr. Bigelow.

The older man nodded. "Could be she's right. I remember Josh Allard very well. He was a fighter where this plant was concerned. And I've just been telling Christie that he always thought the man was more important than the job."

"You're both crazy," John said. "This isn't the way a business is run." But a light had come into his eyes. "Could be I'm crazy, too." He held out his hand to Mr. Bigelow. "Thanks for dropping in, Ed. I'm going to need all the support I can get." Then he looked at Christie. "Okay, young lady, I'll accept this authority you've just called to my attention. I'm in this now till I'm fired and we're going to make things hum. Go put your shoes on. I can use you."

And use her he did all that long, hot day. She typed, made mistakes, erased, and retyped. They studied the files of the workers together and made notes. Sometimes John thought out loud, formulating his plans, drawing up new rules under which the workers would start operating. It was to be a bloodless battle campaign, its objectives to be won smoothly and without clashes. The community of Leola was to be stormed in an entirely new way. The need was all the more imperative now, after what had happened at the public school. The biggest difficulty was that it would all take time. Perhaps quite a long time. And time was the thing of which they had least.

He would want her back at the camp tonight, John said at the end of the day. He was going to hold a meeting of his own and she could help him. Christie fairly tingled at the prospect.

There was an intoxication about taking positive action of some kind. After dinner, tired as she was, she found

168

herself returning to the camp with her step light and her hopes high.

She couldn't remember when she had ever felt so alive, so involved in living. During all her years with Eve she had somehow been a shadow in the background. Now, for the first time, there was purpose to her days. She was able to help with something that really counted. Phil no longer came into her thoughts as he had done. She was too busy now, too interested in matters outside herself. And even when she remembered him, the remembering didn't hurt so much. Though it made her feel faintly disloyal, she suspected that Phil would not have understood all this concern about the migrant workers. When she reached the plant, she found that the trucks had brought the workers back from the fields. The odor of spicy cooking still lingered in the air from the night meal. The men were gathering in small clumps around the yard, while the women hovered in the background, sitting on doorsteps, or leaning against walls, with small babies on their hips. Older children, silenced for once, hovered near their mothers.

Rafael Olivera saw Christie and came toward her as she entered the camp.

"*Buenas noches,* señorita," he said. "The Señor Mac says I am to help you with the notes."

"Notes?" Christie repeated.

Rafael struggled to make himself clear. "The Señor Mac will make the talk tonight. To all the workers. In Spanish. You will take the notes, but I will, what you call—translate—for you. Yes?"

"Why, that's fine," Christie said. "I'll get my notebook and pencil right away."

When she returned, John Macdonald had taken his place on the steps of the office building where he would be a head or so above the men gathered below him. The summer evenings were long now and the sky still light and clear. Christie found a place near the steps and Rafael stood beside her. The boy's tanned, handsome face seemed alive with eagerness tonight. He, too, sensed that something was under way to help his people.

"Where is Aurora?" Christie asked, and Rafael explained that she and her mother had gone to the hospital for the visiting hours, to be with Tomasa. She found herself looking around for Lopez, but the younger Olivera boy was nowhere in sight.

John began to talk and the crowd in the yard quieted. Rafael stumbled in his haste to give Christie the meaning of the words, but he managed fairly well. Christie scribbled henscratchings of shorthand on paper, getting down the gist of what was being said, while Rafael's soft voice whispered in her ear.

John Macdonald minced no words. He began straight from the shoulder with the statement of what every man and woman there knew—that many communities did not want the Mexican-American in its midst. This was a bad feeling and he wanted to see it broken down in Leola. So now some new, strict rules were going into effect.

A murmur ran through the group of men as they stood there in their working clothes, sun-browned faces turned toward him, dark eyes watchful. They liked Señor Mac, they trusted him. But bad things could happen quickly, and today the police had come to ask rough questions.

The new rules, John continued, were not intended to hurt them or insult them, but to help. If the town of Leola did not like Mexican-Americans it was because it did not really know those who came here. So now they were all going to teach the town a lesson. They were going to prove that Mexican-Americans made just as fine citizens and maybe better than many Anglo-Americans.

The first tenseness went out of his listeners. This was something new for an Anglo to be proposing.

Rafael translated hurriedly, getting his words a little mixed, but giving Christie the sense.

From this night on no worker was to appear on the streets of Leola until he had washed and dressed in clean clothes. The new shower building would be ready soon. Many camps did not have showers, so let them be used, before any man or boy or girl or woman, who had been working in the fields, set foot in the town. Clean clothes were to be the rule, and the hair was to be combed. The workers would prove that they could be cleaner, neater than the townspeople themselves. When they went to

170

town, let it be in groups of never more than three together.

Again there was a murmur, and John grinningly admitted that Anglos were a queer lot. Perhaps his people did not know so well how to enjoy themselves as the American of Mexican descent. They did not understand those who laughed aloud at a good joke and talked in gay voices. Perhaps this was because they could not understand the words or the joke. They became uncomfortable when workers stood about on corners in groups of six or eight. That this happened was due, of course, to the fact that there was no place else to go. But for now this feeling must be bowed to.

Reports had reached him, John said, of boys sneaking into the downstairs part of the movie theater, instead of going to the balcony where the town said the Mexican-American must go. This rule was not a good one, but it must be obeyed until it was changed willingly by the town itself.

"What I want," John told them, "is for you to be able to walk into that movie house and sit anywhere you like. If you do these things I am asking of you, that time will come. But first we must show the town how mistaken it has been about the migrant workers."

They would watch their children, he said, and allow none of them to race around the town and go into the stores in droves, or pick over articles on counters. And when there was any meeting between the Anglo and the Mexican-American, they must show the Anglos what true courtesy could be. They would bear themselves proudly and each would be responsible for himself and for his brother, to see that all did the same.

John went on to give some new rules for the fields and for life here in the camp. And then he was finished. The women began to chatter among themselves, and the men broke into little groups.

John smiled at Christie. "Thanks for coming. I hope you got most of it. I want a record of what I said here tonight."

He went down among the men and began to talk to individuals. There was a stirring of pleased excitement

171

throughout the yard and it seemed that the majority of his listeners were warmly behind him. Christie thanked Rafael, returned her notebook to her desk, and started across the camp. As she reached the gate, a small incident revealed that John's plans were already taking effect.

Two teen-aged boys had headed for the gate, only to be hauled back by an older man. He spoke to them sharply in Spanish, rumpled the already untidy head of one, and slapped the sweat-stained shirt of the other, sending them back to clean up before leaving the yard.

Christie took the most direct route home to Aunt Amelia's, the route that led past the house where Tom Webb roomed. Daylight had begun to fade a little, but it was still light enough to see clearly and she glanced up at the house as she went by, half hoping that Tom might be in sight. It would be fun to tell him what had happened out at the plant tonight. But since he was nowhere in view, she walked on past the vacant lot where once more a group of boys were playing baseball.

She recognized the small, lively boy called Bitsy, and the sullen, thin-faced one, Hank, who had seemed the leader of the group. Bitsy had been fresh, but she hadn't minded him. Hank she had disliked on sight. He was at second base now, yelling at the boy who was pitching.

"Make it a good one, Mex!" he shouted.

Christie's attention flew to the pitcher. Out there on the mound stood Lopez Olivera—a confident Lopez who was in complete control of his own motions. He wound up for a pitch that sent the ball sizzling across the plate, while the batter swung at it futilely, striking out. Lopez swaggered a little, permitting the others to tell him how good he was.

She should have been glad to see him playing there, Christie thought; glad that he had finally been accepted and was showing those boys his skill. But instead, she felt worried and uneasy. What had he done—this boy from the camp—to get himself accepted by these boys who had previously rejected him?

Christie walked on quickly, the uneasiness growing in her.

19

Scout Knife

The thought of Lopez returned to worry Christie more than once during the next few days. She mentioned to no one her discovery that he had been unaccountably accepted by the very boys who had treated him so scornfully a short time before.

The vandalism at the school had rocked Leola as it had seldom been rocked before. True, there were those who said the whole thing was the doing of unruly town boys and there was no sense pointing an accusing finger at the camp. But there were others who roused themselves to a state of indignant excitability over the presence of a migrant camp in their midst. No town boy would be mixed up in anything so uncivilized, they pointed out smugly. Of *course* it was the Mexicans. Who else? For several days the tide of emotion ran high and if there had been an ounce of proof against the migrants it might have served as a spark to set off an explosion. But no evidence of any kind was turned up to connect the camp people with what had happened at the school. And as time passed, tempers wore themselves out and the town sank back into its usual placid indifference, with only a murmuring here and there when Miss Amelia Allard prodded sufficiently.

As Monday night approached Christie felt increasingly uneasy. She no longer had an impish desire to push her aunt into this visit to Mrs. Olivera's "home" out in the camp. Her aunt had not mentioned the matter again except to indicate that, having been so foolishly commited, they would go out there Monday night. Her cool disapproval was not reassuring. She spoke no word of reproach, however, until they were actually in the car on the way to the Allard plant. She had asked Christie to drive, and she herself sat in the front seat, very straight, beside her niece.

"I hope you're beginning to realize," Aunt Amelia said, "just how ridiculous this visit is?"

"I don't think it's ridiculous," Christie answered mildly.

Her aunt ignored her disagreement. "It will be awkward for all of us. Obviously that poor woman regretted her invitation almost as soon as it was spoken. There was no reason for you to bring it up again. Now she will be uncomfortable and I won't have the slightest idea how to put her at ease."

Christie did not answer. But now she felt uncomfortable enough about the whole thing herself.

When they reached the plant, she drove the car into the parking area and she and her aunt got out. The grounds were well lighted and the windows of the housing section were bright. Aunt Amelia looked about curiously, her attention caught in turn by the neat, freshly painted barracks, the small schoolhouse, the old carriage house that was being rebuilt, and finally by the ramshackle sheds which contrasted sharply with John Macdonald's additions.

"What are those chicken coops doing here?" she asked Christie.

"People live in them," Christie said. "Mr. Tidings feels they are quite good enough for temporary shelter. Mr. Macdonald doesn't."

Aunt Amelia let the matter drop, but Christie heard her sigh as they started across the camp.

"It doesn't look the way I remember it at all," her aunt said. "I suppose it's twenty-five years since I've set foot on these grounds. I used to haunt the place when I was a little girl. There was a big green leather chair in Papa's office where I used to curl up for hours, reading his books."

"The chair is still there," Christie said. "I sat in it the other day."

A shadow detached itself from a doorway and came toward them. As he stepped into the light, Christie recognized Rafael Olivera. He greeted them in his usual friendly way, but Christie sensed that something was troubling him.

"I have been watching for you," he said. "So I will bring you to our house."

"Our house" was, of course, one of the shacks which Aunt Amelia had termed a chicken coop. Rafael called to his mother from the doorstep, but it was Señor Olivera who came first to greet them. He was a big, genial man with white teeth shining in a smile of welcome that lighted his swarthy face. The room he ushered them into might have been a drawing room, if his hospitality was any indication.

His wife came forward more quietly, but her desire to make her guests welcome equaled that of her husband, and her pride of bearing was far greater. She wore a black dress, very clean and creaseless, and Christie suspected that it was her one good dress.

At first glance the little room seemed to forbid the entrance of one more person. An oil lamp stood on a small table, and shadows crowded the walls. Most of the space was occupied by a double bed and a narrow army cot. On the wall above the cot, Christie noted that a few magazine photographs had been pasted up. All were of baseball players. This, undoubtedly, was Lopez's corner.

A wire had been stretched high from wall to wall and this served as closet space, with hangers supporting the meager clothing of the Olivera family. Surprisingly, considering the lack of space, a spot had been found for a single straight wooden chair and Miss Allard, as the guest of honor, was invited to take it. Christie seated herself on one end of the cot.

It was only then that she noticed the room's other occupant. Lopez was sidling through the shadows along one wall, moving toward the door. He wore a blank smile, automatically adopted as a greeting for the guests, but Christie could see that his attention was upon escape. Rafael stood in the doorway, blocking it—he had seen the approach of his younger brother.

Rafael spoke softly in Spanish and Lopez answered in the same low tones.

Aunt Amelia noticed none of this. She sat stiffly on the

175

hard chair, her hands, white-gloved as was suitable when making a call, plucking nervously at each other in her lap. For once Miss Amelia Allard was not at ease. Mr. Olivera, obviously not a master of the English tongue, smiled and said nothing, and Mrs. Olivera had suddenly forgotten her guests, her attention on the two boys in the doorway. Apparently considering herself in the role of gentry visiting peasants, Aunt Amelia tried to make conversation in her own way.

"This is very crowded for four people," she said. "How do you manage with only two beds?"

Mrs. Olivera seemed not to hear. Every inch of her listened intently to the muttered argument between her sons. But her jovial husband did his best.

"Is not for four people, two beds!" He laughed wholeheartedly and the sound echoed in the small box of a room. "My Rafael, he is beeg boy. He sleep in—what you call—bach house."

"Oh," said Aunt Amelia. "Bachelor quarters, I suppose. At least you keep things nicely here. The place is quite clean and I suppose a little clutter cannot be helped."

Christie squirmed with embarrassment. Mrs. Olivera must have caught the words this time, for her gaze returned briefly to Aunt Amelia. "Thank you," she said with dignity. Then, as the sound of scuffling rose in the doorway, she flung away all pretense of being a hostess and hurried to the door.

The quick clatter of the Spanish tongue always had an excited sound to Christie. But this was something more. Mrs. Olivera was commanding her younger son, while Rafael used a simpler method. He had bent his brother's right arm behind his back and now he twisted it with a slow, steady pressure. Lopez gave a cry of pain and released the thing he had grasped in his hand. A metal object clattered to the floor and Rafael covered it with his foot.

Mrs. Olivera spoke sharply to her younger son, and Lopez, looking at once hangdog and furious, wheeled back into the room and squatted on his haunches in a

176

corner, like a puppy who had been whipped and would make friends with no one.

It was his father who thrust Rafael's foot aside and picked up the object it covered. He balanced it curiously on the palm of his hand and Christie saw with a start that it was an American Boy Scout knife. Señor Olivera turned angrily on Lopez and asked him a question in Spanish, but before the boy could answer, Mrs. Olivera recovered herself and remembered her guests.

"Later," she said firmly to her husband. "This is not the time." Her husband, too, remembered that to one's guests must be given courtesy, not a display of family troubles. Practically in the same instant that he gave his son a black scowl, he presented Miss Allard with an engaging smile. Rafael smoothed his clothes, which had been mussed by the scuffle, and sat down beside his mother on the big bed. Christie saw that he was trembling.

Only Aunt Amelia was not to be put off from consideration of what had happened. "That was a Scout knife," she said. "Where did he get it?"

"His father has asked him," Mrs. Olivera said. "It was given to him. It is no matter for now. He will give it back. I do not like him to carry a knife."

"I should think not," said Aunt Amelia.

Only Christie saw the dark look Lopez gave her aunt.

Mrs. Olivera regarded her guest gravely. "It has been a dry summer this year, is it not so? Unless we have more rain it will not be good for the crops, for the town."

Aunt Amelia blinked and for the first time that Christie could remember a pink flush rose in her aunt's cheeks. After that a most curious thing happened. It was not Miss Amelia Allard who had to set the humble Mrs. Olivera at her ease, but quite the other way around. Mrs. Olivera turned the conversation with some skill to matters of current interest in Leola. She spoke of the coming of the big town event, the Corn Festival, which would be held in September. Apparently Mrs. Olivera had been present during the last festival and was most admiring of the floats. Aunt Amelia snatched at the subject with nervous enthusiasm. No other town in the Middle West had such a festival as theirs, she was sure. People came from miles away to see the parade and enjoy the various displays. She talked on at some length and the Oliveras listened with their natural courtesy.

By way of refreshment, Mrs. Olivera passed a plate of American cookies, apologizing for the fact that she could not serve coffee or chocolate, since anything that must be heated could be taken care of only in the cookhouse. Aunt Amelia, who did not care for sweet things, munched and made no further personal remarks. When she finally looked at her watch, she seemed surprised at the hour.

"I didn't realize it was so late," she said. "We really must be leaving."

The Oliveras showed their guests to the door with the same friendliness with which they had been greeted. Only Lopez sulked in his corner with a mumbled "Adios." Rafael crossed the grounds to see them to the car. There was the sound of the Spanish tongue in the night and gay laughter. These people had a talent for happiness, Christie thought. Somewhere a guitar played and a girl's voice began to sing softly in Spanish. Rafael turned his head to listen, and in the bright yellow lights of the camp Christie could see the rapt expression of his face.

"Is it Aurora?" she asked softly.

He nodded. "Always she sings sad songs now. I like better when she sings the happy ones."

They got into the car, and this time Aunt Amelia took the wheel. As they drove out of the camp, Christie looked back and saw Rafael standing there, still listening to Aurora's song.

She turned back to her aunt. "Well," she asked, "how do you like the Oliveras?"

Aunt Amelia slowed the car to ease it over the railroad tracks. "The woman is an exception, of course. If they were all like that, there would be no trouble."

"But don't you see," Christie said, "she is educated. She has what so many of these migrant people have no chance to get, an education. That's why she stands out."

"Save your breath," Aunt Amelia said drily. "The thing that really caught my attention was that boy with an American Scout knife. Where do you suppose he got it?"

178

"His mother said it was given to him."

"Nonsense. He probably stole it. I believe I shall make a few inquiries. If you recall, the wantonly destroyed mural in the school building had been slashed with a good strong knife."

"You can't blame Lopez for that!" Christie cried. "There must be thousands of knives in this town. It isn't fair to single out Lopez." But uneasiness stirred in her again. She had to talk to someone about the boy and she had to do it soon.

As she undressed for bed that night she thought about the problem. Alan had done what he could. Despite his kindness and understanding, he did not have the influence with Lopez that he had with Rafael. Marge was liked by everyone out at the camp, but she was a woman and this would take a man's hand. Not even John Macdonald would do. To Lopez he was the "boss."

All along she knew the one she was coming to, the one who had been at the back of her mind from the first. In the morning she would telephone Tom Webb at his paper and tell him there was something urgent she needed to talk to him about. Once Tom had been practically where Lopez now found himself.

20

Door Into the Past

The porch swing creaked back and forth as Christie pushed lazily with one toe. Since the evening was young, the pesky mosquitoes weren't out as yet, and the porch was cooler than the house. Marge leaned against the pillar beside the top step and scratched Fatso behind the ears. With Aunt Amelia out to a club meeting, the elderly bull-dog was in a state of mournful bereavement. From up-stairs Christie could hear the light clatter of Alan's portable typewriter. A minister's life seemed to move from one sermon to the next.

That afternoon Christie and Marge had taken time to run over to the hospital to visit Tomasa and give her some bright new hair ribbons. The little girl was getting along fine and seemed her usual happy self. She had apparently won the hearts of the nurses with her cheerful courage.

"I can't believe it's August already," Christie said. "Things have moved so quickly that it seems as though I got here day before yesterday."

Fatso rose and waddled disdainfully away from Marge, to lie down again, just out of her reach.

"Unrequited love," Marge said sadly. "You silly old pooch! You get much more attention from me than you ever do from Auntie." Then she grinned at Christie. "You know something? You've done a lot of changing in this last month."

"I was pretty poisonous, wasn't I?" Christie said.

"No—not poisonous. Just misinformed, let's say. And overly sheltered. If you'd been poisonous, you wouldn't have changed. It's just that we've given you a chance to get away from a little corner you'd never poked your nose out of before."

Christie laughed. "I'm still learning. I didn't know so much could happen in a small town."

"There's a lot ahead of you," Marge said. "Wait till the pack is on and this town really gets rolling. I haven't spent a summer in Leola before, but I've seen it happen other places."

"What do you mean—till the pack is on?"

"The harvesting of the corn, the packing at the cannery. It will begin any day now because the fields have been planted to ripen at different times. That way the pack is continuous, instead of coming all at one time. The cannery is ready to go. The women and girls who'll supplement the work of machinery are already signed up. When old Mama Nature blows the whistle, this town will hum."

"Sounds exciting," Christie said.

"It is. Too bad people all over the country who take corn in a can for granted can't see what's behind it."

The swing creaked idly and Christie glanced down the street for the dozenth time.

"You waiting for someone?" Marge asked.

Christie was matter-of-fact. "Tom Webb. I asked him to come over because I want to talk to him about Lopez."

"Has that kid been up to something again?"

"No. That is, I don't know," Christie said. "I just thought Tom might be the best one to help."

"He probably will be. Especially since he's getting a bit sweet on you."

"Don't be silly," Christie said.

Marge gave her a knowing look and stood up. "Well, chores to do. So you can have the field to yourself."

She went into the house and Christie looked after her indignantly. Why did people always read the personal into something that wasn't in the least personal? Tom thought she was a brat. He didn't like "little rich girls" even when they hadn't a penny to their names. And she didn't care what he thought one way or another, as far as she herself was concerned.

"Fatso-Shelley, you've got better sense than Marge has," she told the old bulldog.

Fatso did not trouble to open his eyes, but snored impolitely.

She saw Tom the moment he turned down their street, though she pretended not to. She was angry with Marge for making her feel suddenly self-conscious. Ten minutes before she'd have waved to him. Now she couldn't. But when Tom came up the porch steps with his usual fresh grin, she relaxed and forgot about Marge. Any senior class would have voted Tom Webb Least-Likely-Candidate-for-Romance.

"I hope you appreciate the fact that I'm giving up a good book for you this evening," he said. "I expect you to make it worth my while."

"It's worth your while," she said. "But not because I'm going to stand on my head or entertain you with my brilliant conversation. I want to talk to you about Lopez Olivera."

He dropped down on the step Marge had just vacated and sighed deeply. "An ulterior motive. I might have known. No one ever loves me for myself alone."

Fatso stopped snoring and opened his eyes. When he saw who it was, he wriggled across the porch and gave Tom a drooly bulldog grin.

"I didn't mean you," Tom said. "Go away, Slobbery. Abominable creature, isn't he, Christie? You treat him nicely and he spurns you. But push him away and he thinks you're wonderful. Just like some humans. So what about Lopez?"

Christie told him the little things she had been adding together. The boy's anger over Tomasa's injury, the way he had suddenly become friends with boys who had refused to have anything to do with him, the incident of the Scout knife.

Tom listened soberly. "I've seen him playing baseball with the other boys, but I didn't think too much about that. Kids are funny. They can reverse themselves so fast that the action seems illogical to grownups. Anything or nothing might have caused the change. I just wish I'd been around to see it happen."

Christie felt somewhat reassured. "Of course the Scout knife doesn't need to mean anything either."

"That's right. He could have traded something for it. Kids haven't much sense of value. Lopez may have had some knick-knack that caught the interest of another boy."

"I suppose there isn't anything you could do?" Christie asked. "After all, you pulled those boys off him that time. You've shown yourself his friend."

"Trouble is, we can't tell how he feels about that rescue. He might just as easily hold it against me. But I'll think about it. I'll see if I can dig up some approach. Anything else?"

"That was all," Christie said. She considered telling him more about the visit she and her aunt had made to the camp, but while she hesitated, he stood up. She was surprised at the little flash of disappointment she felt over his leaving so quickly.

"I really ought to get back to my book," he mused.

'However, a brilliant idea has just hit me. There are a couple of things in this town I'd like to show you. Care to come for a walk, Christie?"

She hesitated uncertainly and slapped at a mosquito on her arm. It was beginning to get dark and they'd be around in droves pretty soon.

"If we keep moving, they'll leave us alone," Tom said persuasively.

There was no reason why she shouldn't go for a walk with him. She got up and the swing went back with a wail of protest.

"I'll be home soon," she told the indifferent Fatso and went down the steps with Tom.

They turned in the direction of downtown and walked toward Main Street. Christie told him about Aunt Amelia and Mrs. Olivera, and enjoyed the way he relished the story. On Main Street he paused in front of a shoe-store window and looked into it. "I just wanted to check on something. Yes, it's still there. Pretty, isn't it?"

Boldly displayed in the window was a sign that Christie had seen before in Leola:

WHITE TRADE ONLY

"That ought to be stopped," Christie said indignantly.

"Now come on across the street," Tom said. "Have you looked into Mr. Bigelow's window lately?"

She hadn't been downtown since the meeting at Mr. Bigelow's house and she walked up to the window curiously. Here, too, a sign was displayed. The print was even larger on this one, and a little art work had been added. In one corner of the poster was a platter-headed creature with four eyes and antennae growing out of its head. Christie read the sign.

HUMAN RACE ONLY
NO MARTIANS ALLOWED

She laughed out loud and liked Mr. Bigelow more than ever.

"Watch tomorrow's *Record*," Tom told her. "I've sold

my editor the idea of using a picture of that window and a story about it. Mr. B deserves some free publicity. And maybe it will embarrass the white-trade-only crowd. I came over here last Saturday night when the stores were open to see how it was working."

"Were any of the camp people coming in?"

"Were they! And I've never seen them so spruced up. Bigelow was doing a rousing good business. Not just with the camp people. There were plenty of townspeople coming, too, to look at that sign and then go into the store. Everybody seemed to be enjoying the joke. What's more, there was practically a boycott on shoes."

"Mr. Bigelow's wonderful!" Christie said. "I had a lovely time with him the other day, talking about my grandfather."

Tom drew her away from the window and turned toward a cross street. "That reminds me of the second call I want to pay tonight. Last I heard you hadn't been to this place yet and I thought I'd give you a personal tour."

They walked back toward the residential section of town. Christie was puzzled until she saw a vast, dignified old house rising behind big trees, and knew where he was taking her. There was a sign near the steps which announced the building as the Leola Museum. This was her grandfather's old home.

"I've been saving this for a special mood," she told Tom. "Tonight is just right. But I thought it was only open in the daytime."

"To the peasants, yes. But don't forget, you Allards are privileged nobility."

"Don't talk like that," Christie said.

"I apologize. You've really turned out much better than I expected. Anyway, I was giving you credit you don't deserve. Ben Brady, the custodian, lives upstairs and he's a good friend of mine. He said I could bring you over any time. He used to work for your grandfather."

Tom rang the bell and they could hear the shrilling inside. Lights flashed on downstairs and after an interval a chain lock was removed from inside the door and it swung open to admit them to a large anteroom. Beyond, rising into shadow, Christie could see the curve of a graceful staircase.

The man who let them in was bent and elderly. He said, "Evening Tom," and then peered dimly at Christie. "You're the little granddaughter, ain't you? The one he never got to see. Welcome home, Miss Christine. I'm Ben Brady."

Christie gave her hand warmly to the old man. There was no need to ask who Ben meant by "he." Josh Allard was still the most important personage in the world to this man who had worked for him so long ago.

"I try to keep the place up just the way he'd like it," Ben said. "But sometimes the dust gets a mite ahead of me. Would you like to see the exhibits, Miss Christine?"

"I'd like to see everything." Christie said.

Ben Brady took them first into what had once been the drawing room of the big house and was now the general exhibition room. Everything on display had to do with the history of the local country, from Indian days when prairie schooners had first penetrated this rich farm area to a fine diorama of the present-day Allard plant.

"You'll want to come back and take a longer look at everything," old Ben said understandingly. "I'll take you through the place now and then you can come back any time you want."

Toward the rear of the house there was an impressive room done in rich maroons, with an Oriental carpet on the floor and thick velvet draperies at the windows. Again there were bookshelves, and here fine bindings of tooled leather indicated a valuable collection.

Ben unhooked the maroon cord that barred the door to visitors. "Your grandfather's library, Miss Christine. Your grandmother had it all fixed up for him just like this."

It was a handsome, dignified room, but somehow it did not resemble Christie's growing picture of her grandfather.

"Did he like it?" Tom asked with quick perception.

Ben Brady scratched the back of his head thoughtfully. "Funny thing, I don't know's he did. He always carted the books he liked best to the plant and did most of his reading out there."

185

"In a big green chair," said Christie softly. She parted the velvet curtains to look out into the darkness of the garden. A big shadowy elm grew close to the house where it would shade the library windows during afternoon heat. As she touched the velvet a faint odor of long-quiet dust rose in the air.

"I'll light up the pictures for you," Ben said. "Maybe you'd like to see them."

He touched a switch and lights sprang on above two portraits, one above the mantel, one on the opposite wall. Christie crossed the room to a place where she could view the handsome portrait of her grandfather. This painting was a far better picture than the photograph in the sitting room at her aunt's. The eyes which looked down at her from the canvas seemed to meet hers with benevolent understanding. Here was more than an outward likeness— here was the interpretation of a man.

Tom said, "He must have been quite a guy."

"He was," said Ben Brady simply. "That's your grandmother over there, Miss Christine."

She turned to study the second painting of the woman who looked so much like Aunt Amelia. There was an interpretation here, too, for all that the picture was an attractive one. You knew, looking at this proud face, that here was a woman who set great store by wealth, family, and position. Looking up at the picture, Christie could feel no relationship whatever with the woman who had posed for it.

"She was a lady who knew how to get her own way," Ben said mildly, and Christie sensed that he held back more than he spoke.

"Her family was pretty old stock, wasn't it?" Tom asked.

Christie glanced at him. "How do you know?"

"You forget I'm a reporter. First thing I had to do when I hit Leola was bone up on the town's Who's Who. Your grandmother was *very* Who."

"Oh, dear," said Christie, "no wonder poor Grandfather ran off to the plant to do his reading."

Ben Brady gave her an appreciative smile and she knew that she had touched on the truth.

186

He led them quickly through other downstairs rooms. Only the library had been left as it used to be. The rest had been turned into standard museum exhibit rooms. When they came out at the foot of the big stairway again, Ben paused.

"Except for the rooms I live in and one other, the upstairs is empty," he said. "We don't let people up there. But there's a room Miss Amelia wanted left just the way it used to be. Maybe you'd like to see it?"

"Of course," Christie said.

He didn't tell her what room it was, but flicked on lights and led them up the curving staircase with its worn maroon carpet, and down a long hall toward a room at the rear. The door was locked, but Ben took a set of keys from his pocket, fitted one into the lock and turned it.

"There's nothing valuable kept here," Ben said, switching on a light. "It's just that your aunt didn't want strangers coming in. Your grandfather left the room exactly this way, and Miss Amelia wanted it to stay the same."

Ben stepped out of the doorway and Christie crossed the threshold. She knew at once whose room it had been. This was a boy's room. There was a pattern of ships and sails on the faded green wallpaper, and the green carpet boasted ink-spots and other unidentifiable stains. The bed was boxlike and plain, the green plaid window draperies severe. On the wall were framed photographs of city spires—Chicago's skyline from Lake Michigan and the lower end of Manhattan with its clustered towers. Even as a boy Lawrence Allard must have yearned toward cities.

"They built good fireplaces in these old houses," Ben said. "Winter afternoons and rainy Sundays Larry used to light a fire in that grate. Then he'd lie on his stomach in front of it and read. He was a great one for books, just like his father. You'll find a lot of his old favorites on those shelves over his bed."

Christie looked about her in a dream. Somehow she could not picture the boy lying before the hearth the way she could picture her grandfather in his green chair. Her remembrance of her father got in the way. Yet she had an odd yearning to go back through the years and reach that boy whom she did not know at all.

"Last time he slept in this room he was about eighteen," Ben said.

"Just my age," said Christie. She wished she could be alone in this for a little while. She could never go back through the years with other people present.

The bookshelves over the bed attracted Tom and he began to run through the titles. Ben found a spot on the bureau that needed dusting and went after it with the palm of his hand.

Beneath a window in an ell that jutted out from the side of the house stood a desk. The top was scarred and battered, indicating that its former owner had given it hard wear. Idly Christie pulled open the top drawer and was a little startled to find it filled with a jumble of paper, pencils without points, pen nibs, a broken eraser. Somehow the contents of that untidy drawer, left just as it had been when the room had an occupant, made the boy who had lived in it seem more real. With her back to the others, Christie reached into the drawer and picked up the eraser. It felt rough and hard as stone in her fingers. She slipped in into her pocket and closed the drawer. Then she turned back to the others.

"I can't thank you enough, Ben Brady," she said. "I'd like to come here again if I may."

"Any time," Ben said. "Any time at all, Miss Christine."

They went downstairs and he bade them good night at the door. As they walked down the steps they heard the rattling of the door chain behind them, protecting Allard property from the world.

It was hard to come back to everyday Leola. Christie pressed the worn eraser between her fingers and felt that she had a passkey which would return her again to that other, long-ago world. Now she was half afraid Tom Webb would break the spell with his usual irreverence. Strangely, he did not. He was silent for two long blocks and Christie was grateful for the lack of words between them.

"Thank you for taking me there tonight," she said

when the sidewalk beneath her feet once more seemed real.

He gave her a sidelong look, as if he were discovering someone he had never met before. "You *do* have a hunk of family behind you. I guess I never really got the picture before."

Christie laughed. How like Tom to call it a "hunk" of family.

"It's fun getting acquainted with them for the first time."

"Pretty impressive," Tom said. "I'd hate to show you the shanty where I grew up."

"I don't see what difference it makes," Christie said. "Everyone has a hunk of family and the farther back you go the more assorted they get."

Tom said nothing and she was willing to walk along in silence again. At Aunt Amelia's he stopped at the foot of the porch steps.

"Thanks again," she said. "And let me know about Lopez."

"I'll do that," he told her. "Good night, Christine."

He hadn't called her Christine since the beginning and she wondered at the change. But he left so quickly, there was no time to ask.

She went up to her room still holding the bit of eraser tightly between her fingers. It was a lucky piece for her purse, she thought. She wasn't sure why she wanted something that had belonged to that boy her father had once been, when she did not care at all about his grownup self. When she had drawn her first week's pay she had taken out her father's check and mailed it back to him with a brief note saying she wouldn't need it. And she had expected that to be the end of her relationship with him.

21

Half a Lifesaver

The crops were late this year, but by mid-August, as Marge had prophesied, something stirred and came alive in Leola. Almost before the last detasseling of the seed corn had been accomplished, the packing of corn for the table began. There was a feeling of acceleration throughout the town. You could not set foot on Main Street without sensing the quickened tempo.

The pack was on!

It was a race now against Nature. The corn must be "jerked" at the right moment. Left too long on the stalks there was deterioration and loss. And it must be processed for canning with equal speed. The workers were in the fields at the first show of daylight and they worked till light was gone. All a part of the day's labor was the early morning chill of wet corn, the humid heat of noontime, mosquitoes, the razor-sharp edges of green corn leaves, the aching of arms and shoulders from reaching up all day long. And always there was the discomfort of dust and dirt. This portion of a nation's food must be preserved, and everything hung on the speed of the harvest.

Out at the plant Christie found herself in the midst of the quickened activity. Twenty-four hours a day tractors rumbled in and out of the grounds, drawing three, sometimes five rubber-tired wagons to the unloading platform. Conveyor belts moved endlessly. The husks were carted off to disposal areas outside of town, to be fed eventually to cattle. At night lights blazed and shifts changed, the sound of hissing steam, the clatter of machinery was constant. The little town hurried.

Even strong, work-toughened hands were sliced and

swollen from handling sharp corn leaves. Workers wore gloves, but these quickly frayed through and Christie found herself helping at the first-aid station, working over slashed hands till she was ready to drop. Disinfectant seemed to be used up by the gallon and she wound miles of bandage over cuts that weren't serious enough for a doctor, but painful to the worker. Sometimes she felt that she would never, as long as she lived, want to look at a kernel of corn again.

Despite the preoccupation with the harvest, through all the activity and bustle of Leola ran a new undercurrent, a new consciousness of the workers on the part of the townspeople. Some of it was good. A woman buying groceries would comment to her neighbor on how friendly and pleasant the migrants seemed this year. Mr. Bigelow would get into a conversation with a customer buying yard goods and somehow the topic of the natural generosity and good-heartedness of the Mexican-Americans would creep into the talk. Someone else would remark on how clean and spruced up they looked when they came into town.

Gradually, without anyone knowing just how it happened, the talk about the schools began. It was a disgrace to the country, the town librarian said, that here were third- and fourth-generation American children who couldn't make use of the library because they couldn't read English. Others agreed that something should certainly be done about it. Why couldn't these children be brought into Leola schools for the months they were here?

Yet the real heart of the problem had not been truly reached. There were those among the workers who were as skeptical of good intentions on the part of the Anglos as they had ever been, and with old, long-justified reasons. There was no sudden acceptance of the migrants by the town as a whole, no concerted attempt at integration or understanding. This was only a beginning.

The reverse side of the coin had an ugly gleam. What had happened to Marquette School had not been forgotten. The fact that nothing definite had pointed to the boys of the camp had not lessened suspicion in many quarters.

While no positive move had been made against the migrants, the seeming indifference was only a layer deep. "Just let those Mexicans step over the line once more." That was the tune to which many people danced. Christie knew that her aunt was marshaling the forces on her side, but so far there had been no outward clash. It was possible that the basic quarrel might be forced into the open if the eventual town meeting was held, and Christie was afraid that those whom Alan termed "men of good will" might easily be in the minority.

At least there had been no further talk on Aunt Amelia's part about sending her niece back to Chicago. Possibly because her aunt realized that she wouldn't go. With a regular check coming in from the plant, Christie could simply move out and get a room elsewhere. And that was something Aunt Amelia did not want to have happen.

At the plant no attempt had been made to interfere with whatever John Macdonald chose to do. The production manager was interested only in results. So long as the harvest problem was met and cans of corn rolled off the conveyor belts at the end of the long operation, he had no quarrel with John's new edicts. They were all to the good. He had none of Mr. Tidings's curious twist of mind when it came to the migrants.

Spencer Tidings had, as Marge blithely put it, conveniently developed complications from which he was mending slowly. He was still in the hospital and too weak to be bothered with plant business. If no serious trouble developed, there was no reasonable objection he could make to John's handling of matters while he was away. Now, with the end of the harvest a few weeks off, and the big event of the Corn Festival approaching, it seemed unlikely that anyone would interfere with him. There had, of course, been no further word from Lawrence Allard.

Even the unruly younger element in the town was quiet. Since the trouble at the school, only minor vandalism had been reported. Lopez still played baseball in the vacant lot with the other boys on those occasions when he could escape from the work in the fields. Of Alan's group, Marge remained the most pessimistic, though she worked as hard as ever.

"It's just the quiet before the storm," she warned Alan. "You wait, the roof will crash in any minute now. It always does when things like this go too well for too long."

The morning after she made this dire prophecy, Marge woke with the sniffles, a blinding headache, and mounting temperature. Despite all this, she tumbled wheezily out of bed, intending to go about her usual duties. Aunt Amelia looked at her flushed face and promptly took matters in hand.

"You'll go right back to bed and stay there, young lady," she ordered, and hurried off for a thermometer which she thrust between Marge's lips.

Marge removed the glass tube. "I can't stay in bed. The children need their school today. This is just a silly summer cold."

"Humph!" said Aunt Amelia. "So you'll go out there and infect all those helpless children. Not that they haven't probably infected you first. Anyway, you're staying in bed while I call Dr. Hunter. And that's settled."

Christie came to the door of Marge's room while the other girl tumbled weakly back into bed, the thermometer in her mouth.

"I wonder if I could take over the school for once?" Christie asked.

Marge merely looked at her and closed her eyes. Her expression was not encouraging.

"Certainly you can't," said Aunt Amelia. "You've been killing herself out there as it is. And you couldn't possibly handle those wild children when you can't even speak their language."

"They're better behaved than most children," Christie said patiently. "Maybe I can get Aurora to help me. Her hands were so bad yesterday, I don't think she'll go to the fields."

Ignoring any further objections, Christie went to her room to get dressed. John Macdonald would recognize the urgent need for the school to go on and he'd let her off her somewhat haphazard job. She didn't need to consult anyone else.

Before she left she dug into Marge's closet and pulled out the big picture of the fly which Marge had never quite

193

finished. It was close enough to completion to use. The carelessness of the workers over the matter of keeping screens closed troubled Christie and this monster might help the children to realize the disease-carrying properties of the fly. Perhaps she could even use Marge's illness to make the point, since they all loved Marge.

When he heard of her plan, Alan was cheerfully encouraging and even loaned her a small Spanish-English dictionary to take with her. She went off with it in the pocket of her summer dress, the fly drawing tucked under her arm. When she reached the camp and went to look for Aurora, she found the girl getting up. The old lackluster look was back in her eyes these days and she seemed indifferent to what happened to her. Tomasa was home now, still on crutches, but developing an agility with them that was surprising. Aurora tended her little sister lovingly, but about all else she was apathetic.

Mr. Gomez had gone early to the fields and Mrs. Gomez was busy in the washhouse doing the laundry.

Christie came to the point at once. "Will you help me with the school today, Aurora? Marge Molloy is ill and I'm going to try to do her job."

Aurora shrugged without interest. She still wore bandages on her hands, but her fingers were free, so she wasn't helpless.

"Nobody thinks I can do it," Christie said. "And I don't think I can either, without your help."

Tomasa had picked up a little English at the hospital and understood more than she was able to speak. She scrambled over to Christie with the queer spider-legged gait she managed on crutches and balanced herself so that she could put her hand into Christie's the way she had done that very first day.

"Mees Titchur," she said.

Aurora almost smiled. "Okay, I will help," she said.

When Christie had cleared the matter with John Macdonald, the three of them went over to the school building. From every direction children swarmed after them, shy but friendly, chattering eager questions. By this time they were used to seeing Christie around the grounds and did not feel her a complete stranger. Once the usual

194

screening had been accomplished to separate the older children from the young ones, Christie took over the class. She taught them tunes from her own childhood and let them hum without words. She even started teaching them the English words to *Farmer in the Dell,* which was a tune and game they already knew. The strange sounds that resulted set them all laughing.

Then came the dramatic moment when Christie produced the fly. She sat the children in a semicircle around her and even the smallest watched her with round-eyed solemnity. She held the black-and-white picture up to view and let them look at it. Aurora translated into Spanish her question: "What is this?"

There was no hesitation at all on the part of her audience. Practically with one voice they screamed, *"La Cucaracha!"* Christie shook her head and turned helplessly to Aurora, who explained that this was not a *cucaracha,* but a fly. Christie pointed to the hairs on the fly's legs and explained the fearsome dangers to health when filth clung to them, and Aurora translated into simple Spanish. How well the lesson went over, Christie could not be sure, but she was pleased later in the morning when she saw one little girl banging at the screen door to chase away the flies outside, shouting *"Vamos!"*

Eventually Christie ran out of ideas for organized games and songs and Aurora suggested a play period. Along one side of the room were several cardboard cartons which were filled with a conglomeration of broken toys. When the signal was given, the children rushed for these boxes, each to capture his favorite toy. Christie saw one little girl pull a doll from the box. Its nose was bashed in; it was bald and unbeautiful and retained only one battered arm. But the child carried it over to a bench and sat down with it in her arms. While other girls played house, while small boys whooped and yelled and ran their three-wheeled plastic trucks over her feet, the child sat there raptly, the battered doll held to her heart.

Christie turned her back on the uproar of the room and went over to a window. But she did not notice the scene before her because of the mist that clouded her eyes. She could remember the beautiful dolls Eve had bought her, the expensive toys that had been all her own. And suddenly she felt miserable and angry because these children must play with wretched junk that anyone else would throw away.

Something touched her arm lightly and she glanced down to find Tomasa balancing on crutches, looking at her with big brown eyes. The little girl held up a book and tugged at her hand. Christie sat down on a bench and Tomasa numbly put her crutches aside and sat with the bandaged foot thrust before her. While neither understood the other's language, they had a wonderful "conversation" over the pictures in the book. Tomasa looked with wonder at a child washing her face at a porcelain bowl in a beautiful modern bathroom. Such a bathroom was remote from Tomasa's experience and Christie turned the page quickly. Most of the pictures were wrong for these children. They dealt with things other Americans took for granted, but which were foreign to Tomasa and her friends.

It was growing late and Christie knew the morning session must end soon. But first she wanted to bestow some small evidence of her affection on Tomasa. She searched the depths of her handbag and found exactly one lifesaver. Watching for a moment when the other children wouldn't notice, she drew it from her purse and put it into Tomasa's little brown palm, folding her fingers over it. Tomasa beamed at her delightedly, but she did not keep her treasure hidden. The small fingers opened at once, displaying the piece of candy in her hand. In a second a group of children gathered about Tomasa and Christie, their eyes intent upon Tomasa's treasure. Christie wished vainly that she had stuffed her bag with candy from the dime store.

Any Leola child, Christie was sure, would simply have popped the bit of candy into her mouth and finished the matter. But Tomasa's people had taught her to share what little she had with whomever had less. She took the circle of candy and tried to break it, but she lacked the strength in her small fingers. Only when she failed in breaking it did she put it apologetically in her mouth. The children sighed and went back to their play without resentment. Christie stood up, clapping her hands to signify that the toys must now be put back.

The scramble was not so wild this time, but the children knew what they were supposed to do and some of the older ones picked up those toys which had been scattered by the babies, and a steady back-and-forth scampering from toys to cartons began. Christie, busily helping, forgot about Tomasa. When she glanced back at the little girl she saw her take the piece of candy from her mouth, having sucked it to a suitable thinness. Unaware of Christie's interest, Tomasa again twisted the white circle between her fingers and this time it broke into two pieces. One half went back into Tomasa's mouth. Then she hobbled out to the middle of the floor and gave the remaining morsel to the first child she came to.

When the children had gone and the two teachers were left to the last picking up and sweeping out, Christie found herself solemn and thoughtful. Perhaps Tomasa's action would not have been considered sanitary by Aunt Amelia, but Christie felt that she had had a lesson in generosity that morning which she would not soon forget. She swept up cinders and dried bits of earth, feeling humble and rather small. When, in all her life, had she ever thought of sharing as Tomasa thought of it?

As they worked she told Aurora what her sister had done, but the other girl seemed neither surprised nor impressed. It was natural, she pointed out, when others had nothing and you had more to give your own heart happiness by sharing. Christie found herself watching Aurora as the other girl went about the room. Aurora worked in spite of her sore hands, but all the spark and life had gone out of her. She looked the way some of her elders looked about the camp. These people of Mexican descent were naturally happy and gay. They knew how to make the best of their little and to live joyously the life of each day. But with some the years beat out the spark, the joyousness vanished to be replaced with resentment or dull resignation. This was happening too early for one as young as Aurora.

"Why don't you try to get a job in town?" Christie asked suddenly.

Aurora gave her a startled look. It was the sort of look one might turn on a friend who suddenly takes leave of his senses.

"I mean it," Christie said. "That field work is all wrong for you."

There was no amusement in Aurora's laughter. "What is all wrong for me is what there is. Me, I am not the only one. You think it is right for Señora Olivera, maybe?"

"I can't do anything about her," Christie said. "She made her choice a long time ago. But I have an idea for you. Come into town with me, Aurora. Run and comb your hair and meet me in ten minutes in the office. I'll wait for you there."

Aurora was doubtful, but she obeyed. She had no hope, but she was curious. Christie locked the school for the noon hour and cleaned up in the office washroom. Then she went in to talk to John Macdonald. He listened to her hastily outlined plan.

"Aren't you rushing into this without giving it enough thought? Why don't you wait and talk to a few people before you raise Aurora's hopes?"

"I can't back out now," Christie said, her confidence still high. "And I'm sure I can carry it through."

"Well, maybe. If it does work, you've broken the ice. Of course you can't go pulling all the workers out of the fields to get jobs in Leola, you know. The crops have to be harvested. And machinery still can't do what human fingers can."

"I'm only thinking of Aurora," she told him, and the smile he gave her was suddenly warm and friendly.

"You're doing all right, Christie Allard," he told her.

"I know!" said Christie ruefully. "I'm not as bad as you expected me to be. I've heard that before."

They were laughing together when Aurora came hesitantly through the door. She had changed to a fresh blouse and flowered skirt and there was a look of interest, if not of hope, in her dark eyes. Noon was steamy warm as they set off for Main Street together. Christie walked the sidewalks with a light step and hardly felt the damp

198

warmth because of the words that were running through her mind. Words Aurora had spoken: "To give your own heart happiness."

22

Storm Warning

Christie left Aurora looking into the dime-store window and hurried across the street to Mr. Bigelow's drygoods store. She had to see Mr. Bigelow alone before she brought Aurora into this.

He was measuring out yards of cretonne for slip covers when she came in, but he looked around with his usual friendly smile. When his customer had gone, he came toward her cheerfully.

"What can I do for you, Christie?"

Christie led him to the front window where he could look across the street at Aurora.

"You remember that girl over there, Aurora Gomez? She was at the church supper." Christie didn't wait for his nod. "Do you suppose you could give her a job?"

Mr. Bigelow blinked. "You never lead up to things, do you, Christie? You just leap. Now suppose you go back a ways and give me the story."

Christie gave it to him hurriedly. About how the fields were all wrong for Aurora, but the Gomez family were so terribly hard up that Aurora had to work in them. Mrs. Gomez couldn't work now because she was going to have a baby soon. So every hand was needed. But Aurora was being lost, wasted as an American citizen, and didn't Mr. Bigelow think that was terribly wrong?

"Whoa now," he said soothingly. "I'm not saying no, without giving it a good look ahead of time. How do you suppose the town will react if I take a Mexican girl instead of a town girl?"

"She's *not* Mexican, she's American!" Christie said.

"Slip of the tongue," Mr. Bigelow said, grinning at he indignation. "And you know I'm not unsympathetic. Bu just the same, suppose now I don't need an extra hand?"

"You've been doing extra business because of the camp people. So why shouldn't some of that money go back to them? Why shouldn't you hire one of their own people to wait on them? Somebody who can speak Spanish. Maybe you might even get more business."

"Look, honey," Mr. Bigelow said patiently, "the camp people only get in here during their free hours and it won't do that girl much good if I only take her Wednesday and Saturday nights."

"She speaks English. She could help out other times, too."

"What if some of my customers wouldn't want her to wait on them? Not that I wouldn't be willing to try anyway if it seemed sensible. But we have to move slowly and take a step at a time."

Christie began to see her fine dream crumbling. Perhaps John had been right after all and she had rushed too quickly into this with wonderful intentions, but half-baked plans. It was beginning to look as though she would have to go back across the street and admit her failure to Aurora Gomez.

Mr. Bigelow cleared this throat thoughtfully. "Well now, let's think this thing through. Maybe there's something we can do about it. You wait here while I make a telephone call."

He went off to the back of the store and she heard him talking to someone over the telephone. When he came back his round, pink face crinkled in smiles.

"Made a sale," he said. "First try. Just called up Mrs. Steese who runs the hash house across the street. She was telling me a couple of days ago that she needed a girl and waitresses are hard to get right now. I've been talking to her about this migrant problem and she's interested. She says bring the girl in to talk to her right away."

Christie planted a kiss on Mr. Bigelow's cheek by way of thanks and was in the same breath astonished at herself. The Christie Allard of a few weeks ago would never

200

have stepped out of her protective shell to make so impulsive a gesture. It was rather fun being the new Christie.

She flew across the street to Aurora, who was examining the contents of the dime-store window for the dozenth time.

"How would you like to wait on tables in a restaurant?" Christie asked.

Aurora stared. "I have done that work in the Valley one winter."

"Then this will be fine. Come along," said Christie.

She led the way into the restaurant and, as she and Aurora went down the aisle, she saw Tom Webb at a table and waved at him happily. Mrs. Steese interviewed Aurora in a corner of the steamy kitchen with its odors of mingled cooking rising about them. She was bird-small, but she carried herself with an air of being in charge. Her eyes were bright blue and they missed nothing as they sped over Aurora.

"What's the matter with your hands?" she asked.

"The corn leaves," Aurora said. "In the fields."

Mrs. Steese understood. "Well, you can't wait tables with your hands like that. But you come back in a day or two when you can take off the bandages and I'll put you right to work. Same pay as my other girls get. Hours are kind of long and you'll be on your feet a lot."

"You mean—" Aurora began—"you mean you will let me come to work?"

Christie had never seen a bird smile, but she was sure such a smile would look as bright and chirpy as Mrs. Steese's. "I mean just that," the little woman said. "Now run along, both of you. This is the rush hour. The job will wait for you, Aurora."

She bustled the girls out through the swinging door and Aurora followed Christie in a dazed state. Tom was watching for them and he stood up when they reached his table.

"Hello, girls. Sit down and I'll buy you some lunch."

Christie was willing enough. She felt bubbly with enthusiasm, eager to talk to someone about her morning. But Aurora hung back, looking around the restaurant uneasily.

201

"No, please. In a little minute I must go back to the camp. My mother——"

"Your mother will keep for a little minute," Tom said. "Sit down and talk to me."

Between Christie and Tom there was no escape without making a fuss and Aurora slipped uneasily into a corner of the booth, while Christie took the opposite place beside Tom. Aurora could hardly be persuaded to order, but she finally agreed to a hamburger and a glass of milk. Christie was hungry and ordered more lavishly. "You asked for this," she warned Tom, who made a pretense of groaning.

When the waitress had gone with their orders, Christie turned back to him. "Do you know anything about the woman who runs this restaurant? Mrs. Steese? Her name sounds familiar."

"I know something about everybody in Leola, including you," Tom said. "She's a grand person. Widow. Her husband was a foreman out at the plant. He died a few years ago and she took this place over. Has a couple of kids. A girl around six and a boy who's ten or eleven."

"That's it!" Christie cried. "That boy who was playing baseball. Bitsy?"

"Sure," Tom said. "Bitsy Steese."

There was much to talk about after that. Aurora's job and Christie's morning at the school. Despite her hunger, Christie hardly knew what she ate. It seemed that possibilities were suddenly opening up before her. There was so much to be done for the camp people and apparently she could help a little herself. Like getting Aurora this job.

"We'll have to celebrate," Christie told the other girl. "I'll tell you what, Aurora, come to a movie with me Saturday night. There's a good picture on and——" She stopped because Aurora was shaking her head almost angrily. "What's the matter? I'd love to take you."

Tom answered for Aurora. "You're forgetting, Christie. The theater isn't run by people like Mr. Bigelow and Mrs. Steese. There's the Mexicans-in-the-balcony edict. You couldn't sit together."

"Maybe somebody ought to talk to that theater owner," Christie said indignantly. "Somebody ought to explain."

"Explaining isn't enough," said Tom grimly. "I've a good mind to see him myself. I'll tell you what, Aurora, let *me* take you to the movies Saturday night. And I'd like to see anybody put you in the balcony when you're with me."

Aurora stared at him for a moment, wide-eyed. Then she sighed and gave in to her own better judgment, shaking her head.

Christie was distressed. "I don't think that's the way to go about it, Tom. Alan says any sort of coercion may do us more harm than good. People have to change these things because they want to. He says pressure ought to come through public opinion."

"What's to make public opinion change?"

"Oh, various tactics. But nothing that stirs up a storm."

"That's all right if you've got five hundred years," Tom said. "But that theater ruling ought to go now. Maybe it's one thing I can accomplish before I leave Leola."

"Leave Leola?" Christie repeated. "Why would you be leaving Leola?"

"You didn't think I came down here to spend my life, did you?" he asked, almost roughly.

Aurora ate her hamburger in silence, her bright gaze moving first to one and then to the other as she listened.

Christie had taken Tom's presence in Leola for granted. He was just part of the town. A part she had somehow come to rely on. The news that he might leave while she was still here gave her a surprising feeling of consternation.

"What's happened?" she asked.

"Finish your ice cream," he said, ignoring her question. "I've got to get back to the office."

For the first time she wished Aurora weren't there so she might question Tom directly. She was relieved when they reached the street and Aurora said she must now hurry home. She went off, leaving Christie and Tom in front of the restaurant.

"Walk you to the office," Christie offered lightly, "since you're in such a hurry."

"And since you're so curious," Tom said. "All right, come along. But don't drag your feet."

For once Christie skirted the problem. Tom wasn't the sort from whom you could demand information. "Did you ever get a chance to talk to Lopez, make friends with him?"

They stopped at the curb to let cars go by. "I've been out playing ball with the gang a couple of times, but that kid is still standoffish. Bitsy is willing to be friends, but Hank Martin is Lopez's hero and Hank doesn't like me. He hasn't forgotten that I threatened to write him up in the paper. Me and my write-ups!"

"You mean you've finally made somebody mad?"

Tom slanted her a quick look and then started across the street, almost as if he might walk away from her. She had to hurry to keep up with him. Why he should include her in his mood of anger she didn't know.

"You might tell me what's happened," she pleaded. "It's not fair to be angry with me when I don't know what I've done."

He slowed a little and his tone was kinder when he spoke. "It's not your fault, Christie. I'm in a foul mood. Suppose you ask your Aunt Amelia about this whole thing."

They'd reached the *Record* office and he was pulling open the door.

"Thank you for the lunch, Tom," Christie said.

"That's all right. Don't be too mad at me, Christie." He managed something of his old grin as he went through the door, but Christie turned away troubled.

That afternoon she returned to the camp school, and once more Aurora came in to help. Now the other girl filled the room with her gaiety and laughter. Since the older children were harder to keep interested, Christie could never have managed without Aurora's help. Fortunately some of them spoke a little English and the language problem was not quite so difficult. By dinnertime that night Christie was limp with weariness. When the meal was over she longed to go straight up to her room and get to bed. But Marge was still ill with what the doctor termed a "virus" and Christie stayed in the kitchen to help her aunt get the dishes into the washer and do the pots and pans. This was her opportunity to broach the

204

problem of what had been troubling Tom. Christie did no beating about the bush.

"What have you done to Tom Webb?" she asked her aunt.

In a less ladylike person the sound her aunt made might have been termed a snort. "I have done nothing to Mr. Webb. I have been trying to persuade the editor of the *Record* to stop these impossible articles that reporter has been writing. The one about the Mexican child's injury in the field was prejudiced and unfair. To say nothing of being sentimental. His write-up about that dreadful destruction at the school implied that our town boys were to blame. And he has been constantly biased concerning the migrants. Instead of doing properly impartial reporting of whatever happens, he has editorialized. And there are a number of influential persons in this town who are tired of it."

"How has Tom's editor reacted?" Christie asked.

"Most stubbornly so far, I must say. But we have started a stream of letters to the paper protesting its policy which can scarcely be ignored. After all, the *Record* wants to continue in business."

"What do you think will happen?" Christie asked, polishing an aluminum pan for the third time.

"That impertinent young reporter will take a more impartial attitude in his writing, or he will leave the paper."

"Then I think he'll leave the paper," Christie said softly.

"Nothing could please me more," said Aunt Amelia. "Thank you for helping me with the dishes, Christie. And don't look so miserable, my dear. You are troubling yourself about matters you are too young to understand."

"I certainly don't understand the sort of prejudice you feel toward the workers at the plant," said Christie stiffly.

"Prejudice? I?" Her aunt closed a cupboard door with what came close to a slam. "I am realistic, not prejudiced. My roots are in Leola and I'm very fond of this little town. When I see scum floating on the surface of good clean water, I want to skim it off in a hurry before the whole pond becomes contaminated. That is what is happening here in Leola, with our own children coming in contact with disease, dishonesty, lack of morals. Christie, I don't believe you realize how strongly I feel about all this. I am not going to rest until the town is closed to these people. Let them do the work they must and be paid for it fairly. But Leola itself wants nothing to do with them."

Christie stared at her aunt, more shocked than she had ever been before. "What about Alan and Marge and the things they believe?"

"Dreamers," Aunt Amelia said. "I am terribly disappointed in Alan. I had great hopes for him when he first came to town. But he is going down a blind alley."

"What about Josh Allard?" Christie asked.

Her aunt dropped the dish towel she was hanging up. "What on earth do you mean?"

"He was your father, my grandfather. And there wasn't a bit of prejudice in him. I'm sure he didn't feel the way you do."

Aunt Amelia crossed the kitchen quickly and put her hand against Christie's forehead. "Your head feels hot. I hope you're not coming down with whatever it is Marge has."

Christie pulled away from her touch. "How can you be Josh Allard's daughter and feel the way you do?"

"There was no scum on the water when my father was alive," said Aunt Amelia.

Christie turned and walked into the hall toward the front door. Alan was coming down the stairs, but she did not speak to him. She didn't dare trust her voice. The screen door resisted when she pushed it because Fatso was lying across the doormat and she had to bump him rather hard with the edge of the door to get him to move. He gave her a look of dignified distaste as she stepped over him and went down the steps. Without choosing her direction, she walked away from the house. All her weariness had vanished under the rising anger that stirred her. She had no idea where she was going and she didn't care. All she wanted was to put distance between herself and her aunt and try to think things out. So stubborn and narrow a reaction made her feel a little ill.

Marge was right. Everything was building surely

toward an explosion in Leola. There was a boiling and a stirring of forces beneath the surface. It had begun to break out as far as Tom Webb was concerned, but most of it seemed to be in preparation for the big town meeting that was to be scheduled in another week or so. If the town turned out and decided against the workers at that meeting, then some quite serious things might happen.

John Macdonald would be through at the plant and Mr. Tidings would run everything in his own twisted way. In the face of the town's avowed disapproval, Mrs. Steese would not be able to hire a Mexican-American girl even if she wanted to. The work of good people like Father Cudahy, Marge, Alan, Mr. Bigelow, Dr. Hunter, and others would be all for nothing. And Tom Webb would go away from Leola for good. Still without noting the path she had taken, Christie turned up a cement walk and stopped before the steps of a house. Only then did she look up in surprise and recognize how surely and instinctively she had come home. The dark mass of her grandfather's house rose before her and there was a light in the upper windows. She walked up the steps and put her finger to the bell. Quite suddenly and surely she knew what she meant to do.

23

"With Love, Christie"

She could hear Ben Brady stirring inside. A few moments later she heard the slap of his slippers on the stairs and the door was opened cautiously on the chain.

"Hello, Ben," Christie said. "You told me I could come back sometime by myself."

"Sure, Miss Christine," Ben said, opening the door wide in welcome to Josh Allard's granddaughter.

It was not the exhibits she wanted to look at tonight,

however, nor the books in her grandfather's library. She went straight upstairs, followed by Ben, and stopped before the door of her father's room. Ben asked no questions. He slipped a key into the lock and opened the door for her.

"Reckon you'll want to stay here a while by yourself, Miss Christine," he said.

She nodded, again not trusting her voice. He flicked on the ceiling light and then went padding off down the hall. Christie walked straight to the desk beneath the window and turned on the bulb covered by a battered metal shade. Then she switched off the bright ceiling light and let shadows fill the corners. The circle of light above the desk drew her and she went over and sat down within its radiance.

For a little while she gave herself to dreaming. It was as if she could reach back now and touch the boy who had grown up in this room so long ago. It was as if he lay stretched out on the bed in the shadows behind her, his hands under his head, staring up at the ceiling while he talked to the daughter who was still ahead in the future. She could almost hear his voice in the whispering silence, telling her how cities pulled him and how Leola held him back. Telling her his dreams, his ambitions. Of how he wanted to grow up and work with books. And how perhaps someday he would marry a girl whom he loved very much and they would have children. A daughter, perhaps. A little girl whom he would take to visit Santa Claus at Christmastime. He and his daughter would be good friends. They would love each other very much and for always.

So much for dreams.

Christie put her arms on the desk, her head down upon them, and cried silently. With the flowing tears resentment and anger washed away, though hurt remained. After a time her tears ceased and she straightened and wiped her eyes. Then she pulled open the top drawer of the desk and began to rummage in its muddled contents.

She found several sheets of slightly wrinkled paper, with a sailboat printed in one corner. So he had liked boats, too, in this little inland town! There was a stubby

208

pencil with no point, but she found a sharpener and turned the stub in it until she had a usable point. Then she spread a sheet of paper on the desk before her and began her letter.

Dear Father:
I am writing this at the desk in your old room in the Allard house. Perhaps you remember this paper which I found in a drawer? Outside the window the branch of an elm tree scrapes the pane when the wind blows. I wonder if you used to listen to it when you sat at this desk doing your homework when you were a boy.

Now and then she paused to listen to rustling elm branches and to think, then scribbled rapidly. She said nothing of her mother, nothing of the years in Chicago when she was a little girl missing her father. Instead, she wrote about Grandfather Allard's office out at the plant, of the books she had dipped into there, and about the way he had been coming to life for her since she had arrived in Leola.

She gave him the story of the migrants briefly, mentioning as few names as possible. She wrote no reproach of Aunt Amelia, since blame was not her purpose. She told him that she was working at the plant. When she'd finished, she hesitated a moment over the signature. Then she wrote, "With love, Christie," and laid the pencil down.

The letter was four pages long and she read it over, not satisfied with it, but feeling that perhaps it was better to mail the outpouring quickly before she lost her courage or changed her mind. At least the letter did not reproach him in any way. It asked for nothing, but merely gave him the facts. She found an envelope and addressed it to his publishing house in New York. Ben Brady gave her a stamp and she left with no more explanation for Ben than she had given him on entering. And he seemed to expect none. His manner implied that it was natural for Josh Allard's granddaughter to spend any time she pleased in this house.

She said good night and went down the steps into the soft summer night. Most of Leola seemed to be out on verandas and porch steps tonight. Children played a last game before being called in to bed. Radios sang and clattered, yet there was somehow an air of quiet over the town. The sounds were not harsh city sounds. Christie walked slowly, her tension gone, at peace with the town as she had not been before. This was strange because nothing had changed. The probability was that her father would receive her letter and do nothing, as he had done before. But having sat at the desk which had been his as a boy, having talked to him out of her heart, she felt released from soreness and resentment.

She passed the post office and dropped the letter in the box outside. Then she went dreamily back to Aunt Amelia's, not hearing radios or children, somehow alone in the summer night, walking the streets of an older Leola where her father and her grandfather had lived when they were as young as she. She had a strange sense of kinship with the past, of being perhaps a connecting link between past and present.

She was glad to find no one but Fatso on the porch of Aunt Amelia's house. Her aunt had gone out to another meeting and Alan was away, too. She looked in on Marge and found her sleeping, so she tiptoed past to her own room. Before she got into bed that night she took out the little snapshot her aunt had left in her room and looked at it for a long time. Then she put it away. There was still so much she did not understand, so much she could not accept.

On Friday of that week Marge went back to her teaching, still a little shaky, but refusing to be an invalid one day more than was necessary. On Saturday Aurora worked for her first day at Mrs. Steese's restaurant. And at noon that day, when Tom Webb came in for lunch, he persuaded Aurora to make a date to go to the movies with him that night.

Perhaps Christie and Alan Bennett would not have known about this ahead of time if Aurora had not nearly burst with the need to tell someone. Not her parents, of course. Her mother would have wept and her father would have strictly forbidden her to set foot out of the camp. He held to the old ways where a daughter was concerned, and would scarcely have permitted her to go anywhere even with Rafael unchaperoned. For her to go out in the evening with this Anglo reporter whom her family did not even know would have caused a tremendous explosion in the Gomez family. Truly, as Aurora pointed out to Rafael, it was hard to be a Mexican daughter in an American world.

It was Rafael whom she told, both because she needed to talk to someone and because she could not resist teasing him a little. Rafael knew better than to remonstrate with her, or utter any protests, but he was far more concerned than he let her know. She had bragged just a little too much over the fact that Tom had said there would be no balcony-sitting for Aurora if she went to the movies with him.

After dinner, when Marge had gone to bed for further recuperation, and Aunt Amelia and Christie were out on the front porch enjoying the summer twilight, Rafael appeared before their front steps. Lopez was with him, but he gave Aunt Amelia a dark look and waited on the walk while his brother asked to see Mr. Bennett.

Alan came downstairs at once to talk to the elder boy in the living room. As Lopez waited idly outside, Fatso ambled around the corner of the house after an evening inspection of the yard. Lopez's aversion to Aunt Amelia appeared not to extend to her dog, for he knelt beside the elderly bull, talking to him softly in Spanish. Fatso, for once, did not spurn this overture, but seemed to listen to these curious sounds with puzzled interest.

Lopez looked up at Christie. "Is good dog," he said. "When I am small in the Valley once I have a most large dog. Not like this one, but good."

Christie said, "What was his name?" but before Lopez could answer, Alan and Rafael came out the front door.

"Thanks for coming to tell me, Rafael," Alan said. "You go on back to camp and I'll see what I can do. I don't think there will be any trouble."

He waited until the two boys had gone before he

211

turned to Christie. "I know this is a bit sudden, but will you go to the movies with me tonight?"

"What has happened?" Aunt Amelia asked before Christie could respond.

"I'll explain later," Alan said. "Will you come right now, Christie, just the way you are?"

"I don't approve of going stockingless to the theater," Aunt Amelia said, but Christie paid no attention.

She knew that whatever Alan wanted must be important and she went down the steps at once. Alan had already gone on ahead to his car. As they drove the few blocks to Main Street he told her that Tom Webb had asked Aurora to go to the movies with him and it was quite possible that he meant to make trouble. Plainly, Alan was worried. "If I'd known in time I might have talked to Tom. He's been boiling over a lot of things in this town, but I don't agree with his idea of the way to handle the problem."

"Is there something I can do?" Christie asked.

"Just come along with me to make it seem casual. If I go alone it will look too obvious. Rafael said Aurora wouldn't let Tom come out to the plant to get her because of her family. So she is meeting him near the theater. If we just happen to stroll in about the same time, well——"

"But what can we *do?*" Christie inquired anxiously as Alan turned the car to the curb on a side street.

"I don't know, Christie. We'll have to see how things go." He turned off the ignition and they got out of the car.

At the corner they paused, looking warily toward the theater.

"I'm not very good at this Dick Tracy sort of thing," Alan said.

Christie touched his arm. "There's Tom now. See him—looking in Mr. Bigelow's window."

"And there comes Aurora," Alan said. "Rafael was right about the time. We barely made it. Wait, Christie. Let them get in just ahead of us."

Aurora was dressed in her finest and she looked gay and a little coquettish. For just a moment Christie felt a twinge of resentment and wondered at the feeling. It

212

made no difference to her if Tom Webb chose to take out another girl.

Then Alan said, "Come along," and they started down the block just as Tom stepped up to the ticket window.

Christie and Alan reached the theater right behind the others and Christie tried not to sound breathless as she joined Alan in greeting Aurora and Tom.

"Well, hello," Tom said, and there was something quizzical about the look he turned on them. Aurora seemed flustered and there was a faint defiance in her manner, as if she dared them to criticize. She and Tom went through the door into the theater as Alan collected his change.

"Wait a minute," Alan called. "How about making this a double date?"

Tom waited for them inside. "It's all right with me, if Aurora doesn't mind. The more the merrier."

They were all in the small lobby of the theater now and an usher was coming toward them, a look of uncertainty on his face.

"Four seats downstairs," Tom said curtly.

The boy hesitated, glancing doubtfully at Aurora. "But, sir——" he began.

"Well?" said Tom.

Tom's meaning was plain and the young usher had no notion of how to handle the situation.

"Will you wait here a moment, please?" he said, and hurried off toward a door with the sign "Manager" above it.

"I understand what you have in mind, Tom," Alan said quickly. "But I don't think forcing the issue will help matters."

"It will help me," said Tom. "It will be a great pleasure to tell Mr. William Broderick just what I think of him."

"Oh, no!" Christie wailed. "Tom, you've got to be sensible."

"If there's one thing I don't like," Tom said, "it's hysterical women. I'm glad you've got sense enough not to interfere, Aurora."

Aurora had lost her cockiness. She looked frightened and sorry to be there.

"Christie," Alan said, "suppose you and Aurora move

213

over there near the center aisle. So you won't be involved unless we need you."

Christie drew Aurora to a spot where they could look down the aisle toward the picture flickering on the screen in the dark theater. The manager's door opened and a big, bristling man came out of the office. He was large enough to make two of Tom, but Christie suspected that his size wouldn't stop Tom from saying what he pleased. She made an attempt to distract Aurora from the scene behind them.

"How did your day go in the restaurant?" she asked.

Aurora glanced at her vaguely. "Was fine, I think," she said, and then looked back at the three men.

After that, Christie watched, too. The manager spoke in a low tone, not wanting to disturb the theater audience, but there was no amiability in the sound. Before Tom could answer, Alan put a restraining hand on his arm and spoke to William Broderick.

"If you will not let Miss Gomez sit with us on the main floor, we will of course have to leave your theater, Mr. Broderick."

"Now look, Reverend," Mr. Broderick blustered, "I got nothing against you, see? And I don't want trouble. But I know how the people of this town feel about Mexicans and I got their interests at heart. After all, Leola residents are the ones who come here all year round."

"You're to be congratulated, Mr. Broderick," Alan said. "Any citizen who is so interested in the good of Leola, however mistakenly, that he empties his own pockets to serve it, is certainly selfless."

"What're you talking about?" the theater manager growled.

Under the pressure of Alan's hand, Tom held himself in check, though still waiting to step in.

Alan beckoned to Aurora and Christie. "Come here a moment, girls."

They went over to him and Alan presented Mr. Broderick with a flourish which made Christie suspect that the young minister was enjoying himself.

"This is Miss Allard," Alan said. "Miss Christine Allard. You may be familiar with her name. And this is

Miss Gomez, who is at present working for Mrs. Steese in her restaurant."

William Broderick gave Christy an uneasy look and a mumble that acknowledged the introduction. Aurora he ignored.

"Aurora," Alan went on, "I wonder if you can make a guess as to how many people from the camp are likely to be up in the balcony of this theater right now."

Aurora shrugged. "Maybe three, four. We do not have much money for movies. But it is only the lazy ones who come here."

"Is the attendance from camp usually so small?" Alan asked.

The girl was quick to catch his point and she tossed her head, setting her earrings adance. "Why we should come where nobody wants us? We take the bus to the next town. In that town we are American, and no rules about go-to-the-balcony."

"You see what I mean?" Alan asked the manager. "You must lose money every summer because of your consideration for Leola's tender feelings. As I say, I feel you are mistaken, but——"

The manager glanced uneasily at the watch on his wrist. "Look, Reverend, in a minute there's a program break and everybody will be coming out. I don't like to block the lobby like this, so why don't you all go in and sit down in main-floor seats? Just for tonight, see. We got rules here, but since it's Miss Allard, and you, Mr. Bennett——"

"That's not good enough," Tom broke in.

Again Alan's calm tone took matters in hand. "That's right, Mr. Broderick. It's not good enough. I have my car outside and there's no reason why we shouldn't drive to the next town where Miss Gomez is more welcome. So if you'll just speak to your cashier, we'll turn our tickets back and be out of your lobby."

Somehow this arrangement did not please William Broderick. But when he started to object, Tom took Aurora by the arm and walked her past the ticket taker to the outer lobby. Alan and Christie followed and there was nothing for the manager to do but authorize the refund.

When they were outside, Alan looked at the others. "Well, how about it? It's a nice night for a drive and——"

But Aurora shook her head. "Please, no. Is better I go home. Sometimes I am a little crazy, I think. Now I have a good job and if I make the papa angry——" She gestured expressively and glanced at Tom.

He grinned his understanding. "It's all right, Aurora. Maybe I wasn't quite bright tonight either. Maybe getting hot-headed hasn't helped matters any. The Reverend here has been good for us both."

"Never mind the titles," Alan said. "Just let me see you in my congregation next Sunday, Mr. Webb."

"I might surprise you," Tom said.

They smiled at each other with mutual liking and led the girls toward Alan's car.

"Just the same," Tom told him, "while you may have avoided trouble tonight, I can't say I approved of your commercial approach. Even if you should get our William to change his rules for the sake of his wallet, you haven't changed his principles. The prejudice is still there, the intent to discriminate."

"You can't knock that out of him with hard words either," Alan said. "But my way you can get him to expose himself to the contagion of good will. Sometimes a fellow can catch that, too, when he discovers that his prejudices make him unpopular."

"I'm not so sure they do make him unpopular in this town," Tom said.

They'd reached the car and Alan was opening the door. "If nothing happens to throw a wrench into the machinery, our town meeting may swing the whole thing. We've got a few surprises up our sleeves for the opposition."

"I'll be there," Tom said. "I expect it will be my last write-up for the *Record,* but I'll manage to stick around that long."

Alan held the car door open for Aurora. "Will it be all right if I drive you back to the camp?"

"For you, yes," Aurora said, and gave Tom an apologetic look.

Tom understood. "But for me—no. All right, Aurora, I

don't mind. Come along, Christie, and I'll walk you home."

They waited until the car drove off, with Aurora leaning out the window on her side, waving at them as gaily as a child. Then Tom and Christie turned down a side street, walking in the shadow of old trees.

"Are you really going away?" Christie asked. "I mean, is it all settled?"

"Just about. The only decent thing to do is let my editor off the hook. He's been fair, and I know he'd never fire me of his own accord. But your aunt's crowd is making things tough for him and right after the town meeting I'll get out of his hair."

"I'll miss you," Christie said.

He glanced at her in the shadowy darkness. "Thank you, Miss Allard."

She ignored his flippancy. "Tonight I wrote to my father," she told him. "I went back to his room and sat at his desk. And I wrote him a letter with an old stub of pencil that used to be his."

"Did you ask him to come home to Leola?" Tom asked.

"I didn't ask him anything. I just told him about how things were here. I don't mean about Aunt Amelia, but about the plant and the migrants and the town. And I mailed the letter."

"You miss your father, don't you?" Tom asked gently.

"I don't know," Christie said, and her voice broke. "I don't want to think about it."

He put his arm about her quickly, lightly, and held her close for just a moment. After that they walked on in silence until they reached her aunt's house and he turned her up the walk.

"Home you go to Auntie," he said, and left her at the front steps.

There was no time to stop him and she stood there looking after him regretfully. Now that he was walking away there seemed to be so much she wanted to tell him, to ask him before he left Leola. She *would* miss him. The town wouldn't be the same without Tom Webb.

24

Letter from New York

By early summer the committee for the Leola Corn Festival had already been appointed, and now as August drew to a close, plans were in full swing. The exact time of the festival always depended on the weather, on the crops, on when the pack started and ended. But now the week had been set for early September and the town buzzed with preparations for floats and displays. A carnival show would come in with merry-go-round and rides and sideshows for the children. More important would be the county fair aspects, with prizes for home-made foods and fancy sewing, vegetables and livestock.

Most exciting of all was the parade which would open the week of festivity. Every merchant of any importance had a float in the parade. Even the school children would have a float, and of course the Allard plant. Christie, listening to plans that buzzed around her, asked Marge if the workers would take any part in the parade, and Marge snorted impolitely.

"I suppose they'll be permitted to stand along the road and watch, providing they don't congest the downtown area. But I'm afraid it has never occurred to anybody that it's their hands which have raised the vegetables and harvested them."

Aunt Amelia, overhearing, said, "You forget that these floats are quite expensive. The Mexicans could hardly afford to take part."

"We might suggest," Marge drawled, "that they use one of the crew leader's trucks and cram themselves into it the way they come up from Texas. That's inexpensive enough and it would make an appropriate exhibit for the parade."

"Don't be sentimental," Aunt Amelia said. "Those people are quite accustomed to that sort of travel."

"Which doesn't make it any more pleasant," Marge said dryly, getting in the last word.

On the day when the two letters from New York arrived, Christie happened to be at home. She saw her father's writing on both envelopes and her heart began to thump. One was addressed to Aunt Amelia, the other to herself.

It had been only a week since she had written to him, and she'd told herself ever since that she expected no answer. But now that one had come, she realized how much she had been hoping to hear from him. Her own was the smaller of the two envelopes and she took it upstairs to read alone: Its brevity was disappointing.

Dear Christie:

Thank you for writing to me as you did. It made a pleasant picture to imagine you sitting there in my room at my old desk.

I have written to Amelia about some of the matters you touched on. Ever since I received John Macdonald's letter I have been pondering the wisest course of action. Perhaps it is time to make some changes. I have thought of a possible solution which may please you. More of that later.

In any event, Christie, I hope to see you before too long. Then we will have to talk about us.

With love,
Your father.

It was not a satisfying note, since it left too much unanswered. If changes were to be made, in what direction would her father be likely to move? Apparently he intended to come back to Leola for a visit and she could not decide whether that was good or bad. What would it lead to, that talk about *them?*

If she had hoped that her aunt would divulge the contents of her own letter, Christie was disappointed. It was obvious that whatever news the letter contained made a curious difference in Aunt Amelia. Overnight she began to brim with mystery and secrecy. There were further exchanges of air-mail letters between Leola and New York and everyone in the house became aware that something was going on.

The town meeting was to be held on a Wednesday night of the week before the Festival, and already the time was nearly upon them. Alan was prepared and confident. Definite proposals were to be made at the meeting, particularly concerning the matter of taking workers' children into Leola schools and opening summer classes for them when school was out. Several of the town's important professional and business men had primed themselves with facts which would answer objections that the opposition might raise.

Dr. Hunter had examined the children at the camp and a good many of the adult workers. He was prepared to show that the incidence of disease was no greater than that in the town itself. Of course any child with a contagious illness would not be allowed in school until well. There were others ready to vouch for the general cleanliness of the camp people and the eager way in which they responded when efforts were made to teach them better ways of doing things.

On all sides praise of John Macdonald ran high. Leola needed him as much as the workers did and it was to be hoped that he would continue as personnel manager of the plant. But whether he did or did not depended in the long run on Mr. Tidings, and perhaps on Lawrence Allard.

Coming home from work on the Wednesday that the meeting was to be held, Christie found herself increasingly uneasy. Her aunt's manner of complete confidence had begun to worry her. But still Alan, Marge, Father Cudahy, Dr. Hunter, Mr. Bigelow—all seemed sure that nothing could happen to defeat them now. As Christie walked home she noticed a boy in a Scout uniform just ahead of her. Glancing at him as she passed, she recognized Bitsy Steese and slowed her steps to his own ambling pace.

"Hello, Bitsy. I didn't know you were a Scout."

He grinned at her. "Sure I am. I started out as a Cub way back. Want to see my badges?"

He held up his arm and she examined his collection with a show of admiration. "You *are* a worker. That other boy you always play ball with, Hank Martin, is he a Scout, too?"

Bitsy shook his head. "Him? Heck, no. He thinks the oath is sissy stuff. But my mom says that's just because he isn't very smart."

On sheer whim she asked another question. "Is Lopez Olivera a Scout?"

"No," Bitsy sounded surprised. "We don't have any of the kids from the camp in our troop."

"That seems a shame," Christie said. "I should think Lopez might make a good Scout."

Bitsy avoided her eyes and looked uncomfortable.

"The reason I thought he might be a Scout," Christie went on, "is because I saw him with a Scout knife a few weeks ago."

"I guess there are plenty of them around," Bitsy said, and suddenly developed an urge to depart. "Well, I gotta be going," and he took off as abruptly as if she had prodded him with a pin.

So there *was* something to that matter of the Scout knife, Christie thought. Something that Bitsy didn't want to talk about. But she had enough else to worry her at the moment and she put the matter out of her mind.

When she reached home, she found Mr. Tidings in the living room talking to Aunt Amelia. He looked pale and a little weak, but quite able to get around.

"I'm glad to see you're out again," Christie said somewhat hollowly, and he gave her a restrained smile.

"Spencer will be able to attend the meeting tonight," her aunt announced. "I shall drive him over myself. A most fortunate circumstance."

Christie couldn't regard it as such and she escaped from their company as quickly as she could.

At dinner that night everyone was keyed up. Aunt Amelia's air of assurance was almost alarming.

"Thanks to your father," she told Christie, "we may have a surprise for the assembly tonight. I had rather hoped he would arrive in town for the meeting himself, but he seems to have been delayed."

Christie looked at her quickly. "You—you mean he's on his way here now?"

"Oh, dear," Aunt Amelia said, "I wanted it to be a surprise. I shouldn't have said anything." But it was evident that this was news she hadn't been able to keep to herself a moment longer.

"Regardless of whether your brother arrives or not," Marge said, "we're going to fight you to the last ditch, Auntie dear. And we've got a very peculiar kind of ammunition we're going to use."

Aunt Amelia's good humor remained unruffled. "I like a good fight, Marjory. What is this ammunition of yours?"

"Something called *right*," Marge said. "The one thing you don't have on your side. And I don't care what Lawrence Allard is planning, you can't tell me might makes right. It never has. Not in the long run."

"A most impressive little speech," Aunt Amelia said. "Will you pass the cream, please?"

The trouble was, Christie thought, that Aunt Amelia had twisted things around so that she, too, believed what she was doing was right. And how could anyone ever straighten her out?

The meeting was scheduled for eight o'clock, which meant that it would probably get under way by eight-fifteen or eight-thirty. Aunt Amelia drove off early to pick up Mr. Tidings, and Alan took the girls over in his car.

The high-school auditorium was beginning to fill when they reached the building. Marge hurried down toward the front to get a seat near the platform, but Christie chose an aisle seat at the rear. Those in the audience would be taking part in this performance tonight and she wanted to be where she could see everything.

"Move over, will you?" someone said, and she looked up to see Tom Webb standing in the aisle.

She slid over one seat and he sat down.

"You don't look too happy, I must say," he commented. "I thought everything was going along pretty well."

She told him about Mr. Tidings's presence here tonight, but he already knew about that. However, he didn't know that Lawrence Allard was supposed to be on his way out from New York and that Aunt Amelia had hoped he would arrive in time for the meeting.

Tom gave a low whistle. "If he's coming today, he could still arrive on the eight-forty from Chicago. Wow! That might make things happen around here."

Christie sighed. "From the way Aunt Amelia's been acting, I'm afraid of the worst."

Tom looked at her. "What about the personal angle? Between you and your father, I mean?"

"I don't know," Christie said. She felt quivery inside at the thought of seeing her father. It was better not to think about that.

By now it was eight-fifteen, but still people were coming in. The interest shown in this meeting was surprising. Christie saw her aunt and Mr. Tidings arrive together and take seats a few aisles away.

"That hat!" Tom whispered. "On top of all that hair! If it was the right season I'd be tempted to take potshots with a snowball."

But Christie couldn't manage a smile. Nothing seemed funny to her tonight.

The man who was to handle the meeting was president of the Leola Men's Club. Alan had said he was in sympathy with the meeting's purpose and that he was a skillful chairman. Now he mounted the platform, and as he stepped to the lectern the crowd began to quiet.

"Hey! Hey, Mr. Webb!" The whisper came from the door at the head of the aisle.

Christie and Tom turned their heads to see Bitsy Steese beckoning furiously.

"You gotta come quick!" Bitsy insisted. "Please Mr. Webb. They're fighting, and—and—I don't know what will happen."

Tom slid out of his seat and Christie went after him, suddenly frightened. On the platform the chairman pounded his gavel to bring the meeting to order.

Bitsy was chattering with excitement. Tom drew him out of the auditorium and took him gently by the shoulder. "Whoa, fella. Slow up so we can tell what you're saying. Where's this fight you're talking about?"

Bitsy nodded at Christie. "It's at her house. Miss Amelia's house. And the dog—"

Tom didn't wait for more. "Get your aunt, Christie, and make it fast. I'm on foot tonight and she's got a car."

25

Fatso Stands Guard

Tom drove because Miss Allard was indignant over being taken out of the meeting and seemed to think this was simply a plot to get her away. Unfortunately, Bitsy had disappeared and there was no further opportunity to question him.

The house looked peaceful enough when they reached it, with the usual lamp burning in the living room. But in the light from a street lamp Christie saw the broken window in the basement, and as they got out of the car sounds of struggle came to them.

Aunt Amelia unlocked the door and Tom dashed through the house with the two women after him and fumbled for the switch at the top of the basement stairs. The scene of battle sprang to life.

A laundry rack had been knocked over and smashed, tools had been scattered from a tumbled workbench, and soap chips had spilled like snow across the floor as two boys rolled over and over, gouging and punching and pummeling each other. One was Hank Martin, with a swelling eye and a cut lip. The other was Lopez Olivera, his nose bleeding copiously.

Tom ran down the stairs, but Aunt Amelia gave the two boys no more than an angry glance. She had seen something else at the foot of the basement steps. There upon the cement lay the old bulldog, limp and unmoving, with a ribbon of bright red from a wound at the base of his skull staining the basement floor.

"Shelley!" Aunt Amelia cried, and for once the name did not seem ridiculous. Christie ran down the stairs after her aunt and bent above the still body of the dog.

Across the basement Tom Webb lit into the fight himself, separating the two boys, shaking each one into a state of sense.

Aunt Amelia paid no attention. "Help me, Christie," she said, and between them they carried the heavy body of the dog up the stairs and into the living room. There they spread papers on the rug and Aunt Amelia bent over him as he lay in a limp heap. After a moment, Fatso opened his eyes, moaned faintly, and tried to lick his mistress's hand.

"Get to the phone," Aunt Amelia ordered Christie. "Call Dr. Burke, the veterinary. You'll find the number on the phone pad. Tell him to come right away. And when you've done that, call the police."

Christie's hand shook as she lifted the receiver. She put the call to the vet through and got his assurance that he would come immediately. Then she phoned the police.

When she left the telephone, Tom was just coming up the stairs with two bedraggled warriors in tow. He thrust each one into a chair on opposite sides of the room and stood between them. To Lopez he gave a clean handkerchief to stanch his bleeding nose.

"Now then," he said, "start talking."

Neither boy said a word. Hank looked sullen and hangdog, but Lopez was smouldering with anger.

"Never mind, Tom," Aunt Amelia said. "The police officer is on his way here. He'll take care of these hoodlums. I knew the Mexicans were in it all along. Come here, Tom, and look at poor Shelley."

Tom examined the dog gently. "Looks like somebody aimed for a skull blow and just missed." He looked at the boys, his voice cold. "Who did this?"

Again there was no answer, and neither boy met Tom's eyes.

The veterinary arrived first. He had only a questioning glance for the two boys as Aunt Amelia explained what she knew of the situation. He went to work at once with cotton and antiseptic. Fatso knew him and endured his ministrations with only a faint complaint.

Then a second car stopped in front of the house and Christie ran to open the door for the police officer as he came up the steps marching Bitsy Steese by the collar.

"I found this kid hanging around the house and he tried to run away when I stopped," the officer said. "So I thought I'd better bring him along."

As Bitsy was marched into the living room, Christie saw that tears had streaked his face and that his mouth was quivering.

Hank looked up sullenly. "Squealer! I'll get you for this!"

Lopez had managed to stop the bleeding, but he was a miserable sight. Nevertheless, there was a certain dignity about him as he straightened in his chair that reminded Christie of his mother.

"This boy, he is okay," he said, motioning to Bitsy. "He does not come here tonight. He does nothing bad."

"Suppose *you* tell us about it then," said the policeman.

Lopez shook his head. "I don't talk so good the English."

"That leaves it up to you," the officer said to Bitsy.

The boy threw a frightened look at Hank and shook his head. Tom Webb leaned past the officer and put a hand on Bitsy's shoulder.

"Look, kid, this is a bad jam you're all in. Your mother's going to be pretty sick about it. But maybe words can straighten out a few things. And maybe you can tell us better than the others what it's all about. Nobody's going to hurt you. You've got a good record behind you until now as a Scout and at school. Everybody knows that."

"I don't want to squeal!" Bitsy cried. "I only came to get you because I thought somebody might get killed. I thought you'd come alone, Mr. Webb, I didn't mean to bring the police and all that."

Aunt Amelia started to speak, but Tom gave her a quick look. "Wait, please, Miss Allard. Look, Bitsy, one of the worst ideas a kid can get is that he is honorably obligated to protect a fellow who is doing something

226

wrong. He isn't obligated. Not even if that fellow is his best friend."

"We got a code!" Hank put in roughly.

"I know all about that," Tom said. "I used to think the same way. But I've found out there's a bigger code. There's a time when you have to choose, Bitsy. You have to think about the most good for the most people. When you begin to injure your mother, your Scout troop, your friends, and the good citizens of the town in order to save the neck of somebody who's off down the wrong road, then, fella, you've got your code pretty badly mixed. You have to have courage enough to put the bigger code above even friendship. Now come on and start from the beginning."

The boy looked at him miserably for a moment longer and then began to mumble his story. The officer knew Tom and he let him prod Bitsy with questions and encourage him when he faltered. Aunt Amelia listened gravely, though she watched the doctor as he ministered to the bulldog.

It wasn't a pretty story, and there was apparently much of it that Bitsy himself did not understand. He did not try to whitewash his own part, but it became evident that his role had been played from the side lines, rather than as a main actor. There had been other boys in on the vandalism, though not tonight.

"Led by Mexican riffraff, I've no doubt," Aunt Amelia put in.

"No, ma'am," Bitsy said. "It was all fellows from town until that day Lopez wanted to play ball with us and we tried to chase him away."

As the boy went on, they began to get a picture of Hank Martin, whose father had died in the war and whose mother worked all day at the cannery and couldn't manage her son. Hank, who failed continually in school and wasn't liked by most grownups, but who had found a way to win respect for himself by bullying boys who knuckled under to him as their leader. Hank, craving an excitement he had found he could get in a dangerous way, and inciting others to join in the same risky game. Lopez had been Hank's meat. Maybe they'd let him play ball with them, Hank said, providing he was willing to prove he wasn't afraid of cops. Of course, everybody said Mexicans were cowards, Hank sneered, and Lopez had almost gone for him right then. But Hank told him there was a better way to show he had guts.

The Scout knife had belonged to Hank. He'd come by it one way or another, but not by being a Scout. Lopez admired it and Hank said he could have it if he'd show he could use it at the school. This, he pointed out, would also be a way of getting even with the town for the way it treated his people. That little girl Tomasa, for instance.

Bitsy had known more of the plans than he wanted to hear. But the night the gang had broken into the school he had stayed home right under his mother's eyes, listening to the radio, trying to get his lessons done. Bitsy's mom wasn't like Hank's. He knew she loved him and he knew also what he'd catch if his mother heard about all this.

It was only the way Tom encouraged him that kept the boy going.

The school had been the biggest "job" the gang had tackled and they laid low after that, apparently having frightened themselves a little. Some of the fellows weren't so proud about what they'd done when it was all over. Lopez had been given his reward, however, and had been accepted on the team. And he was the best pitcher they'd ever had. The only trouble was that Hank had been star pitcher till Lopez came along.

"What started this business tonight?" Tom asked.

Bitsy threw Miss Allard a disgusted look. "I guess she did. She's been going around talking about keeping the Mexicans out of Leola, and about how they're not as good as other people. You can't blame Lopez for feeling sore. But Lopez didn't know it was a double-cross. He didn't know Hank was talking about getting rid of him."

Hank started out of his chair, but the policeman's hand pushed him back. "You're doing fine, kid," the officer told Bitsy. "Keep it up."

Bitsy said he'd come to like Lopez and he was worried when he heard the way Hank was talking and how he was trying to set the camp boy against Miss Allard. Tonight, when Hank and Lopez went off together after the ball game, Bitsy noticed it. He tried to go along with them and when Hank plainly discouraged his company, he became suspicious. He didn't trust Hank and he didn't want to see Lopez get into any more trouble. So he ambled along after them when they started toward this side of town. But he didn't let them catch on that he was following.

This was a good night to pick, of course, since everybody at the Allard house would be over at the big town meeting. And most of the neighbors, too. If Miss Allard came home later and found things smashed up and maybe some kind of evidence around that would point to Lopez, then that would solve Hank's problem. Lopez wouldn't be likely to tell the truth and admit his own guilt, and even if he tried to involve Hank there wouldn't be any way of proving it. The word of a camp boy wouldn't stand up beside that of a town boy, or so Hank had probably figured. They knew about the fat old bulldog, of course, but Bitsy said they weren't worried about him.

Hank hadn't figured on Fatso's valiant heart.

Since this was supposed to be Lopez's job, Lopez broke the basement window and climbed in first. Bitsy, still "tailing" them, as he put it, heard Fatso just about bark his lungs out. The old dog came gallumping down the basement stairs and Fatso still knew what a bulldog's jaws were for. Bitsy, peering in a basement window on the other side of the house, saw that it was Hank who decided to stop the dog. He picked up a wrench and Bitsy heard Lopez tell him to drop it.

"It was getting too dark to see everything that happened," Bitsy explained, "but I know Hank tried to crack the dog in the head and when he did Lopez went for him. Hank still had the wrench in his hand and I was afraid he'd kill Lopez. So that's when I headed for the high school to find you, Mr. Webb."

The policeman prodded Lopez. "Well? You got anything to say?"

"Is all true," Lopez said dully.

"What about you?" the officer said to Hank.

Hank looked at Bitsy. "Think you're smart, don't you?"

"That's more than you've been," Tom Webb said.

But before the policeman could take his charges away to the station, Miss Amelia Allard suddenly remembered something.

"Oh, my goodness!" she cried. "The meeting! Tom, I've got to get back to the meeting."

Startled, Christie glanced at her watch. She had forgotten the meeting completely. It was nine-fifteen and it seemed impossible that no more than forty-five minutes had passed since they had left the school.

Aunt Amelia bent over the dog again.

The veterinarian had finished treating the wound and he looked at her. "Suppose I take him home with me for a few days, Miss Allard. I don't think the damage is serious, but that's a nasty spot and I'd like to keep my eye on it."

"A good idea," Aunt Amelia said. "You let Dr. Burke take care of you now, Shelley. I'll be over the first thing in the morning to see you."

That settled, she started for the door.

Tom spoke quickly to Bitsy. "Don't worry, you're only a witness in all this. I'll go over and see your mother tomorrow. This officer will drop you off at home now, I'm sure." Then he turned to Lopez. "I'll go out to camp tonight after the meeting and talk to your folks. But for now you'll have to go with the policeman. You're in pretty bad trouble, Lopez. And some of it is your own fault."

All the anger had gone out of the boy and he looked so miserable that Christie felt sorry for him. The web he had tangled himself in was not wholly of his own weaving.

The three groups separated and once more Tom drove Aunt Amelia's car, and Christie sat between them in the front seat.

"What will happen to Lopez?" Christie asked.

"I'm afraid he'll have to take his medicine," Tom said. "Just as Hank will have to take his. It's too bad, but it's necessary. I don't hold with the school of thought that excuses everything forever because none of us can help what he is. We'd darn well better help what we are."

Aunt Amelia said nothing.

"The thing that burns me up," Tom went on, "is the

230

people in this town who are also to blame, but who will get off scot-free."

"I suppose you mean me," said Aunt Amelia.

Tom didn't answer her directly. "Well, you have your ammunition now. A camp boy *was* mixed up in this." Then he stepped on the accelerator and gave all his attention grimly to driving.

Aunt Amelia did not speak again until they were once more entering the school auditorium. Then she said, "I'd like to sit at the back, Christine," and Christine followed her to a rear seat, while Tom found a place across the aisle. As they sat down Christie stole a look at her aunt, but there was no telling by her tight-lipped expression what effect the events of the evening had had upon her. As far as Christie could see, everything was worse than it had been before.

Evidently the general discussion was well under way, for the topic seemed to be the matter of opening Leola schools to the children of the migrant workers. Mr. Tidings was on his feet, still a little weak, and holding to the seat in front of him, but managing to speak in a voice that sounded through the auditorium.

"I tell you it is a cruelty to educate these people to a place where they will be above working in their present capacity. There are few other jobs open to Mexican-Americans anywhere. At present they are contented in their work, happy with their lot. I know from long experience what a disservice you will be doing. Besides, they have no desire to mingle with us. They prefer to remain together."

There were several boos from the audience as he sat down, and the chairman rapped for order. Apparently emotion was running high.

Father Paul Cudahy took the floor at once to refute his words. These children had no opportunity to learn English, he pointed out, so how could they be expected to feel at ease among Anglo-Americans? And of course it was an age-old and stupid argument to say that no one should improve his status in society because he might then want more than he had. The ruling peoples of the world had tried too long to operate on just that theory.

John Macdonald was next on his feet to speak for the Mexican-Americans. "I wonder if you all know that some of our newer industries ask for people of Mexican descent because they learn fast, they're honest, and they have more initiative than the average worker when they're given a chance. These people out at the camp aren't asking for special privileges. They merely want the equal opportunity that is the right of every American."

He paused and looked around the auditorium, and the crowd was very still. Christie remembered words of her grandfather's written in the margin of a book—that every man should have, not the *right* to a job—but equal opportunity to get a job.

John went on. "The trouble with the Anglo-American is that while he gives lip service to democracy, he is afraid of true democracy. And this dishonesty is giving us a black eye with the rest of the world at a time when we can't afford a black eye. We have an opportunity here in Leola to counteract some of the wrong that has been done."

When he sat down, Christie glanced at her aunt. Public opinion was quite evidently swinging behind Alan's group, but Aunt Amelia had never bowed to public opinion when it ran contrary to her own. As Tom had pointed out, her ammunition was ready and it was only a matter of time before she got up to take her own place in the discussion. But for the moment she continued to sit stiffly in her seat, alert to everything that was said, but contributing nothing.

At that moment one of the boys who had acted as ushers for the occasion hurried down the aisle and handed a note to the chairman on the platform. When he had read it, the chairman rapped his gavel to silence the murmur that had followed John's words.

"It has just been brought to my attention," he said, "that a Leola man who has long been absent from our midst is now in the auditorium. With your permission, I would like to introduce Mr. Lawrence Allard. We're glad to have you back in town, Mr. Allard."

A gasp went through the room and Christie felt her palms grow damp as her hands lay clasped in her lap. Everywhere about her heads turned and eyes searched the auditorium for the man who had not yet risen to acknowledge his introduction.

Then Christie saw him in the far left corner, rising reluctantly to his feet. Her heart began to thump and sudden tears stung her eyelids. He looked the same, and yet so different from the way she remembered him. His hair had grown a little gray and the lines in his face had deepened. But his quiet manner was the same, and his voice as he spoke was one her heart remembered.

"Thank you, Mr. Chairman," Lawrence Allard said. "It's good to be back and to see old friends. I've been too long away."

He would have sat down but the chairman would not permit him to do so. "Just a moment, Mr. Allard. I don't know how much of this discussion you have heard tonight, but the matters before us concern the Allard plant and can, to a great degree, be influenced by your own attitude. Would you be willing to tell us something of how you feel about these matters?"

Christie saw her father hesitate as if he searched for words. Then he spoke quietly. It was hard for her to follow him because she was so tensely conscious of his presence.

"It has been brought to my attention somewhat directly in the last few weeks that because I have been so long out of touch with affairs at the Allard plant, I have no clear picture of the situation and no right to comment on it. I realize that I have been too far removed from what went on in Leola to do any sort of proper job in the Allard Company. Because of this I have decided that the only sensible course of action was to release my holdings to someone who would be here in town to see that the plant was managed and run to the best interests of all concerned. During this last week I have accepted an offer from my sister. Perhaps, Mr. Chairman, you would like to call on the new owner of the Allard Company, Miss Amelia Allard."

Again the audience gasped, and Christie, startled to awareness of her father's meaning, saw Tom slump despairingly in his seat, saw Marge down near the front

233

holding her head in her hands in an exaggerated gesture of defeat. Lawrence Allard sat down, and once more the chairman rapped for order.

"Miss Allard was here earlier in the evening," he said. "I wonder if she has returned? Miss Allard?"

Aunt Amelia stood up beside Christie, straight as a ruled line, the ridiculous hat topping the high braids somehow failing to make the woman who wore it ridiculous.

"Thank you, Lawrence," she said, and then looked about the room at those who waited so anxiously for her words. "As you know, we have had a serious outbreak of vandalism in Leola. Until tonight it has been my belief that the people at the camp were solely responsible. Tonight my own home was broken into and considerable damage done to my basement. My pet bulldog was nearly killed."

Startled looks turned toward her. The auditorium was very still.

"One of the boys who broke in *was* a boy from the camp," she said. "But the leader of the group proved to be one of our own town boys. It was the town boy who tried to kill my dog, the Mexican-American boy who saved its life. I am not forgiving the action of the camp boy on this account. But is has been thus forcibly brought to my attention that since I have been badly mistaken once in this matter, it is possible—" she hesitated and then went on haughtily—"quite possible that I do not know what I am talking about. Frankly, I am not in sufficient possession of facts to judge both sides. Consequently, I do not feel able to enter the discussion. I do not feel myself qualified to vote either for or against certain resolutions which are to be made here tonight."

With that she sat down, still very straight and stiff in her seat, ignoring the looks of astonishment turned her way. What amounted to a small pandemonium broke out in the auditorium and the chairman had to exert himself to restore order. Across the aisle Christie saw Tom Webb waving his clasped hands at Aunt Amelia in a gesture of fervent congratulations, and she began to understand just what her aunt had done. Without Aunt Amelia's opposition, the resolutions would be passed. Mr. Tidings would not dare do anything but follow her example, and without Aunt Amelia's leadership the opposition would have little force.

Order was restored. The resolutions were now put through quickly and the meeting wound along to an end.

Alan Bennett was called to the platform to offer the closing prayer. He told them simply that he wanted to quote from a prayer that had been written by Stephen Vincent Benét and which was particularly suited to this occasion. As he bowed his head, the audience bowed with him.

" 'Grant us brotherhood, not only for this day but for all our years, a brotherhood not of words but of acts and deeds. We are all of us children of the earth, grant us that simple knowledge. If our brothers are oppressed, then we are oppressed. If they hunger, we hunger. If their freedom is taken away, our freedom is not secure.' "

He added a few words of his own which brought the prayer home and the meeting was over.

26

Father and Daughter

There was a considerable crush as people poured into the aisles, chattering excitedly about the events of the evening. It was impossible to get out quickly. Christie looked across the room, but her father was no longer visible because of those who hurried to greet him. Her heart began to thump again.

Tom wormed his way across the aisle and held out his hand to Aunt Amelia. "I think you're terrific," he said. "I'll bet there's not another soul in this town who would get up and admit in public that he was wrong, the way you've done."

235

"I have not admitted I am wrong," said Aunt Amelia tartly, though she gave him her hand. "I have merely admitted my ignorance. Young man, if you are going out to the camp now I'd like to go with you to see Mrs. Olivera."

"Come along," said Tom. "We'll have to use your car."

They started toward the door and Christie followed them. Others tried to reach Miss Allard, talk to her, but she hardly acknowledged their words. Out in the crowded corridor she turned to Christie.

"See that your father gets home, will you, Christine? He knows he is to stay with us."

Then she pushed ahead of Tom toward an exit. He turned back to Christie for a moment.

"Good luck," he whispered, and gave her arm a little squeeze. He hesitated a moment longer and then said quickly, "Don't expect too much, Christie. No one can really go back."

Then he was gone and she was left puzzling his words. She found a place where she could stand with her back against the corridor wall. Her father would have to come this way and she would manage to catch him. Now and then someone spoke to her, greeted her, and she managed an automatic response.

She saw his head over the shoulders of the crowd and knew he was coming toward her. A moment later his eyes met hers, moved away, and came swiftly back in startled recognition. Nine years had passed, she remembered—nine years more transforming for her than for him. He smiled and raised his hand in brief salute. And after that he came toward her more quickly in spite of the hands reached out to detain him.

Christie braced herself against the wall, at a loss for words, not knowing how to greet him. But when he reached her, the matter was simply solved.

"Hello, Christie," he said. "Do you suppose we can get out of this crowd?"

She returned his greeting gravely. "Hello, Dad. Aunt Amelia said to take you home to the house."

"That's fine. I left my bag at the station. We'll pick it up and get a cab."

But Ed Bigelow, who came along just then and heard his words, would have none of that. He would see Larry Allard home himself. So they followed Mr. Bigelow outside and got into his car. At the station her father retrieved his bag and then Mr. Bigelow drove them back to Aunt Amelia's. Christie sat silently between them in the front seat and let the men do all the talking. The moment of personal recognition between herself and her father was further postponed and the talk was of the meeting and of old times Mr. Bigelow and her father remembered.

When Mr. Bigelow left them at the house, refusing an invitation to come in, Christie led the way into a living room that was still disarranged, reminding her of the disturbing scene that had been enacted there so short a while before. Marge and Alan were not yet home.

"Let's go upstairs," she said, and they went up to her aunt's sitting room. She still felt stiff and ill at ease.

Her father set his bag down and looked around the room. "I see Amelia has kept a lot of the old things. I remember that rocker, and that funny old table with the claws for feet." Then he saw the framed photographs of his mother and father and walked over to look at them.

Nervously Christie turned on lamps and softened the light by switching off the overhead bulbs. Then she sat down in the rocker and waited. It was her father who had gone away. So it was he who must return. If only she could be nine years old again so everything might be as it had been then. But she was beginning to understand Tom's words. You couldn't go back. The years were there between them.

After a moment he seated himself on the couch and leaned forward, his arms on his knees, looking at her gravely.

"You're so far away across the room, Christie," he said. "Come here beside me."

But she had been far away from him across half a continent, and she did not move, though now words came, a rush of words that almost choked her.

"Why did you go away? Why didn't you answer my letters? You never even said good-bye. You—you just went away and never came back!"

237

"Come here, honey," he said.

She went to him then and sat beside him on the couch. But she sat stiffly, feeling no closer to him than before.

"I don't want to go into all the reasons that lay between your mother and me," he said. "Divorce isn't a pretty business. I wanted to save you from the sort of thing I'd seen happen to other children whose parents separated."

"What sort of thing?" Christie asked. "What sort of thing could be worse than not hearing from you?"

He was silent for a moment. "There were two courses open to me. I could hold you to me with your own love. I could let you be torn by divided loyalties. I think Eve would not easily have let you go on loving me. I knew the harm such a pulling apart might do you. So I chose the other way—a quick break that would leave you free to stay with your mother. If you were angry with me, that would make it all the easier for you. Don't you think that was better than to be torn in two directions?"

Christie turned her head in denial. "Nothing could be so bad as—as not having you answer when I wrote to you."

"It hurt me, too, Christie. You know that, don't you?"

Now she could know it. But she had not known it then. She had not known it in time.

"After Eve was gone, I had to move slowly," he went on. "Your letters were understandably cool and you seemed to want to have nothing to do with me. I had to give you time. When I knew you were coming to Leola I decided to come here, too, so that we could have a face-to-face talk. Your letter gave me the opportunity I wanted. It moved me very much indeed."

There were footsteps across the porch downstairs as Alan and Marge came home. Christie heard them talking in the living room, heard the chairs being moved back into place, but it was like something happening in another world.

"How—how long are you going to stay?" she faltered.

"I'll have to go back day after tomorrow. But I hope you'll come East very soon after that. For a visit, at least. Mary is anxious to meet you, and so is your small sister Janey."

238

She shrank away from the thought of those other two. Later would be time enough to think about them, learn to accept them, but now there was only the problem of the years which still lay between herself and her father.

"After a while perhaps you'll want to start college," he continued. "I'll be more than happy to send you anywhere you choose to go."

She sat very still, not thinking about college. He was her father, and he was not her father. And there was an old aching inside her.

He reached out and took her hand, held it lightly in his own. "We can't go back, Christie." The very words Tom had said! "That's the hard thing to accept, I know. But, Christie, starting now we can go ahead. We can get to know each other again. Don't you think that's possible?"

A little of the tenseness went out of her. If he was willing to give her time, not to expect too much of her right away . . .

"I'd like to come to visit you," she said.

He nodded, and she saw that he was too moved to speak. Tears choked her throat. You couldn't go back; that was true. There was no replacing the lost years. But what he had just said was also true; you could go ahead. There would be a new, developing relationship between them, and it could be companionable and very sweet. But there would be an emptiness it could never fill. She understood that now.

She could hear Marge coming upstairs and she went to the door. Standing there, listening to steps approaching, she knew that she could now accept the reality. Now she could live with it.

"Marge," she called, and there was a note of pride in her voice, "come in here. I want you to meet my father."

27

Corn Festival

A grandstand had been erected in front of the courthouse and there were seated the town officials, prominent citizens, and visiting celebrities, waiting to enjoy the parade that would open the week of the Corn Festival.

Christie had not expected or wanted to sit in the grandstand. But Aunt Amelia was there and Miss Christine Allard's presence was also expected. The day was blue and beautiful and, by good fortune, not too hot. All the stores on Main Street had closed and Leola citizens, well supplemented by visitors from towns and country around, waited along the line of march. There appeared to be the usual delay over getting the speeches and parade started, and there was a restless movement up and down the sidewalk before the stand.

Christie watched the throng alertly, waiting for Tom Webb to appear. Just that morning Marge had told her the news about Tom. In spite of the success of the town meeting, he was planning to leave for Chicago and a new job tomorrow. So far, he had not come around to say good-bye, and Christie had an idea that he might run in at the last minute for a quick "so long." She didn't want it to be like that. She wanted to talk to him before he left. As a reporter, he would certainly turn up here sooner or later, and so she watched the crowd as it gathered, moved about, waited.

Loud-speakers had been set up around the stand and now the Festival director began to talk. The moving throng quieted to listen, but Christie did not hear a word of his introduction of the mayor because that was the moment when she saw Tom raising his camera for a shot.

No one was paying any attention to her and she managed to slip quietly from her seat and get down the few steps to the ground without disturbing anyone.

Tom saw her coming and waited for her, grinning. "That's no way for an Allard to behave. Don't you know you have a position to uphold?"

"I wanted to talk to you," she told him. "Do you have to cover His Honor's speech?"

"I already have a typed copy," he said. "But this is no place for a cozy little chat. Come along." He started through the crowd, his camera under one arm, making a path for her to follow. "In case you don't realize it, this is the last Leola affair I'll be writing up."

"I know," she said, and was surprised at the twinge of feeling behind her matter-of-fact words. "You might have told me."

He didn't answer. Behind them Christie could hear the mayor's voice booming over loud-speakers, but Tom turned down a side street where they could walk along in comparative quiet.

Christie groped for safer, less personal grounds. "What's going to happen to Lopez Olivera? Have you heard anything new?"

"The case will come up the end of this week," Tom said. "Your auntie did herself proud out at the camp the other night. She talked to Mrs. Olivera practically like one human being to another. She's going before the judge when the case comes and give him some of the extenuating circumstances. Lopez isn't bad and his mix-ups can be straightened out with the proper handling. Alan's going to try to get him paroled into his custody. So maybe things will work out. Aurora's family is going back to the Valley right after the Festival, but the Oliveras will stay on for the pumpkin pack. So they'll be around for another month or so."

"What about Hank?"

"That's more serious. He's been in trouble before and I'm afraid he needs more help than can be given him in Leola. It may be necessary to send him away to a boys' school. The community has to be protected from the real lawbreakers, and he's been a bad influence for the rest of the boys. How is everything between you and your father,

Christie? I liked him a lot when I went to interview him before he left."

"He liked you, too," Christie said. That had been important to her. She remembered how anxiously she had waited to see if her father would make any comment after the interview. When his remarks were favorable, she had sighed inwardly in relief. Somehow she had *so* wanted these two to like each other. "We're getting acquainted again," she went on. "I'll be going East for a visit very soon. Maybe I'll even go to college in the East."

"Smith, Vassar, or Bryn Mawr, I presume," Tom said.

Christie laughed. "They're quite good schools, I hear. But I don't think they'll want me. My marks weren't always top of the class. No, we don't know yet. It's late to get in anywhere, but what about you, Tom?"

"Neither Harvard, Yale, nor Princeton," he said lightly. "Just night classes in Chicago. I've got a crazy idea that I want a degree, Christie. Maybe because my father never finished eighth grade."

"Good for you," said Christie. "Your new job is in Chicago?"

He nodded. "A city paper saw that story I did about Tomasa and they think they can use me."

"That's wonderful," Christie said warmly. "I knew that story was tops."

"Thanks, lady," he said.

The sounds from downtown were more indistinct now and the side streets seemed deserted. Practically all Leola was down on Main Street to see the parade.

"I'd like to hear how things turn out for you," Christie said. "I'll answer if you write to me."

They'd reached a corner and Tom stopped at the curb, not going on. "What good would that be? Look, Christie, it's been fun knowing you, but let's face it. I go one way and you go another. Now let's get back to that parade. I don't want to fall down on my last write-up for the *Record*. I can get copies of the speeches, but I need to see the floats."

She would not turn back, however, and he was forced to wait. This was harder than she had expected, but she wasn't going to give up until she understood what lay behind his attitude.

"First you have to tell me one thing," she said. "Is it because of all that silly Allard business that you don't want to write to me?"

"Don't be ridiculous," he said. "The reason I don't want to write to you is because you are a giddy little thing with a silver spoon in your mouth. Now, are you satisfied?"

"So it *is* my ancestors," she persisted. "You know something, Tom, I started counting them up the other day. My ancestors, I mean. And I certainly was impressed."

"I'm sure," he said dryly, and started back toward Main Street.

This time she had to go with him if she had anything more to say. He looked so stern and resolute that she wondered if she could ever break past his guard. She mustn't sound serious, she must keep this light.

"You know what I found out?" she asked, and went on quickly, waiting for no encouragement. "I had two sets of grandparents; that makes four altogether. Each of them, oddly enough, also had two sets, which adds up to sixteen great-grandparents. Am I right?"

"You've lost me in higher mathematics," Tom said, but he sounded faintly curious.

"If I go back a few hundred years I've got ancestors by the thousands. And so have you. So don't you see how foolish it is to talk about Allards, or Webbs, or anybody else? Everyone has such a huge mixture behind him that it's silly to boast about family, or take much stock in it. The only thing that matters is what *I* do with what they gave me."

"Gosh!" said Tom, exaggeratedly awed. "All this as a build-up to get a fellow to write to you!"

"But I want you to write to me," said Christie simply.

The brassy blare of the Leola band burst upon them with a crash. Tom glanced toward the summoning clamor and then looked at her. He pulled her to him and kissed her lightly on the tip of her nose.

Then he shouted, "Come along, woman, the parade has started!"

He caught her hand and she ran with him breathlessly, so that they reached Main Street in time to see the first float go by.

It was filled with pretty girls in Indian dress, with Father Marquette on a mound above them. Tom got busy with his camera almost as if he had forgotten that Christie was there. But she knew that he had not forgotten and that after a while he would come back to her.

The Boy Scouts marched by and Christie applauded hard for Bitsy Steese who saw her and grinned as he went past. Then came the float for the Allard plant and Christie called to Tom happily.

"Look! Look up there!"

Corn was queen of the Allard float—a blond Leola girl dressed in golden robes and wearing a green crown. There were cannery people on this float, but there were also workers from the field.

Mr. Gomez sat jovially at the queen's feet, strumming his guitar, while Aurora, dressed in her gayest skirt and blouse, with Rafael beside her, sang Mexican songs to the delighted crowd.

"It was Aunt Amelia's idea," Christie told Tom. "You should have heard her announcing to John Macdonald that it was a disgrace to think that the workers weren't on a single float, when they were the ones who did most of the work. Tom, did you know that Mr. Tidings has decided to retire on account of his health, and John is staying on?"

"Yes, I know," said Tom. "Cheers for Aunt Amelia!"

"Everything's going to be all right!" Christie cried, waving both hands at Aurora, who saw her and waved back.

"Come on down to earth," Tom said, plucking her sleeve. "This is just a beginning. You don't break down years of prejudice in one puff of enthusiasm. But anyway Leola's made a start in the right direction, and maybe we've helped a little with the first push."

There was a break in the ranks before the next float came along and Tom lowered his camera.

"Christie," he said, and she looked at him quickly. Just as she had known, he had come back to where she was. "I forgot to mention something a while back."

"Yes?" she said, and felt a little breathless.

"I'm not much of a letter writer, but you might as well give me your address. Could be I'd get in touch with you."

But Christie had just made up her mind about something. "You don't need it," she told him. "You won't need to write to me because I've just decided where I'm going to college."

He stared at her. "Don't tell me; let me guess!"

"That's right," she said. "Chicago. It's my home town, too, you know. Boul Mich on winter evenings, and the aquarium, and the subway that isn't long enough, and——"

"I know an Italian place on the near north side," he broke in. "You've a date with me to have dinner there some Saturday in November."

"Some Saturday in October," she said. "Oh, Tom, you're missing the floats!"

He went back to work then and she stood beside him happily, unnoticed again. But she hardly saw the bright pageant because of the brink of discovery that had opened before her.

It was quite true, you couldn't go back. You didn't need to go back because life itself went ahead. You outgrew one relationship, but you grew into another that might be even more important. That was what was beginning now, and Tom was a part of it.

They both had so much time—time in which to show all those millions of ancestors what Tom Webb and Christie Allard were made of. Time to find out about each other.

About the Author

PHYLLIS A. WHITNEY was born of American parents in Yokohama, Japan, where her father was in business. Later the family lived in the Philippines and China. After her father's death, she and her mother returned to the States, which she saw for the first time at age fifteen. In this country she has lived in Berkeley, San Antonio, and Chicago, and presently resides on Long Island, New York.

Phyllis Whitney has been writing since the age of fifteen, first short stories and then her first book in 1941. To date she has published over fifty novels, many of which are for young people. Her books have been translated into seventeen languages, with millions of copies in paperback and hardcover in more than two hundred editions. In recent years she has published some eighteen adult suspense novels. Her own daughter loved to read her books when she was growing up, and now enjoys the adult novels. Phyllis Whitney's three grandchildren are presently following in their mother's footsteps.

The author has spent much time in travel, with many of her books set in areas she has visited or lived in. She works six days a week at her writing, usually mornings from 8 to 11; after time out in midday, she returns to writing until 4:30 or 5.

She has won a number of awards for her books for young people, twice receiving the "Edgar" Award of the Mystery Writers of America. She spent a year with the Chicago Public Library and has been Children's Book Editor for both *The Chicago Sun* and *The Philadelphia Inquirer*. She was instructor in Juvenile Fiction Writing at Northwestern University and taught for eleven years at New York University. Presently all her time is given to writing, usually two books a year, one for young people and one for adults.